I0761210

PRAISE FOR

CITIZEN ORLOV

A 2024 IBPA Benjamin Franklin Award Silver Medal Winner
A 2024 IPPY Award Bronze Medal Winner

"[An] enjoyable comic fable—one that may cause readers to think twice about ever answering someone else's phone."
—***Wall Street Journal***

"The blend of action and picaresque buffoonery flatteringly calls Conan Doyle's Brigadier Gerard tales to mind, and Payne pulls off a genuinely surprising conclusion. This auspicious debut announces a bright new voice in comic suspense."
—***Publishers Weekly*, Starred Review**

"This is the most fun spy thriller we've read in ages . . . First-time novelist Jonathan Payne mixes Franz Kafka's surreal absurdism with the ingenious plotting of Graham Greene's spy novels, then adds a hilarious layer of deadpan comedy. Written in short chapters filled with exciting left turns, *Citizen Orlov* barrels along. We wouldn't mind at all if this turned out to be the start of a series."
—***Apple Books Review***

"Jonathan Payne's *Citizen Orlov* is a stunning debut! A page turning, down-the-rabbit-hole delight, told with equal measure of wit and suspense. A timeless classic for our current moment; a paranoid and comic thriller with a surprise on every page. I loved it!"
—Don Scardino, Producer/Director, *30 Rock*, *New Amsterdam*

"A triumph—and an answer to that age-old question of what would have happened had Gogol, Kafka and G. K. Chesterton collaborated on a thriller. A timeless work which will, I fear, be forever timely."
—Dixe Wills, author of *Places to Hide* and *New World Order*

"Highly engaging, and written with an engaging lightness of touch, *Citizen Orlov* marks the debut of a comic novelist to watch for the future."
—Dr. Adam Lively, Senior Lecturer in Creative Writing & Programme Leader, MA Novel Writing, Middlesex University

"*Being There* meets *Catch-22* in this by turns raucous, nail-biting and hilarious send-up of government corruption and bureaucratic incompetence. With an assured voice and wit to spare, Jonathan Payne is a writer on the rise."
—E.G. Scott, international bestselling author of *The Rule of Three*

HOTEL MELIKOV

JONATHAN PAYNE

CamCat Books
2810 Coliseum Centre Drive, Suite 300
Charlotte, NC 28217-4574

Hardcover ISBN 9780744311808
Paperback ISBN 9780744311815
eBook ISBN 9780744311822
Audiobook ISBN 9780744311846

Library of Congress Control Number: 2024949371

Book and cover design by Maryann Appel
Artwork by Grandfailure, LesyaD

5 3 1 2 4

FOR STANLEY AND ARTHUR

PART ONE

An Account of the Coronation of His Majesty, The King

CHAPTER ONE

In which our hero attends a ceremony

If, in the first days of spring, one were to leave the residential area of the city in the hour before dawn and stroll across the cobbles of the Grand Plaza, continuing over the tram lines and down toward the river, across the bridge and into the government sector, one might expect to complete such a walk largely undisturbed by other citizens. Perhaps one might catch a glimpse of the baker arranging the first loaves of the day in the window of his quaint shop on the corner of Grunplatz, or a delivery driver pulling up to the tradesmen's entrance in the narrow alley behind Hotel Melikov. The delivery driver might doff his cap to acknowledge a fellow early riser, and one might decide it courteous to return the gesture with a firm *Good morning, Citizen*. On a good day—that is to say, a day in which the peak of Mount Zhotrykaw is not engulfed in ominous clouds—one might pause on the bridge to smoke a cigarette and await the first glimpse of sunrise over the mountains.

Such is the preferred morning routine of one Citizen Orlov, a simple fishmonger who, at least temporarily, is now properly to be addressed Minister Orlov, owing to his rapid and surprising ascent to the considerable position of Minister of Security. The unusual circumstances in which a fishmonger rose to such a position are recorded in detail elsewhere; no doubt a reader not yet familiar with that strange tale will be able to locate it in a public library or acquire it from a purveyor of books at a reasonable price.

In his twenty years or more as a fishmonger (all of which were spent in the Grand Plaza as the sole employee of his old friend, Citizen Vanev), Orlov established the firm custom of an early morning walk to his workplace, and he has no intention of breaking such a habit now, just because the Ministry of Security does not shake itself into life for an hour or more after the market is in full swing. Sometimes, a second lingering cigarette on the bridge is necessary in order to avoid the wrath of the security guards for arriving before the building is open.

On this particular morning, Minister Orlov lingers over his second cigarette for a different reason. He waits for the pale early sunlight to warm his face, stubs his cigarette on the bridge, throws the butt into the river, and turns to stroll back up the hill into the Grand Plaza. The familiarity of the scene warms him far more than the pale sunlight ever could. In every corner of the square, and all along its edges, market traders are opening shutters, shaking the overnight rain from awnings, and laying out their wares for the day ahead. The greengrocer's whistling of a patriotic song echoes between the ornate stone facades of restaurants, hotels, and townhouses. Although Orlov's eyesight is not what it once was, nevertheless he feels sure he can make out in the distance, at the northern edge of the square, the considerable figure of Citizen Vanev, fishmonger, erstwhile leader of the People's Front, and now deputy leader of the newly-formed People's Party.

As he strides across the cobbles of the Grand Plaza, Citizen Orlov is gripped by a sense that this is his rightful place of work.

He really has no business masquerading as the Minister of Security, trapped in an ornate office with piles of paper that he can scarcely understand. He should by rights be spending his working days out here in the market, in his filthy apron and heavy boots, with the stench of fish on his hands and a cigarette never far from his lips, exchanging pleasantries with the greengrocer and the haberdasher. This is his place and these are his people. He is acting temporarily as the Minister of Security only because the Crown Prince—soon to be installed as the new king—asked him personally to do so. He determines to return to his old life just as soon as he can find a way to extract himself from his governmental obligations.

Approaching the fish stall, Orlov does what the two old friends have always done in lieu of a handshake: he holds out his cigarette case. Vanev takes a cigarette and gestures that Orlov should sit on a barrel.

"Good morning, Minister," says Vanev.

"Citizen, please," says Orlov, leaning over to light Vanev's cigarette.

"Good morning, Citizen, if you prefer," says Vanev. "How is the oppression business treating you?"

"It's much overrated," says Orlov.

"I daresay that's true," says Vanev, pausing to cough heavily. "To what do I owe this honor?"

"Things have taken a turn for the worse," says Orlov, grimly. "Political parties are outlawed, with immediate effect." He looks at his old friend, awaiting a response.

Vanev points to a nearby lamppost, which is adorned with a paper notice carrying the royal crest. Orlov cannot see the details from this distance, but he already knows what it says. Only now, he realizes that these signs are attached to every lamppost in the square and beyond. "Your functionaries have been very efficient in ensuring the news is out," says Vanev.

"I'm sorry," says Orlov. "I honestly thought there was a chance His Majesty could be persuaded."

"Imagine the monarch not listening to the advice of a fishmonger," says Vanev, shaking his head in mock surprise.

"It seems he listened to the generals," says Orlov.

"So, you visited me just to bring your apologies?" asks Vanev.

"I'm here to ask a favor. Can you persuade the People's Party to lie low, at least for a while? Until this blows over."

Vanev grimaces. "Minister." He waves his cigarette toward Orlov deferentially before continuing. "The People's Party has no intention of ceasing its operations, whether they are legal or not. We will keep struggling—fighting, if necessary—until this corrupt dynasty is crushed and our great nation becomes a truly democratic republic. So, Minister, the question is not whether I can persuade them to lie low. The question is whether you will get out before it's too late. The question is whether you will join our struggle, not because these crooks have kidnapped your mother but because you genuinely believe in our cause."

Orlov sighs heavily. He blows out a cloud of smoke and watches it disperse. "I have no intention of continuing in this role for longer than absolutely necessary. I just need a little time to extract myself."

Vanev turns to look at Orlov with an intense glare. "There is no time. If things unfold as Comrade Volf has predicted, no one in the government or the royal family is safe. If you are a government minister when the revolution comes, the firing squad will not ask politely whether your heart was in it. They will not inquire about whether you were appointed on false pretenses before riddling your body with holes."

Orlov is taken aback at the venom in Vanev's voice. On the other hand, his old friend has been telling stories about the revolution for years. This is simply the way he speaks. He is a passionate man with a particular view on how the country should be governed. He is entitled to his view. That does not mean Comrade Volf's predictions are about to come true.

"I understand your concern," says Orlov, "and I am grateful for it. I will look for the earliest opportunity to speak to His Majesty about my position."

Vanev's intensity does not falter. "My advice is this: stay away from the coronation."

Orlov stands up. "Security arrangements for the ceremony are in place. I can assure you that ministers will be absolutely safe."

Vanev stands, wipes his hands on his filthy, fish-stained overalls, and pours a bucket of ice into a wooden display box. "For your sake, I hope so," he says.

Orlov is turning to leave when he spots something curious. An army of craftsmen is hard at work on the huge, stately townhouse that forms the centerpiece of the eastern edge of the Grand Plaza; they are painting, plastering, and repairing. In itself, this is unremarkable, since the work has been ongoing for some weeks. But Orlov's eye is drawn to the ornate, brass lettering now being affixed above the front door, which reads *Hotel Milekov*. He glances across to the western edge of the square, which has—for as long as Orlov can remember—been dominated by Hotel Melikov, and back at the new Hotel Milekov, which sits precisely opposite, the two buildings facing each other across the cobbled grandeur of the Grand Plaza.

Orlov turns back to Vanev. "A strange choice of name, would you not agree, citizen?"

Vanev has begun to spread the day's supply of carp across an ice-filled display box. He looks up at the sign-making activity and says, "Count Milekov."

"What's that?" says Orlov.

Vanev is still flinging carp. "That house belonged for generations to the family of Count Milekov. So, a natural name for the new hotel, I suppose."

Orlov glances again at Hotel Melikov and back at Vanev. "Would you not agree it could cause some confusion?"

Vanev glances at each hotel and turns back to Orlov. "Confusion?" he says.

"Never mind," Orlov says and trudges away across the square toward the government sector.

As he walks, Orlov ponders the gravity of Vanev's remarks. If he is going to tender his resignation, he needs to do it urgently. But he can hardly ask for an audience with the monarch today, given that it is coronation day. He determines to locate Citizen Galin, the private secretary to the Crown Prince, and demand an audience with the new king at his earliest convenience.

Perhaps, given the urgency, he could offer his resignation to Galin, in lieu of a meeting with the king. He will ask Galin if it is possible for a minister to submit his resignation to the private secretary, or whether a personal meeting with the monarch is strictly necessary.

As he strides through the grand entrance of the Ministry of Security, Orlov is greeted by Citizen Bartova, his private secretary, hovering in the lobby in an agitated state.

She hops from foot to foot.

"Ah, Minister, thank goodness," she says breathlessly, "it's time to leave. I will accompany you to the palace."

"Very well," says Orlov, and he turns back toward the door.

Bartova lays a firm hand on his shoulder. "Sorry, Minister. This way. We need to use the rear entrance. Your military escort vehicle is waiting."

Orlov is unsure what to make of this. "Can't we walk to the palace? It takes only a few minutes."

Bartova hesitates. "A change in security posture, I'm afraid. The generals are insisting that all ministers are escorted to and from the coronation ceremony. No exceptions."

They march swiftly through the rear entrance of the ministry into a secluded yard surrounded by high walls. A green armored car stands idling inside the gate.

"Don't we set the security policy here at the ministry?" asks Orlov.

"A good question," says Bartova. "The generals always have a say in operational matters concerning the royal family."

They cross the yard and climb into the rear of the military vehicle. It is bare and uncomfortable but obviously heavily armored. Two soldiers sit up front; the one in the passenger seat grips a huge rifle between his knees.

"Good morning, Minister," he says.

"Good morning," says Orlov.

The gate swings open and the vehicle pulls out slowly onto the cobbled street.

DESPITE THE EARLY hour, crowds are now gathering across the government sector, seeking a good vantage point for a glimpse of the new king as he emerges from the palace later in the day. Police and soldiers line the streets, directing the crowds. The atmosphere is both tense and festive.

Orlov is expecting to be driven to the foot of the palace steps, but instead the vehicle trundles to the back of the palace and through heavy iron gates into a secluded courtyard he has never seen before. The gates are closed by members of the palace guard before Orlov and Bartova are allowed to emerge from the vehicle and are ushered quickly into the palace through a rear entrance.

The palace guardsmen display a hushed urgency, constantly glancing around as though expecting threats to emerge from every direction. Orlov wants to ask what they know, but none of them seem open to a conversation. Instead, he stays silent and allows himself to be marched to the door of an elegant anteroom where, it seems, the entire company of ministers and generals are mingling expectantly.

Before Orlov steps inside, Bartova says, "One moment, Minister, if I may." She leans in to straighten his tie. "When you go in, General Varga will ask you for a decision about the procession."

"The procession?"

"Yes, Minister. General Varga will ask you to agree that we should cancel the open carriages and the horses, even for the king. He proposes armored military vehicles for everyone."

"Isn't it a little late for that?" says Orlov.

"In fact, the general has already made the arrangements."

"So, there is no decision for me to make."

"It would be best if you agree with him, Minister, if I may say so, and pretend you don't know it is already arranged."

Orlov glances into the room full of ministers and generals and back at Bartova. "Do you not think this entire company leaving the palace in armored vehicles will look rather," he searches for the right word, "aggressive?"

"I cannot disagree, Minister," says Bartova, "but security must be our first consideration."

Just as Bartova has predicted, as soon as Orlov steps into the anteroom, he is accosted by a stocky general with terrible breath and a chest full of medals. Above his medals is a nameplate reading VARGA. Orlov does his best to appear surprised by the request and reluctantly agrees.

Before the general dashes away again, Orlov sees an opportunity to make a request. "I hope you will do everything in your power to avoid any confrontations with the crowds," he says.

General Varga seems almost affronted. He lays a beefy hand on Orlov's shoulder. "That is the last thing anyone wants," he says, his awful breath accompanied by a patronizing grin.

Varga disappears and Orlov takes a coffee in an ornate china cup and saucer from a uniformed waiter. He glances around the room at the sweaty, eager throng of ministers and generals, all of them engaged in breathless chatter, and all of them prepared to stab his neighbor in the back for an extra crumb of power. Orlov does not belong in this place or with these people. He belongs in the market, sharing a cigarette with the greengrocer and the haberdasher. This thought causes him to scour the room for Citizen Galin, the private secretary. After completing a circuit of the room, being careful not to spill his coffee, Orlov finally spots Galin in a corner, deep in conversation with two ministers. He approaches the group and tries to catch Galin's eye.

The three keep talking for a painfully long time. Orlov smiles benevolently at no one in particular, sipping his coffee slowly and desperately searching for an opportunity to interject.

Eventually, Galin turns to Orlov and says, "Good morning, Minister. I trust you are well."

Now that the opportunity has presented itself, Orlov does not want it to go to waste.

He glances at the two ministers and then back at Galin before replying. "Perhaps we could talk privately for a moment."

Galin smiles at the two ministers, turns back to Orlov and guides him deftly into a quiet corner. "I am at your service, Minister," he says.

Only now it occurs to Orlov that he has no idea how to phrase what he wants to say. He sips his coffee to buy some time, then clears his throat, then sips more coffee.

Eventually, Orlov says, "Well, citizen, I have a question. I hope you don't mind."

"Not at all," says Galin.

Orlov continues. "Supposing a minister needed to leave his post—to resign, I mean to say—how would that normally be done, in terms of the protocol?"

Galin frowns. "I trust you are not planning to leave us so soon, Minister?"

"Well," says Orlov, "I do not believe I am the most qualified person for the position."

Galin shakes his head. "No one does, at first. But I am quite sure you will find, after a little time, that you have become a most effective minister."

The conversation is not going the way Orlov had intended. He tries again. "You are most kind. But I believe it would be better for me to return to fishmongering."

Galin nods, apparently undeterred. "It is quite natural to remember one's trade with fondness, after arriving in government service."

Orlov sighs. Just as he is about to reply, a waiter appears at the door ringing a small bell. Everyone in the room looks over at the waiter and stops talking momentarily.

Galin sets his own coffee cup down on a table and lays a friendly hand on Orlov's shoulder. "It appears the ceremony is about to start," he says, and promptly disappears into the hallway.

Frustrated at his failure to make any progress, Orlov finishes his coffee and determines to find Galin again as soon as the formalities are over.

The ceremony in the grand Throne Room is painfully formal but thankfully short. The archbishop—whom Orlov has never before seen in person—wears an enormous hat and reads from a dusty tome before placing the crown on the king's head. The king reads some words to the archbishop, and suddenly it's over.

Palace guardsmen appear from nowhere and begin to usher the ministers and generals out into the courtyard, where a long line of armored vehicles is waiting. Orlov searches again for Galin, but cannot see him. He finds himself being ushered outside with Boch, the Minister of Intelligence.

"Have you seen Galin?" asks Orlov, as they emerge into the courtyard.

"I have not," says Boch.

"I must speak to him again urgently," says Orlov.

Boch gestures to invite Orlov to climb into the armored vehicle first. "Please," he says. "No doubt you can speak to Citizen Galin after the procession."

"Yes, of course," says Orlov. "I'll speak to him after the procession."

Orlov and Boch squeeze into the windowless rear of the vehicle. At the front sit a driver and a second soldier gripping a long rifle between his knees. They sit for a long time in silence, waiting for the convoy to move out. The leading vehicle carrying the new king is larger than the rest, including an open roof through which His Majesty can stand and wave to the crowd. A gaggle of officials and generals has gathered around the royal vehicle and there appears to be a heated discussion.

"What is going on up ahead?" says Boch impatiently.

The driver turns to face the two ministers. "A disagreement, Minister," he says, in a matter-of-fact tone. "His Majesty objects to having two armed officers up on the roof with him while he is waving to the crowds; the general is insisting on it." He turns back to watch the altercation. "I believe His Majesty will be persuaded any moment now."

Sure enough, the gaggle disperses with two soldiers still on the roof, the iron gates to the courtyard swing open, and the convoy begins to roll slowly out into cobbled streets lined with excited, expectant, flag-waving citizens.

Orlov leans forward to peer out through the windshield. All he can see are the ruddy, delighted faces of men, women, and children cheering and singing patriotic songs with all their might. As the convoy passes, the crowds lean in closer, held back by a line of soldiers.

The convoy moves painfully slowly. After five minutes, it seems to Orlov that they are still in the middle of the government sector, and slowing down even further as the crowds press in around them.

Minister Boch appears agitated. He leans forward to speak to the driver.

"Sergeant," he says, but gets no further.

The sharp crack of gunfire rings out nearby. Boch leaps back in his seat. Orlov ducks.

The vehicle stops. The officer in the passenger seat shouts, "Down!" and raises his rifle.

Another crack of gunfire. Then several shots in quick succession.

The driver shouts, "Don't move!" at the two ministers, grabs a rifle, and exits the vehicle. The other soldier, unable to open his door because of the pressing crowd, follows his compatriot through the driver's door, rifle in hand.

Orlov and Boch stay low in the back seat, breathing heavily but saying nothing.

The sound of more gunshots is followed by angry shouts nearby.

Suddenly, the crowd surges against the vehicle, causing it to rock violently. Boch shouts something unintelligible. Orlov covers his head with his arms.

A second surge causes the vehicle to tip again, but this time it keeps tipping. Orlov is squashed into the side of the vehicle.

Slowly but surely, the vehicle tips onto its side with a disturbing crunch. Boch falls on top of Orlov.

Now the sound is deafening. Scores of feet are clattering over the vehicle.

If Orlov is not mistaken, the people are dancing.

CHAPTER TWO

In which our hero steps out into a new world

For an unidentified length of time, Minister Orlov cowers in the overturned vehicle, his eyes closed, and his arms wrapped protectively over his head. Minister Boch lies on top of him, breathing heavily but saying nothing. While this is most certainly uncomfortable—Boch being a heavy, muscular fellow—Orlov concludes that Boch is providing an additional layer of protection and consequently does not ask him to move.

The sound of heavy boots dancing on top of the vehicle eventually dies away, replaced by intermittent gunfire and indistinguishable shouts of either anger or celebration, perhaps both. It is not clear to Orlov whether these sounds are nearby or far away, but they have an eerie echo that suggests the crowds have dispersed.

Eventually, Orlov unwraps his arms from around his head and opens one eye. Through the inverted windshield, he can see only cobbles and—worryingly—the green boot of a palace guardsman, lying horizontally in the street. Given his restricted view, it is not clear to Orlov whether or not this boot has been separated from its owner.

Orlov coughs, his throat suddenly troubled by acrid smoke such as might be produced by a grenade. "What do you think is happening?" he whispers.

Boch groans and lifts his weight off Orlov, grabbing onto the front seat of the vehicle to pull himself clear. He peers through the windshield. "I imagine the situation is under control now," he says, with calm confidence.

"Are you sure?" says Orlov, his gaze fixed on the stationary boot.

"Only one way to find out," says Boch, almost breezily. He clambers into the front seat of the vehicle and reaches for the passenger door.

Orlov is alarmed. "Hold on," he says, urgently. "Anything could be happening out there."

Boch scoffs, pushes the door open, and stands up so that his head and torso are outside.

A single shot rings out; a deafening crack nearby. Orlov wraps his arms around his head again but keeps an eye open. Minister Boch slumps heavily onto the door frame with a sickening thud, his head and torso remaining outside. His legs and feet—still inside the vehicle—twitch violently before coming to rest in a lifeless dangle.

Orlov silently gulps air in an attempt to slow his breathing. Twisting himself in the back seat in order to free a leg, he gingerly pushes Boch's leg with his boot. There is no response and no resistance.

"Boch," whispers Orlov, and he kicks him again. Still no response.

Unless Orlov is very much mistaken, Minister Boch is dead.

Urgent thoughts of survival race through Orlov's head. Clearly, it is not yet safe to leave the vehicle. But he cannot stay here forever. How will he know when it is safe? Will someone try to enter the vehicle from outside? Can he remain undetected until dark?

With his arms still wrapped around his head, Orlov takes deep, silent breaths and listens intently for clues as to what is happening outside. He has not heard gunfire for a while, save for the single shot that spelled the end of Minister Boch.

Bursts of indistinguishable shouting sound out in the distance. Orlov focuses in an attempt to hear what is being said, but he is too far away. Given the unfortunate demise of Boch, he concludes that anyone out there issuing orders is more likely to be a revolutionary than a royalist. But which one is he? Orlov considers himself to be neither. He is still today, as he has always been, simply an honest, hard-working fishmonger attempting to play his part as a patriotic citizen. He does not want to belong to either camp. Moreover, he wishes there were no camps. But here we are. It seems his beloved country has finally arrived at the precipice long predicted by Citizen Vanev.

Someone outside appears to be organizing others into action. A group passes nearby and for the first time Orlov can hear what is being said.

"Quickly, quickly," says the first voice, agitated. "We don't have long."

"Are reinforcements on the way?" says someone else.

"Of course," says a third voice. "They'll be here in no time."

The conversation continues but dies away as the group walks past Orlov's vehicle and progresses in the direction of the palace. The third voice is familiar. Could this be Comrade Rozum, the former military officer and member of the Workers' Party who assisted Orlov in planting the disarmed bomb that was subsequently armed by Zelle and which killed the king? The former king, that is.

Orlov cannot be sure, but he would wager that this was, indeed, Rozum. Having said that, he currently has no one with whom to agree a wager. He is very much alone. He does not want to be discovered by the People's Party, or any other revolutionaries, given his formal position in the government. Neither does he want to be discovered by the authorities, for fear of what the police and military might now be planning and what he himself might be required to participate in, given that he has, to date, singularly failed to resign his position as Minister of Security.

Another hour or so passes, and then another. The voices he heard earlier do not return. Indeed, the commotion dies down to almost nothing, and an eerie silence hangs over the government sector. Given what he heard earlier, Orlov fully expects a wave of police or military to appear at any moment and sweep through the area but, hour after hour, no one arrives.

Orlov is still pondering how many hours of inactivity need to pass by before it is safe to move, when he notices through the windshield that the light is fading. He determines to wait for dusk, in the hope that it will provide sufficient protection such that he could make a move in the shadows. Once the scene through the windshield appears sufficiently dusky, Minister Orlov gingerly lifts himself from the back seat of the vehicle and clambers slowly into the front seat. From this position, he can see that the green boot outside is still connected to a palace guardsman who lies dead in the street.

Looking at the dead body of his former ministerial colleague, Orlov wonders if it might be possible to climb out of the vehicle while keeping his eyes closed, so as not to see the precise details of Boch's demise. One brief attempt at this approach causes him to hit his head hard against the door frame, and he abandons it.

Orlov opens his eyes and rises just far enough so that his head emerges outside. The scene is like nothing he has ever witnessed: bodies lie in the street, vehicles are overturned and smoldering, some government buildings are burning.

Since he can see no people nearby—no living people, at least—Orlov lifts himself slowly through the door, trying but failing to avoid touching the corpse of Minister Boch. He looks away quickly, but not before noticing that Boch suffered a single gunshot to the head.

Orlov climbs down from the vehicle and sits on the cobbles, cowering against the side of the vehicle to get his bearings. Only now he realizes that the convoy had progressed an even shorter distance than he had thought; he is, in fact, only just beyond the Ministries of Security and Intelligence. And his own Ministry of Security is on fire, smoke pouring from the second-floor windows above the grand entrance. There is no sign of anyone attempting to deal with the fire, military or otherwise. Orlov wonders if the building will be left to burn to the ground.

Still seeing not a living soul nearby, Orlov stands slowly and peers around above the overturned vehicle. To his horror, the palace is also burning, a curtain of fire cascading down from a higher floor into the cloisters below.

A terrible thought arrives in Orlov's brain: if there is no palace and no Ministry of Security, is there still a government? Is the new king still in charge? Why has the army not arrived already to fight these fires? Orlov is reminded of the terrible language Citizen Vanev has used for years to predict the coming of the revolution. Not for the first time, he must admit that his old friend might have been correct all along.

Minister Orlov determines that his only sensible course of action is to head toward home, staying in the shadows as far as possible and avoiding everyone. He stands and turns toward the bridge. Just as he is about to set off, he hears voices and sees a group of figures—perhaps with guns—running toward him from the bridge.

He briefly considers climbing back into the vehicle, decides against it, and ducks down, pressing his body into the filthy prop shaft which should, by rights, be underneath the vehicle but is now temporarily on the side. Orlov holds his breath as the group approaches him. They continue past him at speed, running fast and panting heavily. Their plain clothes suggest these are members of the People's Party, but Orlov does not recognize them.

Once the group is out of sight, Orlov stands again and, staying low, begins a careful dash between dead bodies and abandoned vehicles onto the bridge, across the river, and up the hill into the Grand Plaza. Here all is quiet, but Orlov notices something very strange: a group of men—he cannot see if they are uniformed or not—is working rapidly to build a wall of sandbags outside the entrance to Hotel Melikov. Another man is dragging a roll of barbed wire into position at the top of the steps.

Orlov stays in the shadows at the eastern edge of the plaza, moving as silently as he can past the entrance to the new Hotel Milekov, which sits in darkness.

Once he exits the Grand Plaza again, the scene returns to something approaching normal, except that the streets are deserted and the streetlamps are dark. He cuts down two side streets and breathes easier as he arrives at his apartment building. Unusually, the lobby is completely dark and, looking up, it appears this is true of the whole building.

Orlov decides that he does not object to the darkness, in all the circumstances, and stays close to the wall as he navigates his way up the stairs to his apartment. He dashes inside, locks the door, and then—without knowing why—makes a circuit of his home to ensure that all is as expected.

Once satisfied, he slumps into a chair by his kitchen window, which affords a partial view toward the government sector. Although it is now late in the day, several pillars of smoke are clearly visible. It seems that the palace and his own ministry are perhaps not the only official buildings on fire.

Although he has eaten nothing since the morning, Orlov finds that the shock of what he has just witnessed has suppressed his appetite. He puts the tea kettle on the stove and returns to the window. While waiting for the kettle to boil, he wonders what happens next. He is no expert in history, to be sure, but he does not believe his beloved nation has ever witnessed anything like this. He wonders who—if anyone—is in charge.

Orlov pours his tea and sits for a while watching the pillars of smoke swirl above the government sector. In all the circumstances, he determines to avoid both government officials and People's Party comrades for the foreseeable future. He does not want to be associated with either group. He is concerned for the safety of Citizen Vanev, naturally, but is unsure that it would be safe to be seen fraternizing with him. In any case, it seems unlikely that the market will open tomorrow, given the current state of affairs.

Minister Orlov—or perhaps he is now Citizen Orlov again—cannot remember feeling so isolated and confused ever before.

As he reaches the dregs of his tea, he remembers something significant: his neighbor at the end of the hall, Citizen Nowak, is the proud owner of a wireless radio, the first one in the building.

Orlov cautiously opens his front door and pokes his head out. There is no one around, and no noise save for distant sirens. He closes the door behind him and tiptoes to the end of the hall, where he knocks tentatively on Nowak's door. There is a long wait before the door opens slightly and someone peers out. But the someone is not Citizen Nowak; it is a much older man, another neighbor from downstairs whose name Orlov does not know. He waves Orlov inside urgently and closes the door behind him.

Orlov is greeted by a curious scene lit by candles: neighbors from perhaps half the building are huddled in Nowak's living room nursing glasses of slivovitz. In the center of the room, Nowak's wireless crackles loudly as it delivers an urgent, frantic news bulletin. The announcer's voice echoes curiously, as though he is broadcasting from a hole in the ground. Since his neighbors are all listening to the wireless with hushed reverence, Orlov says nothing and takes a seat on the floor under the window. Without speaking, Nowak pours a glass of slivovitz which is silently passed around the group until it reaches Orlov. He gratefully takes a swig and focuses on the news bulletin. For a moment the broadcast is lost in a storm of static, but soon it is audible again.

We must emphasize the seriousness of the situation that presents itself this evening. Citizens should not assume conditions will return to normal in the near future. Indeed, we must ask whether normality can even be identified, given the tragic events that have unfolded in the capital since this morning. Reports are now arriving to suggest that similar chaos is unfolding around the country. To answer the most urgent and pressing question, at the moment it is not clear who is in charge. The whereabouts of the new king are unknown. We have no firm evidence of any functioning government. We have attempted to contact government spokesmen, without success. Neither has it been possible to contact the leaders of the new People's Party. It may be some days before questions of governance can be answered, or perhaps even weeks.

The broadcast is interrupted by muffled noises, as though the announcer has smothered the microphone with his hands. A few seconds later, he speaks again.

We are being told the situation here is too dangerous to continue broadcasting. Apologies, citizens. We are being asked to move to a safer location. Please stay tuned in and we will resume our broadcast just as soon as we have moved our equipment to the new position.

There is another storm of static, and Citizen Nowak leans into the wireless to turn the volume down a little. He is careful to ensure that the sound is still audible, so that they will know when the broadcast resumes.

Most of the neighbors continue to look down into their slivovitz with concerned expressions. Nowak addresses Orlov.

"Welcome, Citizen Orlov," he says.

"Thank you," says Orlov, raising his glass in acknowledgement of his neighbor's kindness.

Nowak continues, "Just before you joined us, the announcer said the new restrictions that sparked the chaos during the parade could be placed squarely at the feet of the new Minister of Security, one Minister Orlov. I assume he is no relation of yours?"

There are a couple of grim half-laughs from other neighbors. Orlov looks slowly around the room to see everyone staring at him in expectation of an answer. He takes a sip of slivovitz to buy some time. Although it appears Nowak has no knowledge of his recent change in occupation, he has no way of knowing whether this applies to the rest of his neighbors. Prior to his surprising ascent to ministerial rank, Orlov never paid attention to the workings of the government; he hopes the same is true of the assembled company. He thinks carefully before speaking.

"In fact, my elderly mother is my only living relative," he says.

Nowak smiles. "Just as I thought."

Still casting his eyes around the room, Orlov senses that most of his neighbors are content with his answer. But a serious young man standing in the corner—a recent arrival on the top floor—eyes Orlov suspiciously. Orlov braces himself, believing the young man is about to speak, but they are interrupted by a loud crackle from the wireless, followed by the return of the announcer.

Citizens! We appreciate your patience as we relocated our equipment. We will endeavor to continue broadcasting from this location for as long as possible. We will remain on the air throughout tonight and into tomorrow, if it is safe to do so. Indeed, we aim to continue broadcasting uninterrupted until the situation becomes clear.

The broadcast is interrupted again briefly by muffled voices speaking urgently but unintelligibly.

Citizens! We are learning of another remarkable and unexpected development. On a day of shocking revelations, here is another. I have just been handed a report claiming that Prison Zhotrykaw is empty. That's right, citizens. It seems that, earlier this evening, the prison gates were flung open and every one of the hundreds of men and women incarcerated at Zhotrykaw have walked to their freedom. We don't know if those gates were opened by revolutionaries or whether, perhaps, prison officials simply deserted their posts. We will attempt to discover how this shocking development came about and provide confirmation in due course. For now, however, it appears that hundreds of convicted criminals have walked free.

The broadcast continues, but the assembled neighbors begin talking over it, obviously shocked by the latest news. All Orlov can think about is Agent Zelle and Citizen Molnar; as if things were not serious enough already, the two plotters responsible for the death of the old king are apparently free, and they will no doubt be well aware that Orlov was responsible for their incarceration. What is to stop them coming directly to find Orlov to exact their revenge? His mind spins with the confusing combination of threats and dangers. In his mind's eye he sees Zelle in her favorite disguise: a headscarf and dark glasses; a young woman attempting to appear older.

Nowak shakes his head. "Shocking," he says.

"Awful," says someone else.

"Unbelievable," agrees another neighbor.

Orlov's mind is still spinning so hard with thoughts about Zelle that he does not immediately notice what is happening in the corner of the room. While everyone else is focused on the news about

Prison Zhotrykaw, the serious young man has bent down into his satchel and produced a copy of *The Sentinel*. By the time Orlov notices him, the man is holding out the front page of the newspaper for everyone to see.

Even in the flickering candle light, it is clear that the two large photographs filling half the page are of Ministers Orlov and Boch. The caption beneath the photographs reads *New Ministers of Security and Intelligence Appointed.*

Now the serious young man speaks for the first time. "This is the Minister of Security, right here in this room," he says, with venom.

Unsure what to say, Orlov stands abruptly.

Nowak gasps. "What?" he says.

"That's him," barks someone else.

Orlov holds up both hands. "Now, look here," he begins, but is interrupted by the serious young man lunging forward toward Orlov. Nowak stands and intercepts him.

"Citizens!" snaps someone else.

The young man dodges Nowak and attempts to lay his hands on Orlov.

Orlov darts toward the door, but is grabbed by another neighbor he doesn't know. Orlov breaks free and lurches through the door. Nowak shouts something unintelligible. In the hallway, Orlov looks back to see the young man and two other neighbors pursuing him. He rushes to his own front door, but fumbles for his key and realizes the group is about to catch him.

"Stop," cries the young man.

Fearing for his life, Orlov abandons his attempt to open his door and instead darts down the stairs, out through the lobby and into the darkened street. Only once around the next corner does he pause to look back. The three attackers emerge into the street and split up. Orlov turns and dashes around another corner and into the Grand Plaza.

Marching swiftly along the eastern edge of the square, Orlov hears the footsteps of one of the pursuers behind him. He stays in the shadow of the buildings and hurries in the direction of the river. The earlier activity outside Hotel Melikov is no more; the square is empty and quiet.

As he reaches the new Hotel Milekov, it's clear that the pursuer is gaining on him. Orlov looks at the hotel entrance and notices that the doors are unfinished, without handles or locks. With a brief glance behind, he dashes up the steps of the hotel and—placing his hand into the hole where the new handle will sit—he pulls the door open just a few inches, ducks inside, and pushes the door closed again. He holds his breath and looks out through the hole; his pursuer runs past in the direction of the river.

Orlov stays behind the door for some time, watching through the hole to ensure that none of his neighbors are nearby. Once satisfied he has not been spotted, he turns into the cold, dark building.

The hotel smells of sawdust and glue. Although illuminated only by moonlight through the front windows, it's clear that this is still a building site: he sees no furniture and no carpets. As Orlov creeps along, his heavy boots sound out too loudly on the bare wooden floors, sending echoes around the empty halls. He climbs the central staircase, exploring each level. On the top floor, he finds a huge, splendid room with large windows looking down onto the square. No doubt this will in due course be the most coveted and expensive room the new hotel has to offer.

Orlov begins to feel weary and senses that the safest option might be to spend the night here in the new hotel. He prefers the room with views down onto the square and across to Hotel Melikov, but it is completely bare. He makes another circuit of the top floor, hoping to find a bed, but it becomes clear that none of the furniture has arrived yet. In a smaller bedroom nearby he finds a stash of decorator's equipment: a ladder, pots of paint, brushes, and several heavy tarpaulins. With some considerable effort, he drags the tarpaulins into the bedroom at the front of the hotel and makes a makeshift bed under the window. His bed smells strongly of paint, but it is preferable to the bare floorboards.

Exhausted after a long and confusing day, Citizen Orlov lies on his tarpaulin bed, looks up at the stars, and tries to make sense of his new situation. He may or may not still be a member of the government, officially speaking, but he has no idea where any of his colleagues are, and the government sector is still smoldering. He is most certainly not welcome in the revolutionary movement—including the People's Party—and that animosity apparently now extends to his own neighbors. Even worse than that, it seems that Prison Zhotrykaw is empty, meaning that Agent Zelle and Citizen Molnar are now free to exact revenge on him for tricking them into confessing to their part in the assassination of the former king.

Although this city has been Orlov's home for the whole of his adult life, he has never felt more alone.

CHAPTER THREE

In which our hero renews some acquaintances

In the early hours of the morning, Citizen Orlov is woken by voices outside. He sits up sharply and is initially confused about where he is, before remembering that he had made a makeshift bed on the top floor of the future Hotel Milekov. His pocket watch tells him it is a little after three o'clock in the morning. Sleepily, he pulls himself up to the window and peers out.

There is frenetic activity in the Grand Plaza. Two military vehicles have parked near Hotel Melikov and people are now disembarking from the vehicles urgently while hissing to each other in fervent whispers. It takes a while for Orlov's sleepy eyes to adjust to what he is seeing. After a few seconds, it becomes clear that some of the people are palace guardsmen, rifles by their sides, organizing the disembarkation. But—to Orlov's great surprise—those disembarking are, for the most part, nuns. Not just a few nuns, but fully twenty-five or thirty nuns, dressed head to toe in matching habits.

The scene is surprising to Orlov because there is, to his knowledge, only one religious order in the entire nation: the Sisters of

Our Lady of Perpetual Sorrow Convent of Mount Zhotrykaw. The convent is well known by all citizens for two reasons. Firstly, it occupies the highest inhabited location in the whole nation, clinging precariously to a rocky outcrop on the eastern face of the mountain, high above the prison. Secondly, the sisters are almost never seen in person, for the good reason that the convent is not served by a road. The final stretch of the journey is a dangerous one, possible only on foot, and for that reason the sisters rarely receive visitors, nor are they ever seen in the city (their supplies being delivered to a small hut at the end of the steep, winding mountain pass that peters out some several hundred feet below the convent).

Orlov does not remember seeing any of the sisters in person before. And now—unless Hotel Melikov is hosting an international convention of nuns, which seems rather unlikely—most or perhaps all of the Sisters of Our Lady of Perpetual Sorrow have arrived in the capital. Why?

He watches as the soldiers escort the nuns from the vehicles and march them up the steps of the hotel, rolling back the temporary barbed wire fence and slowly swinging open the wide doors. Once all the nuns are inside, the doors are closed again and the barbed wire is replaced, several armed guardsmen remaining at the top of the steps, where they stand to attention. With that, all is quiet.

Orlov lies back on his bed and wonders what it all means.

HE IS NEXT awoken by footsteps and whispering. His pocket watch tells him it is almost six o'clock. He sits up and looks out at the Grand Plaza, which stands quiet and undisturbed. The sounds are coming from inside the hotel. Orlov covers himself completely in the tarpaulin and listens intently. Several voices can be heard, now more loudly, perhaps on a lower floor, the sound carrying up the grand central staircase. The frantic shuffling of feet on dusty floorboards is interspersed with urgent whispers, as though someone is issuing orders. Eventually, the shuffling stops when a door is closed. The voices continue but are now muffled.

Confident that his unwelcome visitors are on a lower floor, Orlov emerges quietly from his tarpaulin and tiptoes to the staircase. Checking the cavernous stairwell, he sees no one, but the voices are now a little clearer, emanating either from the floor below or the one below that. He presses his body into the wall—to reduce the chances of being seen in the stairwell—and treads slowly and quietly down to the lower floor. Sensing that the voices are still below him, he continues down another floor and stops.

On this floor, a grand ballroom stands centrally, with sweeping double doors opening onto the staircase. The doors are closed, but it's clear that the visitors are in the ballroom, now speaking more openly, as though they have grown confident of not being overheard.

Orlov stands for a while, holding onto the wooden banister, wondering what to do. He could sneak down the stairs and go home, but is it safe to do so? He has no reason to assume that the anger of his neighbors has subsided. He could go to the market, but there would almost certainly be no traders and no customers, given that the security situation is still uncertain and everyone seems to be in hiding. He cannot go to the Ministry of Security, since the government sector is a smoldering ruin.

While pondering these terrible options, Orlov senses that at least one of the voices drifting from the ballroom is familiar; it is Citizen Vanev.

Orlov feels as though he is paralyzed. He grips the banister tighter as though this might assist in clarifying his choices. He forces himself to think. There is no doubt that some in the People's Party—perhaps most—want him dead. By that measure, he should avoid them at all costs, even more than he wants to avoid his neighbors and his fellow ministers. But there is perhaps only one person in the whole nation whom he trusts at this moment, and that person is in this ballroom.

Citizen Orlov straightens his jacket, takes a deep breath, and opens the door.

Initially, Orlov sees no one. The cavernous ballroom is dark, and the central dance floor stands empty. It takes him a second to realize that the inhabitants—a dozen people or so—are huddled together around the window to his left.

At the sound of the door opening, someone at the back of the group swivels around, draws a pistol expertly from his belt, and points it at Orlov's head. Orlov raises his hands. The rest of the group turn to see who has entered.

"Don't move," hisses the gunman.

"Steady," says Vanev, and he steps in front of him, placing his considerable bulk between Orlov and the gun. "Calm, please." He raises both hands to warn his comrades against reacting.

Only now Orlov sees that the man pointing a gun at his head is Comrade Weisz, the former soldier who once tried to drop him into one of Mount Zhotrykaw's infamous ravines, before being laid out by a ferocious right hook from Vanev. "He's one of them," says Weisz. "Let's kill him."

"Better still, capture him," says someone else.

Vanev pushes Weisz's pistol down until it points at the floor. "No," he whispers, "Comrade Orlov might be just the person we need."

"He's no comrade," hisses Weisz, still gripping his pistol.

Vanev keeps his hand on the gun.

"He's a government minister," says someone else.

"There is no government," says Vanev, sharply, and he beckons Orlov to join them at the window.

Orlov waits until Weisz's pistol is back in his belt before approaching cautiously. In the light of the window, in addition to Vanev and Weisz, he recognizes Comrade Nemeth, another former member of the People's Front. The others are presumably comrades in the People's Party who were formerly members of the Workers' Party.

Weisz bristles and moves away from Orlov. Vanev greets his old friend with a warm handshake. "I was worried about you," he says.

"Likewise," says Orlov.

"I told you this day would come," says Vanev. Orlov is well aware of this and does not wish to get into a conversation about it. He says nothing and Vanev continues, "Look, here."

Vanev maneuvers Orlov into the middle of the group so that he can see through the window. Now Orlov, along with everyone else, is looking out across the Grand Plaza at Hotel Melikov, opposite. All is dark and quiet in the square. The front of the hotel is still protected by sandbags, rolls of barbed wire, and four soldiers standing to attention.

"What?" says Orlov.

"This is where they're hiding," says Vanev.

"Who?" says Orlov.

"Your cronies," says someone.

Vanev interjects. "What's left of our wretched former government is holed up over there."

"With the nuns?" says Orlov.

"Nuns?" says Vanev.

Everyone turns to look at Orlov.

"At three this morning," he says, "two trucks arrived, full of nuns. They all went into the hotel."

Vanev looks puzzled. "Interesting," he says. Then, as if jolted into life by an idea, he whispers, "Comrades. This way. Step away from the window, please. We need to talk."

The group moves into a huddle in the middle of the ballroom. Orlov stays close to Vanev and keeps an eye on Weisz.

Vanev addresses the group. "Comrades, I believe the unexpected arrival of Comrade Orlov gives us just the advantage we need. We cannot take Hotel Melikov by force, at least not without considerable reinforcements from outside the city. We can return to that issue in due course. The immediate issue is that we are still in need of information. What better way to find it out than to send in a member of the government to join his colleagues?"

Orlov looks at Vanev and then at the group. His heart sinks into his stomach. What is Vanev talking about? The others nod sagely. "Information?" says Orlov.

Someone says, in a matter-of-fact tone, "We need to know if the king is still alive."

"And where he is," says someone else.

Vanev turns to Orlov. "What do you say, comrade?"

Now the whole group looks at Orlov expectantly. He feels his face flush. "I don't believe I understand what you are asking."

Vanev lays a hand on Orlov's shoulder. If this is intended to be reassuring, it fails. "We cannot plan the next step of our operation until we know who exactly is inside the hotel," says Vanev. "Most importantly, we need to know if the king and any members of his family made it out alive and are hiding out over there. We know some generals and government ministers are in there. We need to know if the king is with them, or if they have spirited him away somewhere."

The whole group stares at Orlov, waiting expectantly for his reply. He has the horrible sense of having walked into a situation from which he now wishes he could retreat again. He wants to rewind the last few minutes, until the moment when he was standing by the staircase deciding whether to enter the ballroom. He could then decide against it, tiptoe outside and then attempt to go home, or attempt to take a train to his mother's house. He wonders if trains are running at the moment. In any case, it is too late, since—on hearing Vanev's voice—he foolishly decided to step into the ballroom, and now he is knee-deep in a situation that he doesn't fully understand and from which he can see no escape.

"But," Orlov says, falteringly, "I'm not a member of your party."

Nemeth jumps in assertively. "You are, comrade."

Orlov thinks back to the ravine on Mount Zhotrykaw, where he would certainly have met his death had Vanev not intervened. He had assumed that an attempted execution was, in effect, an expulsion from the party. But, since he survived the ordeal, Nemeth must be right: he still is, in fact, a member of the People's Party. He decides to change tack in terms of his argument.

"Well," says Orlov, "as Comrade Vanev says, there is no government any more. I was the acting Minister of Security only, and only for one week. I was fully intending to offer my resignation yesterday but, well, the king was hardly in a position to take a meeting."

"So, you know what happened to him," says a comrade, aggressively.

"I have no idea," says Orlov. "I'm simply saying that my plans to offer my resignation to His Majesty after the coronation were," he waves his hand in the direction of the smoldering government sector, "overtaken by events."

Someone spits onto the ground. "Don't use those words here," he says, and it takes Orlov a second to realize that he is complaining about the phrase *His Majesty*.

Vanev ignores this and speaks to Orlov. "But now you are here and—since you can still claim to be the Minister of Security—you are the only member of our company with any chance of walking into Hotel Melikov alive."

The eyes of the whole group are still on Orlov. There are murmurs of agreement with Vanev's contention. The assembled company, even including Weisz, seems to be warming to the idea that Orlov should present himself at the hotel opposite. He needs to think quickly of a reason why this plan will not work.

"But what use is it if I go over there," says Orlov, "if I can't get out again? If I present myself as the Minister of Security seeking shelter with his colleagues, they might force me to stay there for days or even weeks. Perhaps I might learn all sorts of information regarding the royal family and so on, but I will have no way to pass it to you."

Orlov is pleased with this argument, but Vanev appears unperturbed. "Exactly," he says. "Which is why you will need to leave again this evening. It need not be for long. You just need to present a reason for leaving—on your own, not accompanied—and then walk around to the alley behind this hotel. Our comrades are down there right now building a bunker in the kitchen and servants' quarters. That is where you will find us. You can deliver the information and then you will be free to go."

"You will let me leave?" asks Orlov.

"You will have done your part for our movement," says Vanev, "and you would be free to leave or to stay with us and continue the fight."

"I have no idea how I will persuade the generals to let me leave the hotel," complains Orlov.

Vanev ignores this. "Let's vote on it," he says. "Those in favor?"

A chorus of *ayes* rings around the group.

"Against?" says Vanev.

Sheepishly and slowly, Orlov raises his hand.

"You have to say *nay*," says someone.

"Nay," says Orlov.

Vanev quickly scours the group. "The ayes have it," he says.

CHAPTER FOUR

In which our hero embarks on a dangerous mission

By seven o'clock in the morning, Orlov is stepping out of the kitchen of the future Hotel Milekov into the narrow rear alley, having tidied up his appearance to the best of his ability in the bathroom of the servants' quarters. A People's Party comrade moves the hastily assembled barbed wire to let him through. Other comrades are working in the alley, stacking sandbags against the hotel wall.

Citizen Vanev stands by the back door. "Be careful, comrade," he says, "and whatever else you do, come back here this evening."

Orlov looks back at him, a grim expression on his face. Not able to think of anything to say, he gives a brief wave and turns along the alley.

As soon as he is out of Vanev's sight, it occurs to Orlov that he could now simply walk away from this whole affair. He does not want to be a member of the People's Party or the government. He wants only to be a fishmonger. He longs for the situation in the country to return to normal, and then his own life will return to normal, too.

He will be able to leave both these organizations that have snared him on false pretenses and return to the good old days, when his only concerns were the health of his mother and the weather (a constant preoccupation for those who make their living standing out in the Grand Plaza all day with only a simple market stall for shelter). However, he still has nowhere else to go; nowhere safe at least. He has no way to contact his mother and no way to know whether trains are running. Even the walk to the railway station could be a life and death affair.

By the time he reaches the end of the alley and is preparing to take a left turn into the Grand Plaza, Citizen Orlov reaches a surprising conclusion: the least terrible option open to him is to go along with Vanev's scheme. If he can discover the fate of the king and deliver that news to the People's Party, perhaps that will hasten the end of the revolution and the start of whatever happens next. Orlov would much prefer to be associated with neither side in this conflict, but if he can make some small contribution to encourage the return of peace, well, that is what any patriotic citizen would do.

Before he emerges into the square, Orlov straightens what remains of his hair and attempts to look ministerial. As expected, he catches the attention of the guards almost immediately. All four of them train their rifles on him. Orlov stops and raises his hands. He is only a few steps from the east side of the plaza.

"Who goes there?" calls the soldier nearest to the entrance of Hotel Melikov.

"Orlov, Minister of Security," calls Orlov.

"Sshhhh!" calls another soldier.

"Quiet!" calls the first soldier.

Orlov remains in his place with his hands raised. "You asked me a question," he says, a little softer.

Now the first soldier speaks in a stage whisper that is barely audible. "Step into the middle of the square," he says.

Unsure whether he has heard this correctly, and not wanting to be shot for disobeying orders, Orlov decides it might be wise to clarify the order before moving. “I can’t hear you.”

“Sshhhh!” repeats the other soldier.

The first soldier repeats the order a fraction more loudly. “Step into the middle of the square.”

Keeping his hands firmly aloft, Orlov walks slowly until he is right in the midpoint of the Grand Plaza. For just a second, he looks across at the cathedral and, behind it, the snow-capped peak of Mount Zhotrykaw. This is a scene he has admired many times over the years, most often from the fish stall or while taking his daily constitutional. Never has he admired this view in such peculiar circumstances, with the square almost empty, smoke rising above the government sector, and most citizens in hiding for fear of their lives. Only now it occurs to Orlov that he is standing right in the middle of his nation’s history, a situation he did not ask for and is not enjoying.

“Don’t move,” barks the first soldier, before moving across to consult his colleague, who has produced a document of some kind from his pocket. The other two soldiers keep their rifles trained on Orlov. After a few seconds, the first soldier speaks again. “Orlov, you say?”

“Yes, Orlov. Minister of Security.”

They confer again, before the soldier says, “You’re not on the list.”

“What list?” says Orlov.

There is a pause before the other soldier says, “It’s confidential.”

Unsure what to say, Orlov says nothing. The first soldier speaks again. “It says Minister Zelle is the Minister of Security.”

Orlov rolls his eyes but keeps his hands up. “Until a week ago. Then I took over.”

“A week ago?”

“Yes.”

The soldiers confer again. Orlov is wondering how long he will be required to stand in the middle of the square with his hands up when, to his surprise, the door of Hotel Melikov opens slightly and a tall man in a suit marches out. He ignores the soldiers and approaches Orlov, his hand outstretched. It is Citizen Galin.

"Good morning, Minister," he says. "My apologies."

Orlov drops his hands in order to shake. "Good morning, Citizen."

"Quickly, let's go inside," says Galin, glancing around the square. He guides Orlov toward the hotel with a hand on his shoulder.

As they walk, Orlov is reminded that he expected his next conversation with Galin to be another attempt to resign, but that plan has been overtaken by events. Instead, he sees an opportunity for a natural, reasonable question which could garner the information he needs right at the beginning of this strange assignment. "How is His Majesty?" he says.

"Not here," says Galin. "I will arrange a briefing for you inside."

The soldiers return to their places and salute as the two officials pass them.

Galin ushers Orlov into the lobby of the hotel. A soldier stationed in the lobby closes the door behind them and locks it.

As Galin marches him across the grand lobby, Orlov takes the opportunity to survey the scene. Perhaps a dozen soldiers are working in the lobby, some standing guard and others piling up sandbags against the inside of the windows. Another soldier is guarding the elevators. Two generals march across the lobby as though on an urgent mission. Orlov sees only two uniformed hotel staff, standing behind the reception desk and gaping wide-eyed at the veritable hive of military activity going on around them.

They turn off the lobby and into a familiar space: the ballroom where Agent Zelle performed as Mata Hari on the night before the National Day disaster, when the unarmed bomb planted by Orlov and Rozum was subsequently armed by the zealots, killing the former king and two of his generals.

The ballroom is buzzing with activity. Perhaps forty or fifty people are engaged in urgent business, huddled in whispered conversations or hunched over maps spread across long dining tables. The atmosphere here reminds Orlov of the military bases he passed through during national service. Most of the people are in military uniforms, but he also spots a few civilians and, in the corner, two nuns whispering to each other across a small card table.

Galin marches to a table overflowing with papers, behind which is seated a distinguished, middle-aged gentleman in an expensive suit with a floral tie and matching pocket square. He is ensconced in paperwork, so Galin coughs. The man stands.

"Citizen Bastarache," says Galin, "we have a new arrival. May I introduce you to Minister Orlov? Minister Orlov, the owner of Hotel Melikov, Citizen Bastarache."

Bastarache extends his hand. "Minister, a pleasure to meet you." He has a foreign accent that Orlov does not recognize.

Orlov shakes. "The pleasure is mine, Citizen."

"My apologies for the mess," he says, indicating the piles of papers. "My office is temporarily a bedroom for three of the sisters from the convent."

"I see," says Orlov. He sees an opportunity to find out what the nuns are doing here, but Galin speaks first.

"Might it be possible to find a room for the minister?"

Bastarache smiles at Orlov with the expression of someone who loves nothing more than solving problems. "I will ask the staff to look into it right away. We are technically full already but"—he waves a hand theatrically—"I daresay we can work some magic."

"Thank you," says Orlov, only now realizing that, despite the strange circumstances, at least tonight he might have a real bed; a welcome alternative to paint-stained tarpaulins spread on a hard floor. Then he remembers that he has to find out what has happened to the king, find an excuse to leave the hotel on his own, and then return again, all by this evening.

"If you will excuse us," Galin says to Bastarache, and he indicates to Orlov that they are to proceed to the back of the room.

Galin leads the way to a familiar stage door and into the backstage room where Orlov met Zelle on the evening before National Day. This little room is full of cigar smoke.

At a small table sit three generals and two ministers (whom Orlov has met but whose names he cannot remember), hunched over some papers. As they enter, the papers are hastily tidied into a pile and turned face down.

"Ministers, generals, we have a new arrival. I'm pleased to report that Minister Orlov has found his way here safely."

The five men at the table stand and shake Orlov's hand politely, but their unenthusiastic grunts suggest they do not know who Orlov is or did not care about his survival. Once the shaking is completed, however, one of the generals appears to think of something.

"Minister Orlov," he says, "were you not accompanying Minister Boch during the coronation procession?"

"I was," says Orlov.

"And are you aware of his whereabouts?"

Orlov looks momentarily at his shoes and then back at the general. "I'm sorry to say he was shot on leaving our vehicle."

"Were you able to provide assistance?"

"He was killed instantly," says Orlov.

The general's grim but stoic expression suggests he has received news of this type on too many occasions. "I see," he says. "I see."

Galin finds a chair for Orlov and invites him to join the meeting. They all sit.

One of the generals speaks first. "So, Minister Orlov, what intelligence do you have for us from the field?"

Orlov is unsure how to answer this. "I'm afraid I know very little," he says. "I spent the whole of yesterday just trying to avoid the fate of Minister Boch. It wasn't even safe for me to return home."

"So, where did you spend the night?" asks another general.

Now Orlov wishes he had not mentioned this and racks his brain for an answer that is both plausible and safe. "I was forced to take shelter in an abandoned building," he says, hoping that is the end of the matter.

But the general continues, "And where was this, Minister?"

Orlov waves his hand vaguely in the direction of the government sector. "Near the railway station," he says.

This seems to pique the general's interest even further. "And it was safe? We believe the revolutionaries are controlling everything from the palace down to the station."

"Well," says Orlov, wishing he had chosen a different location for his story, "it was certainly dangerous outside. There was chaos everywhere. But once I had locked myself inside the building, I didn't see any more of the"—he hesitates—"revolutionaries."

The general still appears unsatisfied and Orlov is concerned he is going to ask about this further, when they are interrupted by the loud arrival of General Varga accompanied by another minister. They march in from the ballroom, pull up chairs, and join the meeting.

Varga sits next to Orlov and slaps him on the back, a little too hard. "Welcome, Minister," he says, "good to see you are not dead. What news of Boch?"

Orlov explains the story again and Varga grunts a noise that sounds closer to disappointment than sorrow.

"A damn shame," says Varga, shaking his head.

"Yes," says Orlov. "Very sad."

General Varga appears to shake this news off as he peers at his colleagues around the table. His gaze fixes on one of the other generals sitting opposite.

"What news on ammunition?" says Varga, suddenly.

The other general glances at Galin, who shuffles in his chair before replying to Varga. "Well, General, if I may speak frankly."

Varga cuts him off. "Don't sugar coat it."

"The situation is already critical," says Galin.

"Meaning?"

"Meaning another day or two at most before we need new shipments."

Varga stands up in his place and then, apparently not knowing why, sits down again. He sighs heavily. "We can't win a war without bullets," he spits.

"No, indeed, General," says Galin.

"Can't we make the factory work faster? What is that place called?"

"Machak's Munitions," says Galin.

"Yes, Machak's," says Varga. "I trust they are working overtime."

"Machak's is closed," says the other general.

"On account of the war," says Galin.

"Someone has contacted Machak and told him to open again, I'm sure," says Varga, sounding unsure.

"Citizen Machak has fled the country," says the other general.

"On account of the war," says Galin.

Varga's face is flushing with color. "What about the stockpile? We have a stockpile, do we not?"

Galin, apparently reluctant to answer, glances at the other general, who says, "We did. But, when our warehouse is full, Machak's is permitted to make private sales."

Varga stands and begins to pace around the gathering. "And do we know who they've been selling to?" He waves his hands frantically to prevent anyone from offering an answer. "No. Let me guess. They've been selling to the People's Front and the Workers' Party and now the People's Party."

Galin answers in a whisper. "Yes, General."

Varga continues to pace. "So, what you're telling me is, the government was just brought to its knees by a bunch of hairy revolutionaries using weapons and ammunition that we manufactured and that we sold to them?"

No one wants to answer this. Eventually, Galin says, "Yes, General."

"Is someone looking for imported shipments?"

"Our best people are working on it right now," says Galin.

Varga runs both hands down his face and sits back in his place. "Let's move on," he says. "Intelligence. What do we know?"

Now another general—a thin, stern fellow—chimes in for the first time. "The picture is confused. We have some ideas on when the revolutionaries will make a move, and where, but hard intelligence is difficult to obtain."

Varga is still agitated. "If we can't discover what these socialists are planning, they will control the whole nation by the end of the week."

There is a brief pause, then Citizen Galin appears to think of something. "Well, generals," he says, "if I might be so bold, I believe the arrival of Minister Orlov presents an opportunity." He turns to Orlov. "With your permission, Minister."

It becomes apparent that Galin expects Orlov to speak, but Orlov has no idea where the conversation is going. He knows only that he does not like the sound of it. Unsure what to say, he says nothing, and simply holds out his hand, palm up, to invite Galin to continue.

Galin leans into the table and continues in a conspiratorial whisper. "Minister Orlov here has experience with these revolutionaries. Prior to joining the government, he worked as an asset to expose the People's Front. Is that not so, Minister?"

Now Orlov likes the direction of this conversation even less, but he cannot deny it. "It is," he says.

Galin continues, "So, given the lack of intelligence—and the unfortunate demise of our Minister of Intelligence—here is an alternative plan." He sits back.

This piques the interest of those around the table. One of the other generals addresses Orlov. "Did anyone see you arrive here this morning, Minister?"

Still unsure what precisely is being proposed, nevertheless Orlov feels confident that it would be safer to say that no one was aware of his arrival at the hotel. "Indeed, not, General," he says. "I was very careful to move here from my hideout without being observed. For my own safety, of course."

General Varga chimes in. "And how did you know that we had chosen Hotel Melikov for our temporary headquarters?"

Orlov did not expect this question and must think quickly. "Well, I did not know for certain. But there are only a few venues in the capital large enough for such an operation and—when I saw some of our brave soldiers guarding the hotel—I felt it was my duty to present myself."

There are nods of approval around the table in response to this answer.

One of the ministers speaks for the first time, addressing Galin. "So, what exactly is the plan?"

Galin glances at Orlov and then back at the group. "Here is my suggestion, for your consideration, ministers. Since Minister Orlov has connections with certain individuals in the People's Party, he contacts them immediately and declares that he wants to join their struggle. He will then be invited to their hideout, no doubt, or at the very least will begin to learn of their plans, and then he can return here to share the intelligence with us. If the conflict drags on for some time, we will set up a safe system for Minister Orlov to visit us here as often as necessary—perhaps via the rear entrance—or otherwise to send messages."

Galin sits back, waiting for a reaction to his plan. The generals and ministers are pondering it. Now that Orlov has heard the plan spelled out, he feels the need to put an end to this idea before it takes hold. He must think quickly of a reason why it cannot work.

"Well, if I may comment," says Orlov, smiling at Galin before turning back to the group, "Citizen Galin's suggestion is interesting, but it has a serious flaw. Although I have been Minister of Security for only one week, nevertheless this fact is well known to certain senior members of the People's Party. I cannot simply present myself to them now as an ordinary citizen wanting to join their movement, when they see me as a member of the government they are seeking to overthrow." Confident that he has dealt the idea a fatal blow, he sits back in his chair.

One of the other ministers chimes in immediately, holding out both his palms to emphasize the simplicity of his point. "There is no government," he says, with a smile. "As of yesterday, the government has fallen and the country is in a state of civil war. All previous allegiances are history. Whether we like it or not, we are all ordinary citizens, starting today."

Someone else agrees. "Yes, yes. Galin's idea might just work. In the circumstances, Minister Orlov simply needs to tell the revolutionaries that he no longer feels any allegiance to the fallen government."

It occurs to Orlov that this is, in fact, an accurate summary of his actual feelings on the matter. In this company, he cannot say so, of course. Unsure what to say, he hesitates.

Before he has the chance to speak again, the idea appears to catch on with the whole group. They nod sagely and congratulate Galin on his ingenuity.

The conversation around the table continues in an animated fashion, the ministers and generals warming to the idea and discussing the advantage that an insider will give them, especially if the conflict is extended. In those circumstances, a trusted intelligence source could be the difference between victory and defeat.

Orlov's attention wanders; he is reminded of his first day at the Ministry of Security, when he stumbled by mistake into a briefing of new recruits addressed by Agent Zelle. He was fascinated by her stories of life in the field. And one of those stories now comes back to him in some detail. Zelle talked about staying alert to the risk of *double agents*, a term he had not heard—or at least not understood—before that day. She said that assets recruited by the ministry to collect information on radical groups sometimes became sympathetic to those groups and might be persuaded by them to collect intelligence on the government, while maintaining the pretense of working for them. In the worst cases, such deceptions had continued for months or years before being discovered.

Only now, Orlov realizes the full implications of what is happening to him. In the span of one morning, he has been recruited by the revolutionaries to spy on the rump government in hiding, and he has been recruited by the government to spy on the revolutionaries. The whole business is so perplexing that Orlov feels a headache developing. His attention returns to the group only when General Varga slaps him on the back again.

"Well, ordinary citizen Orlov," says the general. "Time to get to work. You have some intelligence to collect."

PART TWO

The Fishmonger As Double Agent

CHAPTER FIVE

In which our hero investigates

Citizen Orlov spends the rest of the morning trying to discover if the king is still alive and, if so, where he is. His attempt to gather this information directly from the members of the government currently residing at Hotel Melikov is scuppered when General Varga—having encouraged Orlov to set out immediately in search of intelligence on the People's Party—breaks up the meeting and ejects the civilian ministers so that the generals can discuss urgently whatever it is that generals discuss during a revolution. As the civilian ministers disperse, Orlov attempts to engage a rather odd fellow in thick spectacles who reveals only that he is the Minister of Works, without sharing his name or making eye contact.

"I do hope His Majesty is well," says Orlov, as they walk from the ballroom into the lobby. "Are you aware of his whereabouts?"

"Don't ask me; no one tells me anything," says the Minister of Works curtly, before scuttling away into the labyrinthine hallways of the hotel.

Since Citizen Galin has stayed in the backstage room for the meeting of generals, Orlov has no one else to ask about the fate of the king—or indeed the presence of the Sisters of Our Lady of Perpetual Sorrow—and so he determines to explore the hotel instead. After all, it seems possible that His Majesty is alive and well and simply hiding out within these very walls until the situation becomes calmer. If so, then it is likely there will be some secrecy surrounding his living quarters; a possibility that might best be tested simply by wandering innocently until one is prevented from doing so.

In terms of the amenities inside Hotel Melikov, Orlov is familiar only with the ballroom and the Royal Room (where he had dinner with Zelle and Molnar the night they confessed to arming the bomb that killed the previous king). As he begins to wander the rest of the hotel, he is impressed with the size and grandeur of the establishment, far more expansive and opulent than he had expected. At its center is an ornate staircase, lavishly carpeted, that opens out from both the left and right onto a mezzanine floor housing a long dining room and a lounge with a cocktail bar, both of which look out onto the Grand Plaza. From there, the staircase spirals upwards to seven floors of guest rooms, each of them a veritable rabbit warren of nooks, crannies, and unexpected turns. On one floor he finds a day room with informal chairs where a group of well-dressed guests are huddled around a wireless, listening to reports of the security situation; on another floor he finds an upright piano being played surprisingly well by two small children; on yet another floor he finds a games room—complete with a billiards table—which has been commandeered by members of the palace guard apparently engaged in a briefing of some kind.

Orlov is the target of a ferocious stare from the officer guarding the door and so he moves on at speed along the hallway. For a moment, he considers pointing out to this soldier that he is the Minister of Security and would like to be briefed on what precisely the palace guard is planning, but thinks better of it. Based on his rather confusing entry into the hotel this morning, the armed forces are not intimately familiar with the names and faces of government ministers, and he does not care to get into another conversation in which he is required to explain who he is.

As he wanders, aside from the aromas of thick carpet and polished wood, Orlov is struck most by the strange contrast between the smoldering chaos outside and the relative calm inside these walls. Certainly, the presence of countless military officers gives the hotel an odd atmosphere, as though things might escalate at any moment, but for now the civilian guests seem to be taking their luxurious incarceration with good humor. There are, to be sure, worse places one could be holed up while waiting for a revolution to pass by.

This raises a question in the mind of our hero: what, exactly, is the point of being well dressed and well presented during a revolution? Not surprisingly—given its opulence and prices—Hotel Melikov attracts only the most upper class and wealthy guests from home and abroad.

In normal times, one would certainly expect the patrons of this establishment, and their children, to be seen in immaculate, formal attire at all times. Indeed, during their many years running the only fish stall in the market, Citizens Orlov and Vanev have often fancied they can predict which visitors to the Grand Plaza are guests of Hotel Melikov simply by observing their clothes and mannerisms. Were one to be rounded up and threatened by armed revolutionaries, however, would an upper-class appearance not be a disadvantage? It might be better to be mistaken for an ordinary, working man. And yet, on the second day of the revolution, the civilian guests of the hotel act as though nothing has happened.

Perhaps they feel that maintaining their standards somehow prolongs the status quo; a way of avoiding the inevitable truth that the nation is in chaos.

Orlov reaches the fifth floor before noticing that he has so far seen only one or two nuns. Since no one is permitted to enter or leave the hotel without the express permission of the military, there must be quite a gathering of nuns somewhere, perhaps toward the top floors.

Stepping onto the staircase that will take him from the fifth floor to the sixth, Orlov has a thought; two related thoughts, in fact. Firstly, if one were to hide a monarch for reasons of safety in a large hotel, perhaps the best location would be on the highest floor, where the guest of honor would be farthest from any dangers that might encroach from outside. Secondly, if the arrival of an entire convent of nuns is related to the revolution, and not simply coincidental, perhaps the reason for their presence in the capital has something to do with the safety of the king. Why the monarch might need nuns to protect him, however, versus members of the armed forces, remains something of a mystery.

Finding nothing out of the ordinary on the sixth floor, Orlov steps onto the final staircase that will take him up to the seventh floor. Immediately, he notices something different and interesting. At the top of the staircase sit two nuns at a small desk; one is white-haired and distinguished, the other is young and pale. The younger sister is working in a ledger of some kind, but closes it briskly as Orlov climbs the stairs. By the time he reaches the top, he sees two palace guardsmen, each stationed at an ornate archway, the entrances to the north and south wings. Both are standing to attention and looking impassively at nothing in particular. It seems clear that Orlov will not be free to wander the seventh floor as he has wandered the other floors, so—now breathing a little heavily—he presents himself politely at the desk.

"Good morning, sisters," says Orlov. "I trust you are well." He exhales before continuing. "Forgive me while I catch my breath."

"Good morning, may we help you?" says the older sister.

"My name is Orlov, Minister of Security. I arrived at the hotel this morning. I'm waiting for a room to be allocated and thought I would take a walk around the hotel. The situation outside is not suitable for my daily constitutional."

"Indeed not," says the sister. She continues to look up at Orlov, but says nothing further.

He wonders how best to draw her into a conversation. "I trust you and the other sisters are keeping well."

"Quite well, in the circumstances," she says, with a polite but forced smile.

"It must be rather trying for you all, to be down here in the city while the security situation is so difficult."

"Yes," she says.

"I imagine you are looking forward to returning to the convent in due course."

This time, the nun's smile slips, as though the question is too pointed. "May we assist you with something, Minister?"

"I was wondering if there is any news of His Majesty," says Orlov. "I am hoping he is safe and well."

The sister glances at one of the soldiers on guard and then back at Orlov. "I dare say we should be asking you about that, since you are a minister of the government."

Orlov had not anticipated this answer and is momentarily flustered. "Yes, I see. In fact, I arrived only this morning after a very difficult day and I'm afraid I have not yet heard the latest news."

"I think yesterday was rather a difficult day for everyone," says the sister.

Before Orlov can reply, the younger nun speaks for the first time. "Did you say Orlov?"

"Yes, Minister Orlov."

She opens the ledger, traces her finger carefully along a page that Orlov can't see clearly, then closes the ledger and looks up at him again. "Sister Zelda would like to see you." Unsure what to make of this, Orlov says nothing and the nun continues, "She said to let her know if you were to arrive. And here you are."

"Here I am," says Orlov, intrigued.

"One moment, please," says the younger nun. She marches over to the soldier guarding the north wing and whispers in his ear. He nods. The nun turns to Orlov and says, "This way, please."

In the few seconds it takes Orlov to follow the nun through the archway to the north wing, his mind returns to the instructions from Citizen Vanev and his comrades at the People's Front: by the time he goes back to Hotel Milekov this evening, Orlov needs to know both the condition and the location of the monarch. He has no idea who Sister Zelda is or why any of the Sisters of Our Lady of Perpetual Sorrow would want to speak to him, but he senses that something is afoot up here on the seventh floor, and so the chance to speak to one of the sisters can only be a good thing.

The younger nun leads him in a brisk walk to the very end of the north wing and stops outside a door marked *Suite Krupnik.*

She turns to Orlov. "Please wait here just one moment, minister." And with that she steps inside.

While waiting, Orlov wonders if this suite is named after the same Citizen Krupnik who founded the glass works. Krupnik is well known in the city as a wealthy industrialist, and so it seems possible that he might be the sort of person whose name is attached to a suite on the top floor of the city's grandest hotel. This is only a guess, however, since Orlov is merely a fishmonger and so not well acquainted with such matters.

The nun returns, holds the door, and opens it a little wider. "Please," she says, indicating that Orlov should step inside.

"Thank you," says Orlov, stepping through the door.

The nun closes the door behind them. "Go right ahead," she says.

This suite is by far the most palatial hotel room Orlov has ever seen. He follows a short entrance corridor into a beautifully appointed sitting room with three armchairs and patio doors opening onto a balcony with a spectacular view of the Grand Plaza. On the left, a sliding door—presumably leading to a bedroom—is closed.

"Please, take a seat," says the nun. "Sister Zelda will be with you shortly."

Orlov sits in an armchair. He expects the young nun to leave, but she sits down in one of the other armchairs, resting her hands peacefully in her lap.

They sit for a few moments, smiling vaguely past each other. Orlov wonders what role Sister Zelda plays at the convent, and why she wants to speak to him. Given the splendid suite, she must be a very senior nun indeed, perhaps even the mother superior. He considers asking the young nun about this, but thinks better of it when he hears a shuffling noise from next door. However, the noise does not immediately lead to the door opening, and so Orlov and the young nun are left sitting patiently for a few moments longer.

The nun smiles at him reassuringly. "Not long now," she says.

Orlov smiles back. While they continue to wait, he wonders if Sister Zelda might be sufficiently senior to have information regarding the king. Perhaps she is the person mentioned by Citizen Galin when he said he would arrange for Orlov to receive a briefing on the wellbeing of His Majesty.

To be sure, it would be a little strange for a government minister to be briefed on such matters by a nun—even a mother superior—when one might expect such information to be passed on by a general or a senior official. But these are strange times and it's possible that the government-in-hiding finds it necessary to resort to unusual measures in order to survive. In any case, he feels honored to have been invited to meet a nun as senior as Sister Zelda. If it turns out that she wants to discuss a matter other than the fate of His

Majesty, no doubt Orlov will have the opportunity to ask her about this before he leaves.

The sliding door is flung open. Orlov looks up to see a most unexpected sight. Just a few feet away stands a nun in full habit holding a pistol. The pistol is pointed at his head.

Instinctively, Orlov raises his hands.

Only now he focuses on the face under the veil, staring at him with steely anger.

It is Agent Zelle.

CHAPTER SIX

In which our hero finds himself in mortal danger

Before Orlov has time to move or speak, Agent Zelle flings a short rope to the young nun with her free hand and says, "Thank you, Sister Agnes," all the while keeping her gaze and her gun firmly trained on Orlov.

With surprising dexterity, Sister Agnes leaps up, catches the rope, swivels around behind Orlov, pulls his hands down from their raised position, and ties them behind his back, all before he has managed to speak.

She drags him up off the chair and pushes him hard, face first, into the wall. To protect his nose, Orlov turns his head to the left, affording him a clear view of the Grand Plaza through the plate glass patio doors.

Sister Agnes has a surprisingly firm grip and only now he wonders if she is, in fact, a real nun after all. Perhaps Agnes, like Zelle, is simply wearing a habit as a disguise. If so, who is she?

Orlov begins to say, "Sisters, please," but Zelle is on him in a flash, pushing the barrel of the pistol into his cheek.

"Quiet," she hisses, then opens the patio door with her free hand. She steps onto the balcony and waves the gun to indicate that Agnes should follow suit.

Sister Agnes, still exerting a muscular grip on Orlov, pushes him through the door, across the balcony, and onto the decorative railing so hard that he doubles over the railing at the waist, his head now pointing down toward the cobbles of the Grand Plaza many stories below. He grunts and tries to press his toes into the balcony floor, but it's clear that one firm thrust from Agnes would send him tumbling to his death. He has no doubt she has the strength to accomplish this at any moment of her choosing. He continues struggling to improve his position, until he sees that Zelle's pistol is still trained on him.

The square is empty, aside from the soldiers guarding the front of the hotel, and quiet apart from birdsong. The soldiers down below appear blissfully unaware of what is going on far above their heads.

Still pointing her pistol at Orlov, Zelle says, "So, Citizen, what brings you to the hotel this morning?"

Orlov is unsure that he can talk in this position, given that his stomach is squashed into the top railing. If Zelle wants a conversation, perhaps he can use this to buy himself permission to at least stand up straight. "I can't breathe," he says.

"So be it," says Zelle.

Orlov waits for Zelle to say something else, but she continues to stand dead still, pointing the pistol at him.

When it becomes apparent that she is not going to let him stand up, Orlov continues in strained tones. "I heard ministers were gathering here."

"So, just doing your patriotic duty?" barks Zelle.

"Yes."

"And how do you like being Minister of Security?"

Orlov has no idea what to make of this question. "You would still have the job, if you hadn't killed the king."

Zelle pushes the barrel of the pistol into this side. "Do you want to take the express route into the square, Citizen?"

"It's the truth," says Orlov. "I heard ministers were gathering here. I'm still a minister."

"And where did you hear this?"

Orlov thinks quickly. "From one of the other ministers. Boch."

She snarls. "You heard it from a dead man?'

"Before he died," says Orlov, now genuinely struggling for breath.

Zelle pushes the barrel harder into his side. "Spare me your lies. You were sent by Volf. Or Vanev."

"You know I'm not one of them."

"And yet you're here to spy for them."

"No!" he shouts.

There is a stirring from the soldiers on guard down below.

"Stand him up," barks Zelle to Sister Agnes.

Agnes pulls Orlov's head back up and allows him to stand up straight, still pushing him against the railing. Orlov estimates that—from this standing position—he could probably resist any attempt from Sister Agnes to push him over the edge. But that does him no good, of course, if Agent Zelle decides to shoot him.

Zelle continues, "I don't have time for games. I know they sent you."

"How do you know?" says Orlov, more sharply than he had intended.

He assumes she is simply making an educated guess. But, to his surprise, she answers the question. "We have friends everywhere."

Orlov has no idea what to make of this. If the government already has an informant inside the People's Party—someone who is somehow able to pass intelligence to them at short notice—why are they insisting that he takes on precisely this role?

"I don't believe you," says Orlov, boldly.

"You don't believe me," says Zelle.

"If you have someone in the People's Party, why did General Varga just recruit me?" says Orlov.

Keeping her pistol firmly trained on Orlov, Zelle turns to one side and spits on the balcony floor with surprising venom. "Do you think I share my assets with Varga? That old fool can scarcely tie his own shoes without being briefed by a room full of colonels."

Not for the first time, Orlov wishes he understood more about the murky workings of the government. Is it possible that some government officials are benefiting from information passed on by a mole in the People's Party while other officials are not even aware of the mole's existence? If so, why is Zelle still receiving this information? She was—as far as he knows—in prison until yesterday. He is befuddled about Zelle's intentions and urgently feels the need to clarify them to avoid being shot or dropped from the balcony to a painful end on the cobbles of the Grand Plaza.

"So, do you want me to follow his instructions or not?"

"I don't care about that," says Zelle, as though this should be obvious. "Follow away. If Varga wants you to bring intelligence on the People's Party, I suggest you do it."

Orlov glances down at the pistol and back at Zelle. "So, why am I here?"

Zelle rolls her eyes and looks at Agnes before replying. "You're here because I'm going to tell you exactly what to say to Volf and Vanev. Being a double agent can be, shall we say, taxing. I'm going to make it a little simpler for you." She smiles.

"So," says Orlov, "you're doing me a favor."

"Exactly," says Zelle. "Now, be quiet and listen." She glances at Agnes, who tightens her grip on Orlov. Zelle continues, "Volf wants to know the fate of the king. You will tell him that the king has been taken to safety over the border. He will ask which border; you will say you don't know. He will ask when this happened; you will say last night. By the time you arrived at the hotel this morning, His Majesty had already been moved to safety. You have that on good authority. Tell him you heard it directly from the mouth of Varga, if you like. He will ask if you have any details of the operation: who accompanied the king, what was the mode of transport, was the king disguised, and so on. You will say it was strictly a military operation only; civilian ministers were briefed by Varga this morning on the success of the operation but—to protect the king's safety—the details are known only by those military officers who were involved. Is that clear?"

As far as Orlov is concerned, this is anything but clear. "So, is it true? The king is safe?"

"Wrong question," says Zelle. "You are concerned only with delivering the right message. If you fail to do so, Sister Agnes and I will hear about it, we will track you down, and we will kill you."

This reminds Orlov there is something else he doesn't understand. "What if Volf asks about," he gestures to their gray habits, "what the nuns are doing here?"

This time, Sister Agnes answers. "Tell him the convent was overrun by prisoners escaping from Zhotrykaw. Our food was stolen and some of us were beaten. So, we fled down here."

Orlov looks at Agnes, shocked. "That's terrible," he says. "I'm sorry to hear it."

Zelle glances at Agnes and back at Orlov. "Citizen, are you absolutely clear on what you will say to Comrades Volf and Vanev?"

"Very clear," says Orlov.

"I hope so," says Zelle. "Your life depends on it."

CHAPTER SEVEN

In which our hero delivers a message

By late afternoon, Citizen Orlov has been allocated a corner room overlooking the Grand Plaza, at the end of the south wing, on the second floor. It occurs to him that this is about as far from Zelle's suite as it's possible to be. There is clearly something going on up on the seventh floor. He wonders if someone is deliberately keeping him away from it. He also wonders if someone has been moved out of this room hastily to make way for him. He searches for evidence of a recent inhabitant, but finds none; the room is spotlessly clean.

On the other hand, the hotel was supposed to be full, and so he is grateful for a comfortable room with a good view of the square. He sits at the window for a while, looking for any signs of life at Hotel Milekov, opposite. He sees nothing to indicate that anyone is over there. No doubt the leaders of the People's Party are capable of lying low and avoiding detection.

Orlov eats his dinner alone in the dining room on the mezzanine floor, arriving as soon as it opens. Initially, the only other diners are a dozen or so members of the palace guard, who were lined up at the door of the dining room before it opened. They keep to themselves and speak in low whispers over a dinner of sausages and cabbage. Slowly, the dining room begins to fill up with civilian guests, but the atmosphere remains muted and strange. The civilians give a wide berth to the military diners, sitting in small family huddles and glancing nervously about them. Orlov notices that, aside from the palace guardsmen and himself, most guests stay away from tables by the windows overlooking the Grand Plaza. Perhaps they are concerned about the risk of a bomb or an attack of another kind and have concluded that the doors and windows at the front of the hotel are to be avoided.

That is a logical conclusion. The Minister of Security, however, has some additional information not available to the other diners. He knows that the leadership of the People's Party is pondering its next move and is waiting for news about the king. He knows that the military is seeking intelligence on the whereabouts of revolutionary leadership. He believes there will be no further hostilities for the rest of today. Tonight will also probably be a peaceful one for guests of the hotel.

As he eats, Orlov looks around at the dining room full of nervous, well-dressed patrons, picking at their sausages and cabbage without enthusiasm. At one table, a young child has become tearful and is being comforted by her mother. At another table nearby, a father struggles to prevent his two young sons from rushing over to the windows to look for military activity. At a third table, a small girl whines to her parents about how long they will be trapped at the hotel and whether it will be safe to travel home again.

Orlov feels terrible. He wishes he could speak to these parents to allay their fears, but he cannot see any opportunity to do so, given the presence of so many palace guardsmen. Anything he says in their presence could easily get back to a general, with potentially difficult consequences. He makes a mental note to check if the palace guard falls under the command of General Varga.

Just before he finishes his food, an opportunity unexpectedly presents itself. In a matter of seconds, the palace guardsmen stand, push their chairs under their tables, and disappear through the door in silence. The dining room is now occupied only by civilian guests. The mood remains tense and somber.

Orlov looks down at his plate and wonders whether what he has in mind is the right thing to do. It is difficult to know. All he knows is that he has an opportunity to make some fellow citizen feels a little safer. Before he has time to ponder this question any further, he lays his knife and fork down on his plate and stands up in his place.

"Ladies and gentlemen," he says, falteringly.

There is no response from his fellow diners. Perhaps he is speaking too quietly.

Orlov coughs and speaks more loudly. "Ladies and gentlemen, my apologies for disturbing your dinner."

Some of the nearest diners now look up at him. But—not being the tallest person in the kingdom—it seems that those on the far side of the dining room have not noticed him. Gingerly, he climbs up onto his chair and tries again.

"I am Minister Orlov, Minister of Security." This time, most of the diners look up. He continues, "Please don't let me stop you from enjoying your dinner. Well, if I may say so, it seems that many of you might not be enjoying your dinner very much, which is understandable, in the circumstances. If you don't mind, I have a few brief comments that I think might be of some comfort to you and your children." He waits for a response but, seeing none, decides to continue. "Please be assured that there is unlikely to be any further fighting near this hotel for the rest of the day. Tonight will also be peaceful, I believe. In fact, I think it will most likely be tomorrow before we hear any more bombs or gunfire."

He pauses. A young girl begins to wail loudly. Her mother shakes her head at Orlov, picks up the girl, and carries her briskly out of the dining room.

Orlov feels the need to repair his remarks. "Please don't be alarmed, citizens," he says. "The point I'm trying to make is: enjoy your dinner. I can't promise that there won't be more hostilities in the vicinity of the hotel in the next few days. But today and tonight I believe will be peaceful. I thought you should know. Perhaps that information will improve your evening."

A senior gentleman on a nearby table speaks up. "The hotel will be attacked tomorrow? Is that supposed to make us feel better?"

"No, no," says Orlov. "We will not necessarily be attacked tomorrow. I'm just saying that, well, the war might have a few more days to run. Unless they run out of ammunition, of course. That is a possibility, so I've heard. In that case, it might all be over rather quickly. Let's all hope for that shall we?"

A younger man sitting alone chimes in. He has a rather aggressive tone. "What about hand-to-hand combat?"

Orlov is not sure what to make of this question and is still considering his response when a woman speaks up. "Aren't you the fishmonger?"

Relieved at the interruption, Orlov turns to face the woman. "Yes, in fact I am. Twenty years and counting. Right here in the square." He smiles and points in the direction of the fish stall.

The woman frowns. "What does a fishmonger know about the war?"

Her husband joins in, disdain in his voice.

"I hope we're not relying on fishmongers to defeat these revolutionaries. We need serious military people who are experienced in warfare."

Orlov raises both hands. "Yes, naturally, I am not in charge of the army." He is about to say something reassuring about the experience of the senior generals but is interrupted by several diners talking over each other.

"I'm not wagering any money on fishmongers to win the war," says someone, laughing at his own joke.

"When precisely tomorrow will the hotel be attacked?" says someone else.

This causes a ripple of concerned grunts around the room. "Don't we have a right to know?" says another man, desperation in his voice.

Sensing the conversation is getting away from him, Orlov feels the need to bring things to a swift conclusion. "Sorry, ladies and gentlemen," he says, "that's all I can say."

But the diners are no longer listening to him. Several are still speaking over one another. Some parents stand up, apparently agitated, telling their children to finish their food in a hurry.

"No time for dessert," says a distressed mother to her children. "There's going to be a bomb."

"That's not what I said," says Orlov, but the woman is not listening.

Realizing reluctantly that the situation is irreparable, Orlov heads for the door. "I hope you have a pleasant evening," he says, breathlessly, to no one in particular.

He ducks through the door, closes it behind him, takes a deep breath, and marches as quickly as he is able down the stairs and through the lobby, concluding that his impromptu speech to fellow citizens was perhaps not a good idea.

Arriving in the ballroom, Citizen Orlov asks for a private audience with Citizen Galin. They sit at a small card table. Orlov desperately wants to tender his resignation but knows in the circumstances that he cannot. Instead, he explains that he would like permission to leave the hotel that very evening, because of a possible gathering of the People's Party leadership. This is his first opportunity to gather the information that General Varga is looking for regarding their plans and whereabouts.

"And how did you learn of this gathering?" asks Galin.

Orlov had anticipated this question and has an answer prepared. "I don't know for certain that it's happening," says Orlov, earnestly. "But, when I joined the People's Front as an asset, they would often discuss plans for emergency situations; where they would gather in the event that Tavern Kreminic was no longer safe, and so on."

Galin sits back in his chair. "If you know their location this evening, Minister, you must share it and we can send in a unit to end this conflict right here and now."

Orlov does not like the sound of this. For one thing, it would represent a direct threat to his old friend, Citizen Vanev. What's more, he will be in no position to deliver Zelle's murky messages about the king—on which his own safety now depends—if the People's Party is attacked or otherwise scattered to unknown locations. He must deflect Galin from this line of thinking.

"I don't know for certain where they are," says Orlov, gravely. "I doubt very much they are all together. That would be madness," he adds for emphasis, rather pleased with the logic of this point. "But I believe I can have a conversation that will deliver the sort of intelligence the general is seeking."

Galin leans into the table, conspiratorially. "You're planning to speak to Citizen Vanev, your fellow fishmonger, I suppose."

Orlov shrugs, pleased to be forced to admit this plausible plan which is true, in a sense, but far removed from what he actually has in mind. He decides to be a little coy in terms of his answer. "Let's just say," he says, pretending to consider something, "let's just say that I believe I can manufacture a useful conversation with one or two old friends this evening, and be back here with the information by the early hours, provided that I am allowed to leave and enter freely, without interference."

"Yes, I see," says Galin.

For the sake of clarity, Orlov adds, "And I must not be followed."

"You have my word," says Galin.

He begins to stand when Orlov realizes this is an opportunity to get an answer to the most pressing issue of the day. "Before you go," says Orlov, glancing around them before continuing, "I trust His Majesty is safe and well."

Galin's face remains blank, suggesting he is well practiced in the art of giving nothing away. "If I might say so, Minister, for your safety it is best that such information be restricted to the smallest number of people possible."

"Not including the Minister of Security?" says Orlov.

Galin stands up to leave and rests a hand on Orlov's shoulder. "The situation will be made clear to all ministers, as soon as circumstances allow it."

AT NINE O'CLOCK in the evening precisely, Orlov presents himself to the soldiers guarding the front doors of the hotel. The senior officer on duty explains that he has been briefed on the situation and will ensure that the minister is admitted again on his return. He offers an armed escort, which Orlov politely declines, explaining without elaboration that he must attend his appointment alone.

"Be careful, Minister," says the officer; as the doors swing open, the barbed wire is rolled back, and Orlov marches briskly down the steps. The sun has long since set and the Grand Plaza is empty, dark, and cool. Orlov decides that he should not walk directly across the square to Hotel Milekov, and so devises a deliberately convoluted route, just in case the soldiers (or, more likely, Galin or Varga) are watching him. He turns left and then left again into Grunplatz, walking for a while away from his destination until he reaches the butcher's shop. Then he ducks into a backstreet and takes another right turn so that he is north of the Grand Plaza and is able to navigate his way east of the square away from the prying eyes of anyone watching from the windows of Hotel Melikov. He sees no one en route until he takes a right into the dank alley that runs behind the buildings forming the eastern edge of the square, including the new Hotel Milekov. The wall of sandbags having been completed, two armed comrades whom Orlov does not recognize hover nervously outside.

"Who goes there?" whispers one of them, waving his rifle in a manner that suggests he is not trained in its proper use.

Orlov raises his hands. "Comrade Orlov. Here to see Comrade Vanev. He is expecting me."

"Don't move," he says, as his compatriot ducks inside the kitchen at the rear of the hotel.

Orlov stays still, his hands raised, listening to the sounds of a city on edge. Normally at this time of the evening one could hear music and drinking from hotels and taverns, and people hurrying across the Grand Plaza on the way to a restaurant or theater. But tonight there is almost silence, punctuated only by an occasional siren or sporadic gunfire in the distance.

Eventually, the other guard returns, nods to his comrade, and they stand aside to allow Orlov to step into the kitchen, where Vanev is waiting for him eagerly, hopping from foot to foot as though in a hurry.

"Good to see you, Comrade," says Vanev, holding out a cigarette by way of a greeting.

Orlov sees an opportunity to raise the two issues at the front of his mind. Firstly, he needs to let Vanev know that he is once again under duress from Agent Zelle and will be delivering a message from her (which may or may not be true) on pain of death. Secondly, he needs to warn Vanev of the possibility of a mole in the People's

Party who is providing information to Zelle and perhaps to other current or former members of the government.

Orlov accepts the cigarette. "Comrade, can we speak in private for a moment?"

Vanev slaps him on the shoulder as if to propel him along faster. "No time," he says. "Comrade Volf just arrived. The whole leadership is here. They are waiting eagerly for your report."

Orlov is disappointed, but he has in any case decided to deliver the message to the whole group as prescribed by Zelle. He will need to ensure that he has a private conversation with Vanev before he leaves Hotel Milekov to return to Hotel Melikov.

Vanev whisks him into a cramped room next to the kitchen. In the absence of furniture, a dozen or so members of the ruling council of the People's Party stand in an awkward huddle. Orlov is relieved to see no sign of Weisz or Nemeth; the meeting is limited to the senior office holders, most of whom are former members of the Workers' Party, with the exception of Comrade Sandor, a kindly, professorial fellow who was head of policy in the People's Front and was elected to the same role in the new party. They are smoking heavily and whispering expectantly to each other as Orlov enters. He joins the huddle next to Vanev before Comrade Volf calls the meeting to order.

Volf is even more gaunt and bedraggled than normal, his formal suit looking thoroughly out of place under a long, unkempt beard. "Comrades," he wheezes, "I hereby declare an emergency session of the Ruling Council. Do we have a motion, please?"

"So moved," says Vanev.

"Second," says someone else.

The energy around the group settles and Volf continues, "I hereby declare we are quorate insofar as the surviving members of the Ruling Council. A moment's silence, please, for Comrade Cech. He worked tirelessly for our glorious republican movement, and ultimately gave his life for it yesterday." He looks down at his shoes; everyone else follows suit. After a few moments, Volf continues. "Thank you. We will elect a new membership secretary via the normal process in due course. For now, we have more urgent matters to deal with. Firstly, let me say a few words about Comrade Orlov here." Orlov holds his breath, having no idea what to expect. "Comrade Orlov and I have had our differences in the past, regarding his ties to the government. However, myself and others owe him a debt of gratitude regarding our release from Prison Zhotrykaw. So, when Comrade Vanev told me that Comrade Orlov had been appointed Minister of Security on false pretenses by the wretched zealots, and that he is prepared to use that temporary position to bring us intelligence, I was prepared to accept the offer. Are there any objections to that?" Seeing no objections, Volf continues, turning to Orlov. "Good. Comrade Orlov, please tell us what you can about the state of the government, and in particular the king."

Orlov glances around the room to see a dozen expectant faces awaiting his report. He takes a deep breath and begins. The conversation goes very much as Zelle predicted it would. The council members want to know where the king was taken, when, and by whom. Orlov delivers the answers exactly in line with Zelle's instructions. They also want to know who exactly is holed up at Hotel Melikov and what they are doing. Orlov describes the situation honestly, including the fact that the civilian ministers are not aware of everything the generals are planning. Volf also asks about the Sisters of Our Lady of Perpetual Sorrow; truthfully, Orlov explains that he had asked one of the sisters and shares the answer he was given. The council members nod sagely, displaying some sympathy with the plight of the nuns. Someone mutters that such things are an inevitable consequence of war.

Comrade Volf breaks in abruptly. "Comrade Orlov, we are grateful to you for taking the risk to come here and bring this valuable intelligence. Please keep yourself safe and communicate with Comrade Vanev if you discover anything additional which could be helpful to our cause."

It becomes apparent that Orlov is now expected to leave. He steps back, but says, "If I could have a word with Comrade Vanev privately, please."

Comrade Volf squashes this suggestion instantly. "We are in session. Members of the Ruling Council are not permitted to leave for side discussions. If you have something additional, Comrade, let the whole council hear it."

All the members look at Orlov expectantly. He glances at Vanev and back at the group. His mind goes blank. He must explain the truth to Vanev, but he has no idea how or when to achieve that. He decides it would be best to return to this problem tomorrow. "Nothing additional, Comrade," says Orlov, and he begins to leave the room.

When Orlov reaches the door, another member says to Volf, "Should we not provide a warning, Comrade?"

Orlov stops at the door and turns back to look at Volf.

"Very well," says Volf, turning to Orlov. "Comrade Orlov, this information is for your ears only, no one else. We are expecting reinforcements to arrive soon. Hotel Melikov will become a very dangerous place. You would be wise to be somewhere else."

CHAPTER EIGHT

In which our hero sets out on a journey

For his late-night walk from Hotel Milekov to Hotel Melikov, Citizen Orlov has every intention to use the precise reverse of the circuitous route he took earlier in the evening, when a thought occurs to him. As he leaves the dark alley to turn left into the Grand Plaza, he need only shuffle a short distance along two backstreets to reach his own apartment block. This thought fills him with another pang about when life will return to normal. For a moment, he wonders if he should simply return home and pretend the revolution is not happening. After all, there are plenty of angry and passionate participants on both sides who will continue to fight about their differences whether Orlov is involved or not. Both sides have recruited him to spy on the other, but if he were to disappear until all this is over, they would simply find someone else. On the other hand, Galin and Varga expect him to return to deliver his report on the People's Party; it would look very suspicious if he went to speak to them for the first time since receiving his commission and then failed to return. And he must remember the hostility from his neighbors as recently as yesterday, which might take some time to subside.

By way of a compromise, Orlov decides to return to Hotel Melikov via a brief visit to his apartment. It will settle his nerves to do what he normally does at this time in the evening: he will make tea and sit by the window. As long as he can avoid his neighbors, it should be perfectly safe. He will then return to the hotel as expected to ensure he remains in good standing with what remains of the government.

Pleased with this compromise, he ducks into a familiar backstreet and then another. As he rounds the corner, he decides to pause and check that his neighbors are not in sight before approaching the apartment block. From the cover of the building opposite, he stops and peeks carefully around the corner. Things are very much not as expected.

The entrance to the lobby of his apartment building is piled with sandbags. Next to the pile of sandbags sits one of his neighbors—a heavy, bearded fellow with a history of military service—a long rifle between his knees. Worse still, Orlov's own apartment window is broken, shards of glass and other debris scattered across the sidewalk beneath it.

Orlov ducks back behind the building opposite, now breathing heavily. He quickly revises his plan to visit his apartment. Whatever his neighbors are doing, he wants no part of it. He wonders what state his apartment is in, and whether his own possessions are amongst the debris lying in the street. He needs to postpone these questions until a later date.

Rather than dwell on the state of his apartment, Orlov retraces his steps to the Grand Plaza, marches across the square, and presents himself to the soldiers on guard. They now recognize him, usher him into the lobby, and instruct him that he is expected urgently in the ballroom.

Galin and Varga are waiting at a central table, with a handful of other generals and ministers. The ballroom is otherwise empty. Orlov joins them and takes a seat.

"We are pleased to see you return safely, Minister," says Varga, without conviction.

"What news of the People's Party?" says Galin.

Orlov takes a deep breath. "I had a brief conversation with an old friend," he says, glancing at Galin, to give him the false impression—without saying so—that he has spoken privately to Vanev. "The leadership of the party is scattered in safe houses across the city." Orlov is pleased with this lie, which sounds plausible. "Some of their number were killed in the fighting yesterday. The survivors are determined to fight on. They are currently depleted, in terms of armed men able to fight, and are awaiting reinforcements from outside the city. We can expect those fighters to be put to work immediately, although they were not, of course, prepared to share their precise plans with me." In the hope that that is sufficient information, Orlov stops talking and sits back in his chair.

"Do they know we are here at Hotel Melikov?" asks one of the generals.

Orlov should have anticipated this question, but did not. He thinks quickly. "It was not mentioned to me. I do not believe they are aware that the government has gathered in one place."

"Where did you meet this contact?" asks Varga.

"At a neutral location," says Orlov.

The general continues, "And where did he believe you were coming from?"

"I told him that I had just come from home," says Orlov. "But we could not meet there because my neighbors have set up a round-the-clock guard to prevent strangers from entering the building." He is pleased with this lie, because the last part is apparently true.

"Is Volf still alive?" asks Galin, pointedly.

Orlov hesitates. "I believe so. My contact said they have taken some losses, but would not reveal the names. I expect he would have specified it, if any of the senior leadership had been killed."

Apparently satisfied, Galin glances around the table and back at Orlov. "Thank you, Minister. We appreciate you bringing us this intelligence. Perhaps you will be able to speak to this contact again?"

"At a time agreed by us," interjects Varga.

"Of course," says Orlov.

Lying on his bed in his corner room on the second floor, Orlov goes through both conversations in his head: what he said at Hotel Milekov and then what he said here at Hotel Melikov. He works through which parts were true and which parts were lies. The business of being a double agent is exhausting. He falls asleep worrying about whether he is passing this strange test and wondering what exactly the People's Party is planning. He cannot afford to stay in the hotel, given Volf's warning. He must invent another reason to leave, perhaps an urgent opportunity to collect more intelligence about the movements of the revolutionaries. It is not clear to him how he might have discovered this new opportunity; he will need to invent a plausible reason.

ORLOV IS WOKEN in the middle of the night by a sharp knocking at his door. "Minister, my apologies. Your presence is required urgently, please." The voice is gruff and insistent.

His pocket watch tells him it is almost three o'clock in the morning. Still half asleep, Orlov opens the door of his room to find a tall officer of the palace guard looking agitated. The officer is holding a bundle of clothes which he thrusts toward Orlov.

"Please dress in these, Minister," he barks. "And shave."

"You're asking me to shave?" says Orlov.

"Yes, Minister," says the officer, "and then present yourself in the ballroom. You have five minutes."

Orlov takes the clothes, hesitantly. "What's going on?"

"All ministers are to dress in these clothes, and must be shaven. Those are my orders." With that, the officer marches away.

Orlov closes the door, spreads the clothes on his bed, and turns on a lamp. Only now, he realizes he is being asked to wear a gray nun's habit, just like the ones Agent Zelle and Sister Agnes were wearing. Now he sees why he is required to shave, but that does not explain what on earth is going on. On the other hand, he needs a reason to leave the hotel and has not yet thought of one; perhaps this is such an opportunity. He shaves quickly and then stands in front of the mirror while trying to work out how to wear a nun's veil and then arrange the habit over it.

Two minutes later, still far from satisfied, and feeling foolish, Orlov shuffles down the stairs and into the ballroom, carrying his carefully folded ministerial suit in a pillowcase. Roughly a dozen other people are in various stages of trying to arrange a gray habit around themselves. One of them is the Minister of Works. A number of officers of the palace guard hover nearby, impatiently. Orlov spots one of the sisters assisting people with their habits. She sees him and walks over to help.

"Good morning, Minister," she says. "May I?"

"Please," says Orlov.

The sister picks up his veil, straightens it, and rearranges the habit with expert precision. She steps back to admire her work. "Much better," she says.

"What is going on here?" asks Orlov.

"Everything will become clear," she says, dashing away to assist someone else.

Now the officer who knocked on Orlov's door speaks up and the room falls silent.

"Sisters and ministers, your attention, please. The vehicles are ready. For your own safety, please follow the instructions of the palace guard at all times. Doing so will maximize our chances of reaching the destination safely." Mumbling breaks out amongst some of the men in habits, but the officer talks over it. "If you do not have a name, the sisters will assign one for you. Now, everyone to the front of the building immediately, please."

Now thoroughly confused, Orlov attempts to engage the Minister of Works—a diminutive man drowned in a long habit—who simply shrugs to indicate he does not understand what is happening. Orlov tries to speak again to the sister who helped with his habit, but she marches away to the front of the group as it moves through the lobby.

Outside on a cold, moonlit night, three vehicles stand in front of the hotel. These are unarmed trucks of the sort the military might use to transport troops in non-combat conditions. Orlov remembers sitting in the back of such vehicles during his military service.

He estimates that the party waiting to board the trucks numbers about two dozen; half of them are sisters and the other half are men in habits, like himself. As far as he can tell from the hastily shaven faces, these men are most or all of the civilian ministers staying at the hotel. Each truck also has several armed members of the palace guard who are urgently organizing those boarding in hushed voices.

As Orlov approaches the trucks, he is confronted by a gruff soldier, who points to the pillowcase he is carrying.

"What's this?" grunts the soldier.

"My suit," says Orlov.

Without hesitation, the soldier grasps the pillowcase, pulls it out of Orlov's grip, and flings into the gutter. "Sorry, Minister. No luggage. We're at war."

Even as Orlov tries to protest, he is bundled into the back of the middle truck, along with the Minister of Works. He sits on the hard bench and notices, opposite, the senior, white-haired sister he met yesterday on the seventh floor, along with Agnes. He is about to ask her what is happening when he is interrupted by a stage whisper from one of the soldiers.

"Citizens! Please keep the noise down. No talking until we leave the city. This will greatly improve our chances of moving you safely."

Soon, the strange convoy of nuns, ministers-dressed-as-nuns, and soldiers is rolling across the cobbles of the Grand Plaza. Avoiding the government sector, still regarded as too dangerous, they swing around behind the cathedral and head north out of the city. In the enforced silence, the only sounds are the creaking wheels of three vehicles and sporadic gunfire in the distance.

Orlov looks around to see if he can work out who exactly is in his truck. This proves difficult since the faces of most of the passengers—whether they are nuns or not—are covered with a veiled headdress. In addition to the Minister of Works, he spots the senior, white-haired sister whom he met on the seventh floor. He sees no sign of Sister Agnes or Agent Zelle. He notices that one nun in particular, in the center of the truck, is reluctant to show her face. Unlike the others, she is surrounded by a ring of soldiers, facing outwards, who give angry stares to anyone looking in their direction. Orlov looks away.

Once the convoy leaves the city and is rolling through small villages to the north, whispered conversations begin to break out. They are difficult to hear above the noise of the truck, but Orlov senses people are speculating about where they are going, and perhaps discussing whether the route is safe. He does not like being in the dark about the destination, particularly when the circumstances are so dangerous. He determines to find out for himself.

Orlov stands up, intending to speak to the white-haired nun, when he sees lights in the road up ahead. The convoy screeches to an abrupt halt, sending Orlov tumbling to the floor. He picks himself up in time to see they have arrived at a checkpoint in the road.

Several armed, civilian men begin walking from the checkpoint toward the convoy.

Two of the soldiers in Orlov's truck prepare to jump down to meet them. Before doing so, one of them addresses everyone on board.

"Stay calm, please. Whatever happens, say nothing."

The atmosphere in the middle truck instantly becomes more tense. Everyone glances furtively at their neighbors, then attention turns to the meeting about to take place in the middle of the road. A silence settles on the truck as people try to hear what is being said. Orlov glances over his shoulder to see the two soldiers meet the half dozen checkpoint guards, who appear to be civilians. If Orlov is not mistaken, this is an impromptu checkpoint set up by local civilians to protect their village. He is not sufficiently familiar with politics to estimate if these villagers are likely to be supporters of the People's Party, or the monarchy, or something else.

"Good morning, citizens," says one of the soldiers, with exaggerated politeness.

The politeness is not reciprocated. "Who do you have here?" barks a guard.

"These are sisters from Our Lady of Perpetual Sorrow on Mount Zhotrykaw. We are escorting them back to the convent."

"How convenient for you," shouts another guard.

The soldier continues in the same calm tone. "I can assure you, Citizen, it is not at all convenient for the sisters to travel in the current circumstances. Which is why they asked us to escort them."

"We'll need to check the trucks," says the first guard.

The soldier protests. "Our passengers are nuns and nothing more. They are doing you no harm."

"We'll need to check the trucks," he repeats.

Now the soldier turns to address his passengers. “Sisters, these men will pass through each vehicle briefly. Please remain calm. This will be over soon and then we will be on our way.”

Orlov feels all the passengers tense up. He pulls his veil and hood down as far as possible over his face, covers his hands in his sleeves, and looks down, hoping that he will be able to remain in this position for the entire inspection process. The civilian guards spread out and one climbs up onto the back of each truck, using the barrels of their rifles to prod sisters in the arm, or to lift their veils.

The senior, white-haired nun looks up and tries to engage the guard who joins the middle truck. “Good evening, Citizen,” she says.

The guard ignores her and continues moving along the line.

Orlov holds his breath as the guard approaches him and stops. The tip of a rifle barrel appears under his veil and lifts it, slightly.

“What is your name, Sister?” he says.

Orlov tenses and his brain freezes. He does not know whether to speak or what to say. He does not know if he should attempt a high-pitched voice.

For several long seconds, the guard moves the barrel slowly to left and right under Orlov’s veil. He continues to look down and attempts to stay perfectly still.

He is rescued by the white-haired nun who leans across and announces in a matter-of-fact tone, “Sister Olga is deaf and mute. She cannot understand you.”

Orlov, staying silent and still, is hugely relieved at this intervention. It occurs to him that the sister’s voice is rather masculine, when heard at close quarters, but he puts it out of his mind.

The guard grunts and moves on. He arrives in the center of the truck and stops at the sister surrounded by a ring of soldiers. The guard raises the barrel of his rifle to investigate, which causes one of the soldiers to stand abruptly. He puts his considerable frame between the guard and the sister.

"Sister Karla is sick," he says, sternly. "She almost died. That was the reason for the sisters' trip to the city. Please leave her alone."

The guard looks curiously at Sister Karla, who does not move and whose face remains completely hidden by her veil.

The guard grunts, shuffles slowly along the rest of the truck, and then climbs back down into the road. The sighs of relief around the truck are palpable.

Orlov exhales, finally, and glances over his shoulder to check what is happening in the road. The inspection of the other two trucks is still ongoing, and the atmosphere remains tense until the soldiers are all back on the trucks. There is an exchange between the checkpoint guards that Orlov can't hear, and then the convoy begins slowly to move out.

The atmosphere finally calms only miles later, once the convoy is engulfed in the darkness of the countryside. The white-haired nun stands and begins to walk around the truck, whispering in ears. Orlov is wondering what she is doing, until she approaches him, lays a hand on his shoulder, and whispers, "As you know, you are Sister Olga."

"Yes," says Orlov. "Thank you for rescuing me."

"You're welcome," she says.

"May I ask your name?" says Orlov.

"I am Sister Magda."

"Pleased to meet you, Sister Magda," he says.

"Likewise, I'm sure."

Orlov watches Magda as she works her way through the truck. The Minister of Works is given the name Sister Berta, and so it goes on.

For her final stop before she sits down, Sister Magda stops next to Sister Karla, who does not move or acknowledge her. Orlov notices something curious. Sister Magda says simply, "Sister Karla," and bows her head as she speaks.

The convoy trundles on slowly through dark countryside and it is some time before Orlov realizes where they are. Eventually, the steep, forbidding slopes of Mount Zhotrykaw come into view, closing in around them as they draw nearer.

A half hour later, the convoy rolls past the familiar, infamous sign reading *Prison Zhotrykaw*. Brief, whispered conversations break out between the passengers.

The convoy stops outside the intake room where Orlov was once a newly-arrived prisoner. The passengers climb down from the trucks and follow the soldiers inside.

Once everyone is inside the clammy waiting room—Orlov remembers the peeling paint and overwhelming smell of urine—one of the palace guardsmen makes an announcement.

"Citizens, we will wait here until sunrise. You are welcome to get some sleep. Gentlemen through that door, please, and ladies over here."

As he shuffles into the adjoining room with the other men, Orlov looks around for a sign of Sister Karla and her entourage of soldiers, but they are nowhere to be seen.

CHAPTER NINE

In which our hero learns troubling new information

At seven o'clock in the morning precisely, Orlov is woken by a soldier banging on the door and announcing it is time to leave. He is still exhausted, given only a few hours of sleep on a cold, hard floor. But he is nevertheless pleased at the prospect of leaving Prison Zhotrykaw, a place he hoped never to see again after his incarceration on false charges. He meets the rest of the party outside, where it is a bright but bracing morning. He is disappointed to learn that they are expected to keep wearing their habits, despite being miles away from the nearest settlement. There is some debate about searching the prison for overalls, but the palace guardsmen insist that habits are mandatory.

The soldiers announce that the remainder of the journey will be on foot, and they distribute some bags of supplies among the men. Orlov receives a heavy sack full of potatoes. It takes him a little while to work out how to position this bag on his back without disturbing his habit. Once he has perfected this, he follows the party out of the gates of Prison Zhotrykaw and around the corner onto a footpath which winds up and up above their heads, apparently becoming steeper and steeper until it disappears from view. Although Citizen Orlov does not look forward to such a challenging climb dressed in a habit while carrying a sack of potatoes, nevertheless he is now sure about one thing in this strange episode: their destination is the convent, the only habitable place higher than the prison.

As they climb, Orlov notices that Sister Karla—still completely covered from view in her long habit—stays away from the rest of the party in a separate huddle with her four military minders, who are careful to keep their distance from everyone else.

After they have walked for a half hour or so, Orlov spots Sister Magda up ahead. He considers catching up to talk to her—after all, she was very kind to him at the checkpoint—if he can muster sufficient acceleration to move up through the pack of walkers. The sack of potatoes is weighing heavily on his shoulders during an especially steep section of the path. He is pondering whether a burst of speed is possible when he catches a glimpse of something disturbing. The nun walking next to Sister Magda turns her head briefly; although half hidden by her head covering, this looks like the face of Sister Agnes. Orlov takes a half step back and walks more slowly. He scours the group of nuns surrounding Magda, wondering if Agent Zelle is among them, but he sees no sign of her. Dropping his pace so that others pass him, Orlov gradually works his way to the back of the pack. He had hoped Zelle had stayed in the city, but the presence of Agnes suggests that maybe Zelle is here, too. Given the death threat hanging over his head, he wants to avoid Zelle at all costs. If they come into contact again, he can report that he delivered her message to the People's Party. But, based on his bitter personal experience, Zelle is never satisfied and will no doubt have another task for him on pain of death.

After walking for an hour, the party takes a rest for a while. Orlov stays at the back of the pack, pretending to be having more difficulty with his potatoes than he is, keeping a wary eye on the gaggle of nuns up front that includes Sister Magda.

As they depart again, Orlov spots the Minister of Works, otherwise known as Sister Berta. He moves across to talk to his fellow minister.

"This is a strange experience, Minister," says Orlov. "I hope you are keeping well."

As usual, the Minister of Works fails to look Orlov in the eye. "I will be doing much better once we are permitted to remove these costumes," he says.

"I'm afraid I don't remember your name," says Orlov.

"I believe my name is Sister Berta."

"Your real name."

"My real name is Citizen Budny, Minister of Works."

Orlov thinks about this for a moment. "I see a pattern in what the sisters have done," he says. "They have matched our initial letters. Since my real name is Orlov, my temporary name is Olga. And, for you, Budny becomes Berta."

"Very nice," says Budny, still looking at the path ahead.

After a stretch of steep, treacherous hiking, Orlov is relieved to see buildings up ahead. High above, clinging precariously to the dark, angular cliffs of Mount Zhotrykaw, are three buildings, apparently hewn from the same stone as the mountain itself. The main building, huge and imposing, sits beside two smaller structures, one shaped like a church and the other a small house. From this angle, it seems an architectural wonder that these buildings are able to stand at all, with little obvious to prevent them tumbling down into the deep ravine below. As far as Orlov can see, the buildings appear to be connected by thin walkways hanging between them like ribbons.

There is a sense of relief as the entire party finally rounds a corner and finds itself outside the door of the main convent building. Sister Magda steps up to swing open the main doors and invite everyone inside. The men carrying supplies are directed to a larder next to a huge but basic kitchen. They deposit their goods in the larder and meet the rest of the party in the kitchen. Somehow, it seems to be several degrees colder than it is outside. Everything smells of incense. Keeping his hood pulled down firmly over his face, Orlov keeps his back to the wall and stands nervously next to Budny, scouring the group for any sign of Zelle.

The senior palace guardsman speaks to the whole exhausted party. "Citizens, you may be staying here for some time. Some of our company will stay on to ensure your safety; most of us will need to return to the capital. While living here at the convent, you will be in the care of Sister Magda."

He steps back and Sister Magda addresses the group. "Citizens, it is my pleasure to welcome you to Our Lady of Perpetual Sorrow Convent of Mount Zhotrykaw. I wish your visit was under happier circumstances, but here we are. Since the length of your stay is not yet known, we will need everyone to contribute to cooking and cleaning. I will place two rosters here in the kitchen. I will also assign a room to everyone; some of you will need to share. Finally, even though we may seem isolated here at the convent, there are two rules which the generals have asked us to abide by without exception: firstly, everyone assigned a habit must wear it during the day and must remain well shaven; secondly, real names are banned; sister names only, please."

As the meeting breaks up, Orlov notes there is no sign of Sister Karla and her entourage. Perhaps she has been taken directly to her private room, or even a private building. Perhaps they will not see her again.

Orlov spends the rest of the morning exploring the curious little convent. He is taken in particular with the precarious pathways that connect the various buildings. They are painfully narrow and unprotected by railings or rope. Made from the same dark Zhotrykaw stone as the convent buildings, the pathways are almost perfectly smooth thanks to years of use.

En route from the main building to the chapel, Orlov looks down into the ravine that drops dramatically into nothingness beneath him.

The drop must be one thousand feet. The ravine seems to have its own weather, including swirling winds somewhere down below that make an alarming howling sound, like a distressed animal. He picks up a stone and flings it into the abyss; it disappears without a sound. He hurries into the chapel, being very careful where he places his feet.

Beyond the chapel is a small house clinging to the mountainside, accessible via a similarly treacherous walkway. The house is guarded by a palace guardsman stationed at the front door. Deciding that he does not need to try his luck along any more of the convent's pathways, Orlov returns carefully to the main building, where he finds his name on the roster to assist with food preparation. A half dozen others are already working, including Minister Budny. Orlov begins to slice potatoes and tries to engage Sister Magda in conversation, while she is peeling carrots.

"I am wondering how long we can expect to stay here," he says.

"Well, Minister, that is a good question," says Sister Magda. "I do believe the generals have your safety in mind. Better to be up here than down in the city just at the moment."

"No doubt," he agrees. "I was sorry to hear about Sister Karla. I do hope she gets well soon."

Sister Magda glances around the kitchen and then back at Orlov. "I'm sure we can all agree on that, Sister," she says.

Perhaps Sister Magda wants to move the conversation on to other topics, but Orlov decides to press a little harder. "It must have been very difficult to have a seriously ill sister here. Do you need to travel down to the city for medical reasons very often?"

This is a simple enough question, but the sister looks uncomfortable. She gives him a forced smile. “I’m pleased to say it is very rare, Sister.”

Undeterred, Orlov tries again. “I imagine the visitors would appreciate knowing the nature of the illness Sister Karla is battling, such that we can remember her in our prayers.” Orlov is pleased with this question, which seems to him to be the sort of thing that religious people might say to each other.

Sister Magda puts down her knife and carrot onto the table more firmly than necessary. “The rule here at the convent is that the health of each sister is her own, personal business. I suggest that our visitors should observe the same rule, Minister.”

“Of course. I understand,” says Orlov. On the one hand, he has discovered no new information regarding Sister Karla. On the other hand, he has confirmed that Sister Magda most certainly does not want to talk about it. He determines to raise this issue with another sister, when the opportunity arises.

In the afternoon, when rooms are being allocated, Orlov is disappointed but not surprised to be paired with Minister Budny. It would be easier for him to work out what is going on here if he could sneak around without being observed. However, he cannot think of a plausible reason to complain about sharing a room, so decides not to mention it.

Orlov and Budny’s shared room is a plain, austere affair on the first floor, not far from the kitchen. It has two beds and a limited view of the pathway to the chapel. It transpires that all the men are to be accommodated on the first floor, while all the women will be on the second floor. Someone mentions that only Sister Karla will be housed in an outbuilding, because of her continued convalescence.

At dinner, in the long, cool dining room off the kitchen, Orlov once again scours the group for Zelle or Agnes. He is relieved to see neither of them. He begins to wonder if his partial sighting of Agnes on the walk up the mountain path was mistaken. He has still seen no sign of Zelle. He becomes a little more hopeful that Zelle's nefarious schemes might have kept her in the city.

IN THE EARLY hours of the following morning, Citizen Orlov is woken by noises. At first, he assumes the culprit is the intermittent, guttural snoring of Minister Budny, just feet away in the other bed. As he becomes more aware of his surroundings, however, it is clear that the sounds that woke him are a scratching and scraping somewhere in the distance. He lies still and listens. A short burst of scraping is followed by a break, before it starts again. It sounds as though someone is working away frantically at something, then pausing to take a rest. Some sort of sharp instrument being applied to the wall. This seems an unlikely activity for the middle of the night.

Orlov assumes that he will fall back to sleep when the noises stop, but they do not. The scraping continues in regular bursts, becoming more intense and a little louder over time. It is enough to prevent Orlov from sleeping again. Eventually, he gets up, being careful not to wake Budny. He determines to investigate the noises and, assuming all is well, he will return to bed quietly in due course. Budny need never know.

With Budny still snoring, Orlov dresses quickly in his habit (minus the headdress), maneuvers silently through the door, and treads carefully along the cold hallway. The only light seeps in from a weak moon through the high windows.

He stops just short of the kitchen and listens. The scraping sounds, though still just audible, are now quieter. So, he reverses and creeps back along the hallway past his room and continues to the far end of the building. Again, he stops to listen; this time, the sounds are louder.

He opens a door at the end of the building, but remembers just in time that this door leads directly to the treacherous pathway to the chapel. He has one foot on the pathway and one hand on the doorknob when a blast of freezing wind swirls up at him from the ravine. The pale moon casts just enough light to illuminate the angular, unforgiving cliff face.

He shuts the door and steps back into the hallway. The scraping sounds have momentarily halted, but soon begin again.

Now Orlov notices another door nearby. It is too small to be a bedroom door. He opens it and at first sees only darkness. As his eyes adjust, it becomes clear this is a closet full of brooms and cleaning supplies. He is about to shut the door again when he notices that the scraping sounds are now significantly louder.

Without any clear plan in mind, Orlov steps into the closet and shuts the door behind him. He moves a broom to give himself more space. There is no doubt that the sounds are louder here. In fact, it feels like he is right on top of them.

Unsure what to do next, Orlov waits for his eyes to adjust fully to the darkness of the closed closet, and then begins carefully to move brooms and buckets around, to see if he can work out why he can hear the sounds more clearly. To his surprise, at the back of the closet is another door, albeit much smaller than the one through which he entered. It is a peculiar, half-sized door that appears to have been fashioned for a child. Now that the cleaning supplies are moved out of the way, it seems the scraping sounds are seeping through this unexpected little door.

Orlov takes a deep breath and thinks quickly. He does not know why he and the other ministers have been brought here, nor does he know if Sister Karla is the king, although the thought has occurred to him. He does not know why the nuns have involved themselves in the war. Nor does he know where Zelle is, or what her role is in all this. Something is going on here and he needs to work out what it is. It might seem dangerous and foolish to follow this mysterious noise but, on the other hand, perhaps it will shed some light on these questions.

Fully aware that he might regret it, Orlov leans over and turns the handle of the miniature door. At first, this has no effect, and then the door lurches open, not locked but simply sticky with age or rust. In the semi darkness he sees what appears to be a spiral staircase, winding downwards. Poking his head through the door to get a better look at the staircase, the scraping sounds are now much clearer. He uses a broom to ensure the little door remains open, and then drops onto the staircase, feet first.

Once standing on the staircase, Orlov double checks that the broom will keep the door open, and then begins to descend, steadying himself by holding onto the cool stone walls. Although the staircase itself is in almost darkness, there is a soft light from below that suggests moonlight through a window.

Soon, Orlov is standing in a narrow, damp corridor that appears to be in the basement of the building. Instinctively, he heads toward the end of the corridor illuminated by moonlight through a thin, high window. As he walks, it's clear that he is now very near the source of the scraping sounds.

Under the window is a heavy internal door, barred from the outside by a thick plank of wood. He puts his ear to the door and listens. At first, the scraping sounds continue. When they stop, he hears whispering. Not one voice, but several voices in an agitated, frantic discussion. Shocked by this, Orlov steps back from the door, checks around that he is still alone in the corridor, and then returns his ear to the door. There is no doubt that there are several people in there, at least.

Orlov's mind races. Why on earth are there people in the basement of the convent, whispering behind an apparently locked door? What is going on here?

He takes a deep breath, then knocks gingerly on the door.

"Hello?" he says.

Instantly, both the scraping and whispering stop dead.

Orlov knocks again, this time more firmly. "Hello?"

A woman's voice. "Who's there?"

"Citizen Orlov. A fishmonger. Do you need help?"

Another woman's voice. "Citizen who?"

"Orlov."

"Can you open the door, Citizen Orlov?"

"One moment," says Orlov.

He lifts the heavy plank, lays it aside, and pushes the huge door inward.

Stepping inside into a huge, dank space in semi-darkness, Orlov sees some twenty-five or thirty women, in various states of underwear, staring at him expectantly. Two women who were apparently engaged in working on the inside of the door now step back to make room for him to enter, one of them brandishing some sort of metal poker.

Embarrassed, Orlov averts his eyes. "What are you ladies doing here?" he says.

"Why are you at the convent?" asks the woman holding the poker.

"The military insisted," says Orlov. "We arrived this morning."

"Who's here?" asks another woman, distinguished and commanding, despite her state of semi undress.

"Some palace guardsmen," says Orlov, "some ministers of the government, and some sisters."

The women glance at each other. The distinguished, older woman speaks again. "And which of those are you, Citizen?"

"I'm a minister," says Orlov. "I *was* a minister, until all this started, for the past week anyway. In truth, I'm just a fishmonger. I have no idea what's going on here. Who are you?"

The same nun speaks again. “We are the Sisters of Our Lady of Perpetual Sorrow. And I am Mother Superior.”

Orlov is now even more confused. He tries quickly to make sense of this. “I thought you all traveled to the city with Sister Magda and the others.”

Mother Superior frowns. “Who is Sister Magda?” she asks.

PART THREE

The Sisters of Our Lady of Perpetual Sorrow

CHAPTER TEN

In which our hero frees some prisoners

In the cramped urgency of a convent basement in the early hours of the morning, Citizen Orlov learns some new information from the Sisters of Our Lady of Perpetual Sorrow, once they have filed out from their temporary incarceration into the adjoining corridor. He learns that the entire convent is represented by the twenty-seven sisters now shivering and huddled before him, save for two additional sisters currently on a visit overseas. They have never heard of Sisters Magda, Agnes, Karla, or Zelda. None of them has recently been sick and none of them has had need recently to travel to the city.

They became aware of the current political unrest only when the guards at Prison Zhotrykaw deserted their posts and the whole prison emptied out onto the mountain. Although most of the prisoners escaped down the mountain, a group of perhaps a dozen or so—some armed—arrived at the convent, demanding food from their kitchen before forcing them into the basement, where they were required at gunpoint to remove their habits.

Now shivering in the musty hallway, and having abandoned averting his eyes for reasons of practicality, Orlov listens in amazement to their account. He attempts to assist them in opening the exterior door, but it is locked from the outside. It is agreed that they need to move with minimal noise, so the entire company files back the way Orlov entered, up the spiral staircase and through the cleaning closet.

From there, with Mother Superior in the lead, they tiptoe silently out through a side entrance and drop down onto the mountain path that leads up to the main gates. Peering around the corner, Orlov notes that a palace guardsman is still stationed outside the outbuilding where he believes Sister Karla is staying, but thankfully the main gates are unprotected.

The whole group walks for a while down the path, in the pale light of a weak moon, dropping some distance below the convent before they feel it's safe to talk again.

Mother Superior turns to Orlov, taking one of his hands in both of hers.

"Citizen, we owe you a debt of gratitude," she says.

"It is the least I could do," says Orlov. "Where will you go?"

Mother Superior looks down at the mountain as the wind swirls around them. "We will go to the prison to collect clothes and supplies. After that, we shall see. What of you, Citizen?"

"I need to stay here," says Orlov. "The government still considers me to be one of them, even if I do not."

Mother Superior squeezes his hands. "I understand, Citizen. May God bless you."

With that, the entire company of the Sisters of Our Lady of Perpetual Sorrow shuffles away into the darkness of the mountain, leaving Orlov standing alone.

He watches them go, then retraces his steps through the side door, careful to avoid the angle whereby he might potentially be seen by the guard outside Sister Karla's outbuilding. He tiptoes to the end of the corridor and closes up the cleaning closet before returning to his room, where Minister Budny is still snoring.

Orlov lies on his bed for a while, still wearing his habit, staring at the ceiling, unable to sleep. If Magda, Agnes, and the others are not real nuns, who are they? And why are they working with Zelle? Perhaps they are fellow prisoners Zelle met during her short stay in Zhotrykaw. Sister Magda, in particular, seems such a sweet old lady that it is difficult to imagine this being the case. Her voice is vaguely familiar, although he cannot think why.

IN THE MORNING, after just two hours or so of additional, fitful sleep, and still dressed in his habit from his night-time excursion, Orlov lies on his bed, waiting for Minister Budny to wake up. Having confirmed that not one of the nuns who escorted them to the convent is an actual nun, Orlov is desperate to warn someone. There is some risk to this, certainly. Perhaps it would be safer to keep this news to himself, but Budny does not give the impression of someone involved in sinister plots. He is a quiet, somber fellow who keeps to himself. As far as Orlov can tell, Budny is just the Minister of Works and nothing more.

Orlov visits the communal bathrooms, seeing no one, and spends some time back in the room slowly arranging his head covering in the mirror. All the while, Minister Budny snores heavily.

Eventually, when he can stand it no longer, Orlov approaches Budny's bed and pushes his shoulder.

"Minister, wake up," he says. "It's urgent."

Budny stirs and slowly sits up. "What happened? Are we under attack?"

"No," says Orlov. "But something is going on."

Budny glances through the tiny window and back at Orlov. "I'm listening."

Orlov begins to pace around the cramped bedroom. "Before I tell you what I know, I need to ask you a question."

"Very well."

"Who is Sister Magda?" asks Orlov.

Budny reaches for his thick spectacles and puts them on, blinking at the early morning light before answering. "You mean the mother superior?"

"Yes. Is she, as far as you know, the leader of the nuns who live here at this convent?"

"Who else would she be?" says Budny with a bemused expression.

"What would you say if I said that none of the people who brought us up here are actually nuns?"

Budny frowns. "They wear habits and live in a convent."

Orlov stops pacing and looks at him. "I met the real nuns in the early hours of this morning."

Budny sits up straight on the edge of his bed, still frowning. "There are more nuns?"

"There are real nuns, and there are imposters," says Orlov.

"How can you tell which is which?" asks Budny.

"The real nuns were trapped in the basement. I rescued them. They fled the convent in the middle of the night."

Budny scratches his head. "I'm not sure I understand you, Minister."

"I assure you," says Orlov, "that all the nuns still at the convent are fake."

"Why would anyone who is not a nun pretend to be a nun?"

"That is my question to you."

"I'm just the Minister of Works," says Budny. "I have no idea."

Breakfast is overshadowed by a tense atmosphere.

The ministers are left to their own devices to prepare food in the kitchen, while most of those posing as sisters—including Magda—are apparently occupied, whispering to each other in an agitated state before disappearing for some time, not returning to the dining hall until breakfast is almost over. Orlov keeps an eye on them, while pretending to be focused on washing the dishes.

He wonders if Magda and her cronies have discovered that the real Sisters of Our Lady of Perpetual Sorrow—whose habits they presumably stole—are no longer trapped in the basement. He wonders if they have been out searching for them, only to conclude they have escaped.

He keeps his head down, focused on ensuring that every one of the breakfast dishes is cleaned and dried spotlessly, pondering what might happen next.

After the breakfast dishes are done, Sister Magda summons all the ministers to gather in the dining room. Orlov, Budny, and the rest of the dozen ministers file in from the kitchen and dutifully retake their seats at the dining tables. The women dressed as sisters line the wall; Sister Magda stands at the head of the room with the air of an earnest school principal.

"Ministers," she begins, "your attention is appreciated. Apologies that my sisters and I could not join you for breakfast. We were required to attend a discussion with our military protectors." This sounds plausible, but Orlov does not believe it. He is convinced they were investigating the whereabouts of the real sisters. He hopes they have made a successful escape. Magda continues, "The outcome of that discussion is that one team of four soldiers will remain with us here, while the rest of the platoon returns to the capital tonight. Fierce fighting is still ongoing around the country, and the platoon is needed to return to the fray. However, the platoon leader assures me we will be safe, so long as we stay up here at the convent." She pauses and stares across the assembled gathering. "Any questions?"

One of the ministers raises a hand. He is Minister of Health, or perhaps Welfare. "Do the generals believe four soldiers are sufficient to secure the whole of the convent?" The question is followed by a murmur of support from some other ministers.

Sister Magda seems momentarily flummoxed. Another sister—a fierce woman whose habit does not quite hide an elaborate neck tattoo—steps to her side and whispers in her ear. Magda smiles grimly before answering. "The role of the four soldiers will principally be to protect Sister Karla," she says, causing another murmur around the room. She continues a little louder, speaking over the noise. "But, no doubt—no doubt they will come to the aid of the group, should we need anything."

Now the disgruntled discussion among the ministers becomes unruly and Magda, red-faced, appears to have lost control of the group.

Another minister speaks up. He is a rotund, pompous fellow whose name Orlov cannot remember but believes to be Minister of Finance. "I think we can all agree that Sister Karla needs protection," he glances across the group before continuing, "given her state of health. There's no argument in that regard. The question is whether there should not be additional protection for the facility as a whole."

This comment is met with several supportive comments, some of them rather loud, and it seems the meeting is in danger of becoming a free-for-all.

The tattooed nun steps forward, raising her hands to calm the commotion. "Ministers, please. I'm sure we can all agree that the generals have our safety at heart. They have decided that leaving the whole platoon here is an unnecessary burden on their limited resources. The purpose of bringing you up here to the convent was that it is safe. We do not expect to need any protection at all, given the difficulty of the journey. A convent at the top of a mountain is hardly the place to conduct a civil war. But, in any case, we have the team of four soldiers here, in the unlikely event that anything should happen."

It occurs to Orlov that this fierce-looking, tattooed sister is remarkably assured when discussing matters of national security, which is perhaps not what one would expect of a nun. He scans the group of ministers and guesses they have no idea she is anything but a real sister. On the other hand, he notes that there was no particular surprise or questioning of Sister Karla's need to have four soldiers assigned to her personal protection, which suggests that at least some of the other ministers—perhaps all of them—know exactly who is holed up in the precarious little outbuilding.

CHAPTER ELEVEN

In which our hero steps out

Citizen Orlov spends the next hour pacing the grounds of the convent, thinking. Avoiding the precarious walkways to the outbuildings, he favors instead the gentler slopes between the main building and the gate. Pretending to be taking in the air, he strolls with a casual gait, but his brain is racing. What will happen tonight once many of the soldiers have left? It seems possible that the imminent departure of most of the platoon has been manufactured by Magda and her cronies. Perhaps the platoon leader believes he is dealing with the actual Sisters of Our Lady of Perpetual Sorrow, and they have told him they feel quite safe if only four soldiers remain.

Given that the temporary sister names appear to have been assigned with matching initial letters, it seems that Karla is the king. Everything points to that conclusion. What do these fake nuns intend to do with, or to, the king, once they outnumber the soldiers? And what might the implications be for the outcome of the civil war? For the future of the nation?

As he ponders these things, Orlov deliberately and slowly increases the size of the circuit he is making in front of the convent, so that he passes closer and closer to the main entrance at the top of the circuit, and closer and closer to the main gate at the bottom of the circuit.

He works hard to appear nonchalant, and nods a friendly *good morning* to a passing minister on one occasion, and to two passing soldiers on another occasion, all the while monitoring whether anyone is watching him. He continues in this manner until, at the lowest point of his circuit, he could reach out and touch the gate, if chose to do so.

On his next circuit, as he approaches the lowest point of his circuit, Orlov—now humming an old patriotic song—takes in a deep breath, opens the gate, slips through it silently, and closes it again. A second later he is marching purposefully down the mountain path, away from the convent.

He waits until he has dropped twenty yards or so beneath the gate before looking back over his shoulder. As far as he knows, he has not been seen.

Now with a spring in his step but a lot on his mind, Orlov strides down the rocky, twisting mountain path as fast as his middle-aged legs will carry him. He stops only once, to drink deliciously cold water from a mountain stream. The air is fresh and bracing; he is relieved to be outside, on his own, away from the strained atmosphere of the convent.

Eventually, he sees the grim, forbidding buildings of Prison Zhotrykaw below him, and he follows the now-familiar road as it turns back into the mountain and through the infamous gate. Approaching the prisoner intake area, he is reminded once again of his brief stay here as a prisoner, which makes him shudder. He pauses at the door and turns to take in the view down the mountain, toward the city.

Although empty and quiet, the grimy intake area—with its filthy, peeling walls—still has the distinct aroma of urine, just as it did when Orlov arrived here as a prisoner, and when he subsequently came to the prison to visit Citizen Vanev. Seeing and hearing no one, he ventures farther into the prison, where he finds doors flung open and chairs lying on their side as though a storm has blown through. Wandering alone through such a large, empty building is a distinctly eerie experience and, reaching the cavernous dining hall, he is wondering if this is a wasted trip when he hears voices nearby.

He ducks behind the door to the dining hall and listens. Female voices, quiet but firm, can be heard moving between the dining hall and the kitchens beyond it. Peering through the gap between the door and the wall, he sees what he had hoped to see: the Sisters of Our Lady of Perpetual Sorrow, now dressed in the familiar heavy, gray overalls synonymous with Prison Zhotrykaw, apparently making lunch from supplies they have discovered in the huge larder.

Orlov waits until he spots Mother Superior entering the dining hall, then he removes his head covering and steps inside.

Mother Superior spots him instantly and speaks first. "Citizen, it is good to see you again. Is everything well?"

Glancing around at the growing gathering of sisters, Orlov says, "May we speak in private?"

"Of course," says Mother Superior, and she leads the way into the larder. The cold, moist room is bursting with food; it looks as though the nuns could live here for a month before needing additional supplies. She closes the door behind them and says, "So, Citizen, you decided to leave after all?"

"Only temporarily. I need to return urgently, before I am missed. If they believe I have deserted my position, there could be terrible consequences."

"I see," says Mother Superior. She looks into his eyes with piercing concentration.

Orlov continues, "I was hoping you would still be here because," he hesitates, "I need to send a message. I am wondering if you might be moving down to the city. I do not like to ask for such a favor, but I'm afraid there could be grave consequences for our nation if this message is not received."

Mother Superior looks at him intently for a while before replying. "When does this message need to be delivered?"

Orlov does not hesitate. "Today," he says.

Mother Superior looks shocked. "Citizen, we arrived here only this morning, as you know. We are about to sit down to our first meal in two days. My flock is exhausted and in shock. I have told them we can stay here at the prison for a few days, at least. From what you have told us, it is dangerous on the roads."

Orlov's heart sinks. "It is dangerous; that much is true." He wonders for a moment whether he should reveal his worst fears and quickly concludes that he has no choice. He glances at the door and back at Mother Superior before continuing. "May I share something with you in confidence? Just between you and me?"

"If you must," says Mother Superior.

"I do not believe we should reveal this to the other sisters. For their own safety."

"Very well." Mother Superior nods encouragingly, as though acknowledging that she is ready to hear a secret that cannot be shared.

"I believe His Majesty, the king, is among the group of people who arrived at the convent yesterday." He pauses to assess Mother Superior's reaction; she frowns. He continues, "Someone cooked up a scheme to lock you in the basement, steal your habits, travel to the capital pretending to be you—the whole order, I mean—and then return here. But, on the return journey, some of them remained in the city, I think, and gave some spare habits to a dozen of us ministers, as a means of smuggling us out safely. My guess—although I do not know for sure—is that His Majesty, heavily disguised, traveled with us. So, you see, the whole scheme was really intended to move the king to a safe place, until the troubles are over."

Still frowning, Mother Superior says, "If the king and his ministers are safe, good for them. I dare say the convent is just about the safest place in the whole kingdom. I'm currently more concerned about the safety of my sisters."

"I understand," says Orlov. "But, there's something else." He sighs, unsure how to explain what he is thinking. "As far as I know, the other ministers—some of them, at least—believe they are staying with the real sisters, with you. We just found out that most of the platoon that escorted us up the mountain is going to return to the city tonight. Once they are gone, I have grave concerns for the safety of the king."

Mother Superior appears to be trying to make sense of this. "If the government wanted to bring His Majesty up to the convent, why did they not simply ask for our assistance? We would have cooperated, of course."

"Yes," says Orlov. "I'm sure you would. The thing is, you see, I have learned from difficult personal experiences that the government does not act as one. There are tensions and factions that I do not pretend to understand. Officials claiming to act on behalf of His Majesty are not necessarily being truthful. The same goes, it seems, for people claiming to be nuns."

Mother Superior frowns again. "So, are they protecting the king or threatening him?"

Orlov sighs. "I'm afraid I don't know. My fear is that they're going to kill him. Which is why the message must be delivered today."

"And to whom will the message be sent?"

"To the only man in the kingdom I can trust," says Orlov, gravely. "He will know what to do."

"Can you not simply explain your concerns to the other ministers?"

"I wish I could," says Orlov. "But I do not trust any of them. I don't know who is in league with these fake sisters and who is not. If I am seen to be interfering in their plans, my own life could be in danger." He waits for a reaction.

Mother Superior sighs heavily. "Given the gravity of the situation, I cannot refuse you. But neither can I force any of my sisters to take on such a dangerous task." She appears to be mulling something over. Orlov waits. She continues, "Here is what I propose. You will explain the nature of the task to the sisters, but not the details. You may say that the task has consequences regarding the troubles, but nothing more. If any of the sisters choose to undertake this task, I will not stand in their way. If they prefer to stay here, in the relative safety of the prison, so be it."

Orlov ponders this offer briefly but, in reality, he has no choice. "Very well," he says, "I will follow your lead. Thank you."

They emerge from the larder into the dining room, where the sisters—looking exhausted and disheveled—are seated in front of a makeshift lunch. One sister, standing, announces that she is going to bless the food. Feeling embarrassed, Orlov stops next to Mother Superior and looks down at his shoes. As soon as the blessing is over, the sisters tear into the food like ravenous animals.

Mother Superior projects across the room. "Sisters, I do not want to stop you from eating, but please listen. Citizen Orlov here has a request. He needs someone to perform a dangerous task. Once you have heard what he has to say, you may decide if you want to assist him. This is strictly voluntary; no one should feel any compunction." She steps back and indicates that it is Orlov's turn to speak.

Orlov is not familiar with the word *compunction*, but the direction of Mother Superior's comments is clear enough.

Only now, it occurs to Orlov that he is about to address a room full of nuns while he is the only person wearing a nun's habit. He holds the head covering behind his back in an attempt to lessen his embarrassment at these very strange circumstances. He will emphasize the gravity of the situation and hope that the nuns take him seriously, despite his appearance. He clears his throat and speaks falteringly.

"Sisters; since I saw you this morning, some information has come to light which could have serious consequences regarding the war. Consequences, perhaps, for the future of the nation." He pauses, and Mother Superior nods to encourage him to continue. "Given that I am still, I think, a minister of the government, I must return urgently to the convent. However, I need to send a message to someone in the city. That message must be received today. I believe the message will improve the chances of peace being restored. It might even save lives. I will not announce the details to the whole group. I will, of course, explain exactly what is required to anyone brave enough to take on this task."

Orlov glances at Mother Superior, who speaks again. "Let me repeat, sisters, that this is entirely optional. Citizen Orlov is well aware of our recent ordeal and our plan to stay here for some days. I have explained to him that you all may prefer to remain here at the prison until the security situation improves."

Mother Superior steps back a little and folds her hands. It occurs to Orlov that she knows the sisters very well and he, of course, does not.

From the expression on her face, it seems Mother Superior fully expects there to be no reaction. She will then have been true to her offer, but he will have achieved nothing.

Orlov holds his breath and looks across the room full of nuns in prison overalls, eating enthusiastically, glancing up at him and Mother Superior apparently out of politeness rather than interest.

After several long seconds of silence, Mother Superior turns to Orlov, as though about to confirm that there are no takers. But she is interrupted by movement at the back of the room.

"I'll do it," says a young, strident voice. The smallest person in the room has stood up in her place. A tiny, dark-eyed nun whose face beams with life.

Mother Superior holds up a hand in caution. "Sister Sofia, please. We have spoken before about your tendency to act impetuously."

Orlov, delighted at the offer, is not sure of the precise meaning of *impetuously*, but it's clear that Mother Superior is attempting to pour cold water on things. He tries to interject, but Sister Sofia speaks up again.

"Our vow is to serve, is it not? If we believe this message serves the cause of peace, I will go. If we do not, let us send this fellow on his way." She remains standing, a half-eaten bread roll in her hand.

Orlov is surprised at the blunt tone of these remarks, but apparently Mother Superior is not. She sighs and speaks again.

"I am prepared to believe Citizen Orlov that his message is intended to further the cause of peace. I am not, however, prepared to let anyone travel on their own, in the current circumstances. Your offer is very generous and very brave, Sister, but unless someone is prepared to travel with you, I cannot allow it."

Mother Superior folds her hands again, as though indicating that the matter is closed. Orlov's heart sinks.

Apparently undeterred, Sister Sofia says, "It's not so dangerous. No one shoots a nun, not even in war time." She takes a bite from her bread roll and chews on it while awaiting a response.

Mother Superior's arms are still folded. "No one is traveling alone," she says, sternly.

There is another silence. Orlov holds his breath.

At the opposite side of the room from Sister Sofia, a slim, pale nun with long hair stands very slowly, carefully arranging her plate, cup, and cutlery in precisely the correct formation on the table before looking up at Mother Superior, a beatific smile on her face.

"I'll go," she says.

BACK IN THE confines of the larder, Citizen Orlov stands in an awkward huddle with three nuns, their impromptu meeting taking place between sacks of potatoes on one side and strings of sausages on the other. Mother Superior speaks first.

"Sisters Sofia and Petra," she says, "please remember that what Citizen Orlov is about to tell you is a matter of national security. It must not be shared with any of the other sisters. Is that clear?"

"Yes, Reverend Mother," they say, almost in unison.

Mother Superior opens her hand to invite Orlov to speak.

Orlov smiles grimly at the two young volunteers. "I will say as much as I can," he says. "As you know, some senior members of the government are currently staying at your convent. I believe some of those people are in danger from some of the others, and the trouble might start as soon as tonight. It needs to be stopped, but I cannot do it alone. The person you need to find is one Citizen Vanev, who is currently staying in the Grand Plaza at Hotel Milekov."

Sister Sofia chimes in. "You mean Hotel Melikov, I think."

"No," says Orlov. "It's very important that you don't go to Hotel Melikov. You may not even be safe there. Directly across the square, they are converting the home of Count Milekov into a hotel. You will see the sign above the door. Do not attempt to enter that way. Walk around to the back of the hotel and approach the rear entrance. Tell them you urgently need to speak to Citizen Vanev. If there is any resistance, tell them you have a message from Citizen Orlov, but it is for Vanev's ears only."

Sofia nods gravely. "Citizen Vanev," she repeats.

"Yes," says Orlov. "Like me, Citizen Vanev is a fishmonger. He is a very large man with a beard." He extends his arms to each side in an attempt to demonstrate the size of Vanev's wide frame. "It is absolutely essential that you speak to him alone. Just the two of you and him; no one else. I say this because I believe one of his associates at Hotel Milekov is an imposter."

The nuns frown at this, apparently expecting Orlov to explain, but he does not want to say more about it.

Sister Petra speaks out. "Once we have Citizen Vanev on his own, what is the message?"

"Yes, good question," says Orlov, buying himself some thinking time. "Here it is. Tell him this. Are you ready?"

"Ready," says Sister Petra.

Orlov continues, now speaking with exaggerated clarity, enunciating each word precisely. "The prize halibut did not swim overseas. It is at the peak of the mountain. Come quickly, tonight. Meet at sundown, at the convent gates."

"The prize halibut?" says Sister Sofia.

"Yes," says Orlov. "Can you repeat the whole message back to me?"

He holds his breath while Sister Sofia and then Sister Petra slowly but accurately repeat the whole message.

"Is that everything?" says Mother Superior.

"Yes, that's it," says Orlov.

"Very well," says Mother Superior, "let us join the others."

Back in the dining hall, the other nuns are clearing up after lunch. Mother Superior asks them to gather before saying a prayer on the theme of traveling mercies for Sisters Sofia and Petra. Once again, Orlov stands awkwardly, looking down at his shoes, with the sense that he is intruding on the private business of a family to which he does not belong.

Once the prayer is over, the sisters gather around to say farewell to Sofia and Petra.

"How will you travel?" asks Orlov.

Sister Sofia does not miss a beat. "There are some abandoned prison vehicles in the yard. We found them earlier. The better ones were taken, but I'm sure one of them will suffice."

"And will you travel back here tonight, with Vanev?"

Sister Sofia looks at Sister Petra, who shrugs. "We'll see," she says.

Mother Superior ushers everyone outside, where the two volunteers choose a vehicle from the yard. Their choice is a prisoner transfer truck—a cage on wheels—precisely the same sort of vehicle in which Orlov first arrived at Prison Zhotrykaw. He stands by the other sisters, with a sense of admiration and gratitude, as the two volunteers maneuver the vehicle out onto the mountain path, to begin their precarious journey down to the capital, to the Grand Plaza and, hopefully, to Hotel Milekov.

After the truck disappears from view, Mother Superior turns to Orlov. "I hope this is worth it, Citizen."

"So do I," says Orlov. "So do I."

He bids farewell to Mother Superior and the remaining sisters, and immediately turns to begin the march back up the path to the convent. Checking his pocket watch, he has been away a little longer than intended; he hopes to sneak back into the convent without his absence being noticed.

It is much quicker to walk up to the convent from the prison when one is not part of a large party and not carrying a sack of potatoes. He makes good time, stopping just once to drink from a stream.

As he rounds the corner where one first sees a glimpse of the convent gates, Orlov's heart sinks into his boots. He sees the last thing he wants to see: Agent Zelle and Sister Agnes, each dressed in full, gray nun's habit, each wielding a pistol.

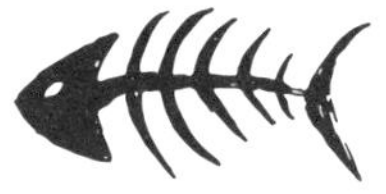

CHAPTER TWELVE

In which our hero is detained

Citizen Orlov freezes, his body momentarily paralyzed while his brain formulates a plan. He attempts to shuffle backwards, around the bend and out of sight of the convent. Before he can do so, however, Sisters Zelda and Agnes step forward, raising their pistols to point at his head.

Despite being petrified, it occurs to Orlov that the three of them make a ridiculous scene: a nun being detained at gunpoint by two other nuns.

"Don't move," says Zelle, the venom in her voice very much not nun-like.

Orlov stops and raises his hands. The two women march swiftly toward him, their guns still trained at his head. He is struck by the contrast between their religious outfits and the menace on their faces.

When they reach him, Zelle sticks the barrel of her revolver into his side, hiding this arrangement from view under the billowing folds of her habit.

"Let's walk," she says. Then she leans in closer to whisper menacingly in his ear, "We're having a friendly stroll in the grounds. Nothing more. Understood?"

Orlov stiffens as the gun barrel digs into his skin. He lowers his hands slowly. "Understood," he says.

They walk up through the gates and into the grounds of the convent, with Zelle glued to Orlov's side and Agnes walking just behind. He cannot see it, but no doubt Agnes is also using her habit to hide the fact that her gun is trained on him.

Breathing heavily, but forcing himself to remain calm, Orlov glances around the grounds, wondering if any of the ministers are nearby. But what would he do if he saw someone? With two guns trained on him, he is hardly in a position to ask for help. As if to emphasize this truth, he spots Minister Budny strolling along some distance away, behind the main building. For half of one second, he considers calling out to Budny, but what does he expect will happen? The Minister of Works is hardly a match for two armed captors.

Zelle leads them around the side of the convent and down some steps to a rear entrance. Only now Orlov realizes where he is: this is the door he tried to open in the early hours of the morning to free the real Sisters of Our Lady of Perpetual Sorrow. Sister Agnes produces a key and pushes Orlov through the door. The two women follow close behind, lock the external door, and push him into the dank dungeon from which he released the sisters just a few hours earlier.

"Look here," Orlov begins to say in protest.

He is cut short by Sister Agnes producing a rope from somewhere, tying his hands and, with considerable speed and skill, attaching him to a rusty metal bracket protruding from the wall. Without warning, she pulls off his head covering and flings it into the corner.

As Sister Agnes works, Zelle begins to talk. "So, Citizen Orlov, you decided to take a little trip out of the convent."

Given his new predicament, Orlov is facing toward the wall. He twists his torso awkwardly in an attempt to look at Zelle. "Only for a walk," he says, a little more desperately than intended. "I was just admiring the scenery."

Zelle scoffs. "There you have it, Sister Agnes. He was admiring the scenery."

Her work complete, Agnes steps back. "There's plenty of scenery to admire from within the grounds of the convent."

Now Zelle is pacing behind Orlov such that he cannot easily keep an eye on her. "Yes. And one doesn't need two hours to admire it."

"There's nothing to do here," says Orlov. "Is it a crime to take a walk?"

Ignoring this remark, Sister Agnes replies to Zelle. "Two hours might be just enough to meet someone at the prison, wouldn't you say so, Sister Zelda?"

"I imagine so," says Zelle. "Perhaps he has been visiting some lady friends."

Since this remark is not directed at him, Orlov says nothing.

Sister Agnes continues, now addressing Orlov. "What did you tell them?"

Now Orlov twists the other way, in an attempt to see Agnes. "You're not a sister. So, who are you?"

He feels the barrel of Zelle's pistol jab sharply into his back. "We'll ask the questions," she says. "This is not the first time you've been down here in the basement, is it, Minister Orlov?"

Exhausted at twisting to look at his two captors, Orlov turns back to the wall. "I don't know what you're talking about."

Zelle continues, "I'd say you were down here recently, assisting some damsels in distress. Was your visit to the prison purely social, Minister, or were you sharing some information with your new friends?"

Still staring at the damp stone wall, Orlov considers this. It is possible that Zelle and Agnes were watching him earlier. They could just as easily have guessed that he assisted the real sisters in their escape. Either way, he sees no advantage in admitting to anything, so stays quiet.

Now Zelle begins to sound agitated. "Sister Agnes, it seems the minister is reluctant to talk. Perhaps you could provide him with some encouragement."

Saying nothing, Sister Agnes delves into the corner of the room and emerges with a long wooden bar that might once have formed part of a dining table or a similar piece of furniture. As Orlov twists to see what Agnes is doing, she drives the wooden bar hard into the wall.

Orlov flinches at the impact. "Please," he says.

"I'll try again," says Zelle, now spitting with anger. "What did you tell them?"

Orlov hesitates before replying. "I like to take walks to admire the scenery," he says.

Without a further word being spoken, Sister Agnes swings the wooden bar with venom. It drives into Orlov's right knee. He gasps and his legs buckle underneath him, so that he is still upright only because his hands are tied to the wall. The rope bites into his wrists.

Zelle leans into his left ear. "Try again," she says.

Orlov grimaces to prevent himself from screaming in pain. Worried that he might pass out, he speaks through gritted teeth. "Beautiful scenery," is all he can manage to say.

Zelle sighs heavily, then speaks to Agnes. "Let us leave the minister to think about his priorities. Perhaps a night down here will concentrate his mind."

In a flash, the two women are gone, locking both the inner and outer doors behind them.

CHAPTER THIRTEEN

In which our hero receives some visitors

Citizen Orlov wakes up in his basement dungeon, his right knee throbbing with sharp waves of pain. It is almost completely dark. Startled, he attempts to stand up but his injured knee crumples and he slumps back onto the filthy stone floor. The tiny window high up in the wall tells him a terrible truth: the sun has already set, the only illumination a weak twilight.

He has no memory of passing out; presumably the result of his knee injury.

His mind races. Did Sisters Sofia and Petra make it to Hotel Milekov? Has Citizen Vanev arrived at the top of the mountain? If so, Orlov has already failed in his promise to meet him at the gates at sunset. If he is here, Vanev could be in mortal danger right now, should he be taken for an intruder by the military platoon or by Zelle and her cronies. Orlov does not even know if the soldiers have left for the capital.

Multiple possibilities race through his imagination, each one more terrible than the last. He begins to work on his ties, pulling this way and that, determined to free himself. The effort causes his knee to complain even louder. Nevertheless, he forces himself to stand up, picks up his right foot, balances on his left leg, and attempts to work on the ropes in that position for several minutes, without success.

Orlov is becoming desperate. Looking over at the tiny window, the sky is darkening by the minute. He pulls on the ropes with renewed vigor, but achieves nothing. Whoever Sister Agnes is, she knows a thing or two about restraining prisoners.

A sound in the distance makes him jump. He stops and listens. A bang that might have been a gunshot. This is followed by two more bangs. This time, he is sure they are gunshots.

Citizen Orlov has never felt more helpless. The future of the nation could be playing out just yards away from his basement dungeon, but he is unable to do anything about it. He wonders who is firing and why.

He hopes that Citizen Vanev is safe. He hopes that Sisters Sofia and Petra did not return here with Vanev; he would hate to be the cause of any harm to the genuine nuns whose formerly peaceful home has been invaded during this strange episode. On the other hand, he would be perfectly content if someone—anyone—is shooting at Zelle and her fake nuns for any reason at all.

The shooting stops and he returns to working on the ropes with renewed vigor but with no more success. He pauses again at the sound of voices nearby. It seems a group of people is rushing past the window, hissing urgent instructions to each other.

A gunshot rings out, this time much closer. Orlov ducks instinctively. It could be just outside the window. He turns but sees nothing. Now he can hear more hissing and commotion nearby.

Seconds later, another gunshot explodes. This one is loud enough to be in the basement. He flinches and looks around. Someone forces open the door and suddenly the basement is full of a gaggle of sweaty, aggravated people, each carrying at least one pistol. They slam the door behind them and pause to catch their breath.

Given the almost-darkness, it takes Orlov a few seconds to register who has joined him in his murky dungeon. He is delighted that Citizen Vanev is leading the way; a huge man sweating heavily in his familiar fish-stained overalls, now looking surprisingly natural with a gun in his hand.

Behind him are Comrades Weisz and Nemeth, former members of the People's Front. He does not like them or trust them, but he can understand why Vanev might have decided to bring them along, given their military background. Beside them is Comrade Rozum, the young explosives expert and former member of the Workers' Party. To Orlov's surprise, the four men have been followed into the basement by Sisters Sofia and Petra, both still wearing their prison overalls but now glowing with the sweaty adrenaline of the moment and both brandishing pistols.

"What the hell are you doing down here?" says Vanev to Orlov.

Orlov nods to indicate his tied hands. "It was not my idea," he says.

Comrade Rozum, ever the soldier, raises his gun and puts his considerable frame behind the door.

The two sisters work on Orlov's rope as Vanev talks to him in low, urgent tones. "I hope this is worth it. Talk quickly."

Orlov nods to indicate the two nuns. "Do you think this is a good idea?"

"They insisted on returning with us," says Vanev.

Sister Petra unties the rope. "He made me carry the gun," she says, nodding at Vanev. "It's not loaded."

Sister Sofia brandishes her gun. "Mine is loaded," she says, proudly. "This is our home, after all."

Vanev looks at Orlov expectantly, waiting for news. Comrades Weisz and Nemeth pace uneasily. Orlov speaks as quickly and precisely as he is able. "Thank you for coming here," he says, adding, "comrades," a little self-consciously. "Here is what I know. Behind the convent are two small outbuildings, accessible only via a precarious, narrow path; one is a chapel and the other is a private residence of some kind."

"The guest house," says Sister Sofia.

Orlov continues, "The guest house is currently occupied by a Sister Karla, who is being guarded by four soldiers."

"Quiet," hisses Nemeth, raising a hand in warning. Everyone freezes as several figures rush silently past the high window.

Nemeth lowers his hand and Orlov continues, "A whole platoon brought us up here, but all besides those four were due to leave tonight. I don't know if they're still here."

"We've seen no military," says Vanev. "We were shot at just now by a nun."

Orlov senses there is a lot to explain and very little time in which to explain it. Having said that, he is still very conscious that he does not understand what is going on.

He continues, "I believe Sister Karla is the king, in disguise. I believe they brought us here mostly to keep His Majesty safe. But something has gone wrong. The soldiers believe—as far as I can tell—that they're dealing with the actual sisters." He nods reverentially to Sisters Sofia and Petra. "But, as you have no doubt heard, that is not so."

Vanev nods. "We have heard."

Orlov continues, "All I know is that Agent Zelle is here and she's mixed up in this. It was she who put me down here."

Vanev scratches his beard and sighs. "They're zealots, I would think," he says.

"You mean Zelle and Molnar?" says Orlov.

"And the rest," says Vanev, waving a hand as though this is well known. "You know they were all arrested?" Orlov shrugs, since he does not know, and Vanev continues, "After National Day, they didn't just arrest Zelle and Molnar; they rounded up all the known zealots—twenty or more—and threw them all into Zhotrykaw. They weren't in there for long, of course."

Orlov's mind is racing. He is unsure what to make of this.

"Hurry," hisses Weisz.

Orlov ignores this. He replies to Vanev. "You think all the zealots came up here and disguised themselves as nuns?"

"Seems so," says Vanev, in a matter-of-fact tone.

"But they're supporters of the king. The new king, I mean. Why interfere with the operation to protect him?"

Vanev sighs. "Imagine you worked for years, risked your life, staked your whole career on putting a leader in power. Then, on the very day he takes over, he throws you in prison."

"I see what you mean," says Orlov. It takes a moment for this to sink in, but it seems to make sense. Not for the first time, political maneuverings that are mysterious to Citizen Orlov are seen much more clearly by Citizen Vanev. "You think, when all the other prisoners were heading down the mountain to the city, the zealots came up here to plot their revenge against the new king?"

"I'd say so," says Vanev.

"But they're all sisters. Women," says Orlov. "Where is Molnar?"

Vanev shrugs. "If the king can dress as a nun, so can Molnar."

Orlov experiences a sudden revelation. "Sister Magda," he says.

"Who?"

"Sister Magda. She's older, white hair. Perhaps it's a wig. I thought her voice was familiar. I can't believe I didn't recognize him. It's Molnar."

Weisz and Nemeth are becoming more agitated. Vanev glances at them before turning back to Orlov. "What now?"

"Quickly," says Orlov, "we need to warn the king."

Vanev frowns. "Warn him?"

"About the sisters," says Orlov, exasperated. "Tell him that they're zealots looking for revenge."

Vanev, Weisz, and Nemeth exchange glances. Vanev lays a heavy hand on Orlov's shoulder. "Comrade," he says, in a grim, somber tone. "We're not here to warn the king. We're here to kidnap him."

CHAPTER FOURTEEN

In which our hero realizes he has made a terrible mistake

Citizen Orlov experiences a sinking feeling in his gut reminiscent of an airplane dropping suddenly from the sky. Instantly, he wants to return to the beginning of the day and start again. Things started so well; it's not every day that one is able to rescue a whole convent of incarcerated nuns. Now, however, things have taken a shocking and tragic turn for the worse. Contacting Citizen Vanev seemed the wise thing to do; he is, after all, the only person in the whole kingdom whom Orlov really trusts. However, he did not factor in the possibility that Vanev might bring with him the People's Party's most experienced former soldiers. Perhaps more importantly, he did not stop to think about why the revolutionaries holed up at Hotel Milekov were so focused on learning the whereabouts of the king. Now, in hindsight, he realizes that he should have given more thought to that question.

In formulating a reply to Citizen Vanev, Orlov decides it would be best to remain calm and buy some time to contemplate his next move.

"Kidnap?" he says.

Vanev shrugs, as though this plan should be obvious. "How better to win a civil war than to capture the monarch?"

Unsure what to say, Orlov says nothing. The two sisters, who have been listening quietly, now step into the pale pool of moonlight in the middle of the basement.

Sister Sofia waves her gun. "We cannot be involved in a kidnapping," she says firmly.

"Do you want to get your convent back?" says Nemeth, sharply.

"Not by force," says Petra.

Nemeth's tone changes, as though he is attempting to be reassuring. "The zealots will kill the king. We will move him back to the city. Which do you prefer?"

Sister Sofia seems agitated by this, but Sister Petra lays a hand on her arm. "He's right, Sister. It is better this way."

Sofia says, "We should let the king leave peacefully. If you people have an argument with these so-called zealots, you should settle it without involving the king, or us sisters, for that matter."

Vanev speaks to Sister Sofia in kindly, fatherly tones. "I understand your concerns, but this is a civil war. It cannot be settled without the monarch. If he tries to leave now, the zealots will certainly kill him. If he comes to the city with us, there is a chance he might survive the journey. That is the most peaceful option available."

Sister Sofia seems unmoved by this. "If the king can leave with you, he can leave with the soldiers. What's the difference?"

Vanev shakes his head. "The difference, Sister, is that the king's security detail believe they are dealing with real nuns—with you—and that leaves the king vulnerable to attack. We know better."

Sister Sofia is about to reply, but Weisz speaks over her in an urgent tone. "We need to move. What's the plan?"

Vanev turns to Rozum, still behind the door. "What do you say, Comrade?"

"Where are the four soldiers?" says Rozum to Orlov.

"One has been stationed at the front door," says Orlov. "The others, I don't know. Perhaps they are inside."

"Is there a back door?" says Rozum, looking at the sisters.

"At the guesthouse?" says Sister Petra. "Just a front door. The path from the chapel is the only way to reach it."

Orlov notices a furtive glance between the two nuns, but says nothing.

Rozum frowns and looks at Vanev. "We can't eliminate four. That's a bloodbath. We need to split them up."

Weisz scoffs. "If their orders are to stay with him, they will stay with him. I say we take them." He looks at Vanev.

Vanev sighs and drags a hand down his face. "I'm with Rozum. We need to give Sister Karla a reason to move."

In the urgency of the moment, in the darkened, filthy basement of the convent, Citizen Orlov has an idea. It is an idea that might save lives. An idea that could help determine the future of the nation. But the idea is only partly formed. It has a beginning but no end. His brain scrambles to play out all the potential consequences, but there are too many possibilities. Since it's clear that the People's Party comrades are about to make a move of some sort, there is no time to ponder the possible endings of the idea. His gut tells him to put it into action as soon as possible. If it goes wrong, the consequences could be terrible. On the other hand, if he does nothing, the consequences will certainly be terrible. The time has come to take a risk.

In order for this idea to work, he will need to persuade Vanev and his comrades of one particular course of action while actually planning something slightly different. It will also be necessary to separate the two nuns from the members of the People's Party.

"I have an idea," says Orlov.

Vanev waves a hand. "Quickly, Comrade. Let us hear it."

"I believe I can persuade Sister Karla to move from the guest-house, but you will need to trust me." Weisz scoffs, Vanev raises a hand to silence him, and Orlov continues, "Let us suppose that the king receives a visit from some of the sisters."

He is interrupted by Vanev, who motions for him to hurry. "Comrade, there is no time to suppose. Please tell us the plan, simply."

Orlov sighs. "Very well. First I need to check one thing." He turns to Sisters Sofia and Petra. "Sisters, is there a store of spare habits somewhere, such that you could change quickly?"

"We have a laundry room," says Sister Petra. "There might be a few habits in there."

Orlov turns back to Vanev. "Here it is. The two sisters here dress in habits and approach the guest house. I will follow along, also wearing my habit. You and the comrades will wait in the chapel." He waves to indicate Weisz, Nemeth, and Rozum. "The sisters will tell the soldier at the door that the security of the convent has been compromised, in that there are some imposters posing as nuns. They do not know who these imposters are, but it would be safer to move Sister Karla down to the prison, temporarily. When Karla and her minders emerge, they must move through the chapel, and at that point you comrades have the opportunity to separate them. After that, you need only to avoid the zealots as you leave the grounds, and you have your prize halibut on his way down the mountain."

Weisz replies to Orlov, "Why do you need to go?"

"I am the back-up plan," says Orlov. "If the soldiers are persuaded by the sisters, I will say nothing. If not, I will remove my headdress and demand an audience with the king. He knows who I am."

Vanev glances at Rozum, Weisz, and Nemeth. "Comrades, any complaints?'

"It's worth a try," says Rozum.

Without waiting for a response from the others, Vanev says to the sisters, "Find those habits, Sisters. And hurry."

"Very well," says Sister Sofia, and the two nuns move toward the door.

Orlov begins to follow them, limping on his bad knee, which prompts Weisz to speak. "You can stay here."

"I lost my head covering," says Orlov.

Weisz is unmoved. "Let the sisters bring one for you."

Orlov does not miss a beat. "I need to try it on for size."

Weisz is about to speak again but is interrupted by Vanev. "Go quickly, Comrade," he says. "Return here with the habits. Do not keep us waiting."

Before anyone can speak again, Orlov shuffles through the door behind Sisters Sofia and Petra, dragging his injured knee behind him and following them through the labyrinthine corridors of the basement until they arrive at a door. Sofia opens it to reveal a small, dark laundry room. Several habits are hanging on a drying rack. Orlov immediately begins to search through a pile of head coverings on a shelf, but notices that Sister Petra has moved into the corner and is whispering something. He looks at Sister Sofia, who is picking out a habit.

"A prayer of contrition," says Sofia, matter-of-factly, nodding at Petra. Orlov is unsure what this means. Sofia continues, "The guest house has a back door."

It takes a moment for Orlov to see the significance of this. "I see," he says. "Thank you." And now his idea is fully formed.

Sister Petra turns, avoids Orlov's gaze, and quickly begins to pull a habit over her head.

"We will go along with your plan," says Sister Sofia, "if you give the king the chance to leave peacefully."

"I promise," says Orlov.

Now dressed in complete habits, the three of them dash back through the dark corridors, collect the four People's Party comrades, and exit up the steps into a cool, starry night.

Vanev turns to Sister Sofia. "You lead the way." He waves his gun at Weisz and Rozum. "You two at the rear." He fishes a spare gun from a back pocket and hands it to Orlov. "It's loaded," he says. To everyone, he adds, "Nothing louder than a whisper."

Sweeping up the folds of her habit in one hand, her pistol in the other, Sister Sofia whispers urgently, "Follow carefully. The path is treacherous."

Orlov holds his breath as the party of seven moves out, weighing the cold, hard gun in his hand. He has rarely handled a gun since national service.

The group scuttles silently away from the convent and up the steep slope behind it, illuminated only by moon and stars. Sofia leads them to a narrow path that loops behind the main convent building, up the severe slope of the mountain and down again, until it joins the path that Orlov took yesterday, from the rear of the convent to the chapel. They walk in a cautious single file, with Sister Sofia leading the way, then Sister Petra, then Orlov, now acutely conscious of the throbbing in his injured knee. The four comrades are behind him. It soon becomes clear that this narrow path, challenging enough in daylight, is a deathtrap at night.

While focusing with all his might on following in the footsteps of Sister Petra in front of him, Orlov feels his right foot sink underneath him. He lurches involuntarily to the right and sees the moonlit slope dropping a thousand feet below him. For half of one second, he expects to fall, until he feels the powerful hand of Citizen Vanev grab the back of his habit and pull him back into the mountain. Sister Petra spins around, grabs his shoulder, and pushes him into the safety of the rock. Orlov stays there for a few seconds, his face pressed against the cold, dank mountain, breathing heavily to calm himself.

"Thank you," he whispers, grabbing his bad knee, before the party continues.

Orlov is mightily relieved to reach the chapel, which is in darkness. He breathes more easily as he follows Sofia and Petra through the cool, stone entrance.

The party of seven gathers in the darkness of the narrow vestibule, breathing heavily but saying nothing. There is a sense of relief that they have reached the chapel without losing anyone into the void below.

"I will light some candles," whispers Sister Petra.

She rummages for a moment on a window ledge next to the door. She strikes a match and lights two candles that illuminate an ancient stained-glass window.

It takes a few seconds for the pale, flickering light to reveal the remainder of the vestibule. As it does so, Orlov gasps and steps backwards.

Emerging from the darkness, pistols extended, are Agent Zelle and Sister Agnes.

CHAPTER FIFTEEN

In which our hero executes a daring plan

In the flickering candlelight of a cramped vestibule at the front of a tiny chapel perched against the side of a mountain at the highest point in the kingdom, nine people stand their ground, faces determined, brows furrowed, each pointing a gun at someone else. Five of them are dressed as nuns and four are not, although only two are actually nuns. Four of them want to kidnap the king, two of them want to kill the king, and three are hoping the king can escape unharmed. Four of them are card-carrying members of the People's Party and two of them are fishmongers. Of the nine guns being thrust forward in a threatening manner, eight are loaded and one is not. Everyone looks at everyone else. No one wants to be the first to make a move. Nor the last.

The stalemate persists for an uncomfortably long time. As he stares around the group at the steely faces and the steel gun barrels, it occurs to Citizen Orlov that this strange, tense moment could be significant in terms of the outcome of the civil war. Most of all, he wants to get out of this chapel alive and in one piece. But he also wants a peaceful resolution to the troubles. He is not especially enthusiastic about the king—or the monarchy, for that matter—but neither does he want to see His Majesty hurt or kidnapped in the name of politics. In the end, there will need to be a peaceful resolution to all of this.

Orlov is beginning to wonder how the immediate stalemate will be broken when the question is answered in front of his eyes.

Since Sisters Sofia and Petra were at the front of the party, they are furthest into the vestibule and so are closest to Zelle and Agnes. Sofia is staring directly into the barrel of Zelle's gun. As Orlov himself knows, this is not a comfortable position to be in. Sofia's own gun is trained on Agnes.

In a flash, however, Sofia pivots to her left like a prize fighter, switching the focus of her gun from Agnes to the side of Zelle's head. In a half second of confusion, Agnes moves her own gun in an attempt to follow Sofia's movement, providing just enough opportunity for Petra to snatch Agnes's gun from her hands and pass it coolly over her shoulder to Comrade Weisz, who takes it and trains both his guns on Zelle. Vanev steps forward, grabs Agnes in a bear hug, and bundles her into a corner.

All guns aside from Zelle's are now trained on Zelle, whose expression reveals that she knows the game is up. She raises both her hands. Rozum steps forward, snatches Zelle's gun from her raised hand, tucks it into his belt, and bundles her into the other corner.

Still pinning Agnes into the corner, Vanev turns to address Orlov over his shoulder.

"Go quickly, Comrades. We will keep order here."

Orlov catches Zelle's eye. To his surprise, a flicker of sympathy runs through him. Vanev must be twice Zelle's size and twice her weight.

And, though he can be intimidating, he is nothing compared with the three former soldiers standing right behind him. Although he has many reasons to be afraid of Zelle and to distrust her, nevertheless Orlov has certain feelings for her which he cannot quite identify.

"I trust violence will not be necessary," says Orlov, his voice rather forlorn and pathetic.

Vanev's answer is urgent and impatient. "Go!"

"Sisters," says Orlov to Sofia and Petra, indicating they should lead the way.

As he steps out into the moonlit night, Orlov is struck by two competing thoughts, both of them unpleasant. He wonders if he will be able to follow the nuns safely to the guest house without plunging to an untimely death because of his throbbing knee. And he wonders if he will ever see Agent Zelle alive again.

As before, Sister Sofia leads the way, followed by Sister Petra, and then Orlov. The path to the guest house is even longer and even more precarious than the path from the convent to the chapel. And much more challenging in the dark. To make matters worse, the wind is now swirling up from the ravine, causing Orlov to sway alarmingly. He tucks his pistol into his belt so that he can focus on balancing. For a second, he looks up at the dim lights of the guest house in the distance, but even this causes him to become unsteady.

He returns to focusing on his footsteps, carefully placing each step in precisely the spot where Sister Petra stepped a moment earlier.

As they creep along, the skirts of their habits pulled up to avoid tripping, Orlov tries to run through what he will say, if he has the opportunity to speak to the king. But he cannot form even one sentence in his head, which is fully occupied with stepping and balancing.

Occasionally, Orlov looks down below his right foot to see flashes of moonlight glinting off the slick cliff face beneath him. These flashes cause him to stumble, so he returns his gaze to the path.

He breathes a little easier when they arrive in the weak glow of the lamp above the front door of the guest house. Only now, a thin wisp of smoke can be seen rising from the chimney. The soldier stationed outside—young and stern—immediately swings his rifle off his shoulder and trains it on them.

"Who goes there?" he barks.

"Just three sisters," says Sofia, without hesitation. "We bring news of a worsening security situation at the convent."

"Stop! Hands up!" The soldier waves his rifle at them to indicate the direction he expects to see their hands moving. "Do you have weapons?"

"We are nuns," says Sister Sofia.

The soldier ignores this. He trains his rifle on each in turn, starting with Orlov. "Take out your weapon slowly and throw it over the edge," he says, nodding to indicate the ravine.

Orlov begins to say, "I don't think that's a good idea," but the soldier jabs the barrel of his rifle into Orlov's chest. Genuinely concerned that this soldier might be on the verge of shooting him, Orlov leaves his left hand in the air while moving his right hand slowly to his belt, fishing out the pistol with two fingers and flinging it out into the darkness beyond the path. It falls without a sound. As the soldier trains his rifle on each of them in turn, Sisters Sofia and Petra do the same.

Once this ceremony is over, the soldier speaks again. "Why are you here?"

"We need to speak to Sister Karla," says Sofia, urgently. "Some imposters have arrived at the convent. They intend to harm the ki—" she changes tack, "the sister."

"No one sees Sister Karla," he says, fiercely.

Sister Petra tries to assist. "We simply want to warn him—her—about the threat posed by the people who arrived here this afternoon."

"Tell *me*," says the soldier.

Sisters Sofia and Petra turn to Orlov, who pulls back his head covering to reveal his face completely. "I am Minister Orlov," he says, "Minister of Security. These ladies are two of the real Sisters of Our Lady of Perpetual Sorrow who live here at the convent. The nuns who traveled with us from the city are imposters who intend to harm Sister Karla. They were simply waiting for the rest of your platoon to leave. What's more, four members of the People's Party arrived just now, intent on kidnapping Sister Karla. For those reasons, we need to speak to him—her—urgently."

There is a pause while the soldier apparently absorbs this information.

Finally, he says, "Wait here. Do not move."

He knocks on the door behind him, which opens. He slips inside and the door is closed and locked again behind him.

Orlov, Sofia, and Petra wait in silence. Only now it occurs to Orlov that it is cold being at the top of a mountain wearing only a nun's habit. He hugs himself and slaps his hands against his shoulders for warmth. The two sisters smile at him, but in a grim, resigned fashion, as though they are anxious about the task ahead.

A scream of anguish rings out in the night.

It lasts only for a second before trailing rapidly into silence.

The three companions swivel around and look at the darkness behind them. The scream seemed to emanate from the path they just traversed. The two sisters cross themselves.

Before anyone has the time to speak, the soldier emerges from the door.

"What was that?" he says.

"Please hurry," says Orlov, "we need to speak to him now."

To Orlov's surprise, the soldier grabs him by the habit and pulls him toward the door.

"Just you," he says to Orlov. To the two sisters, he says, "Wait here."

A second later, the door is locked behind him and Orlov finds himself in a warm, candle-lit house, well-appointed with furniture and the smell of sausages wafting into the living room from the kitchen. He is marched to a small, leather sofa by a crackling fire and told to sit.

His Majesty the king strolls in from the kitchen, dressed in a pristine business suit. Orlov looks down at his habit and feels embarrassed. The king removes an apron and hangs it on a hook by the kitchen door. He joins Orlov in the living room, taking a seat in a grand armchair. This is the first time Orlov has seen the king since his coronation. The monarch's silvery hair and furrowed brow are a constant, but—perhaps not surprisingly—he looks a good deal more haggard now, as though he has had little sleep. Nevertheless, his voice is just as deep and charming as always.

"Minister," says His Majesty warmly. "I am grateful for your visit. Slivovitz?" He takes a small bottle and two glasses down from the mantlepiece.

"Thank you," says Orlov, who is quite sure that a stiff drink will both warm him up and calm his nerves.

The king pours two glasses, hands one to Orlov, and returns to his armchair.

Orlov takes a sip and rests the glass in his lap, enjoying the warmth of the fire. It would be easy to forget that a civil war is raging outside. He wonders what one should say to the monarch in such strange circumstances. He settles on something that he feels would be appropriate.

"I trust your family is safe and well, your majesty."

"I'm pleased to say they are across the border. For rather complicated legal reasons, I was advised against joining them. What of your family?"

Orlov is taken aback. He had not expected the king to be interested in his family. "There is only my mother," he says. "In Havlinik.

I hope she is safe. I will pay a visit as soon as the security situation allows."

The king nods reassuringly. "Things are quiet in Havlinik. Your mother may not notice the troubles at all."

Orlov has no idea if this is true or if the king is simply trying to be comforting. "Thank you," he says.

"So," says the king. "You have news for me?"

"Yes," says Orlov, clearing his throat and sitting up a little straighter on the sofa. "Two security developments that I think you should be aware of." Orlov hesitates; the king indicates that he should continue. "Firstly, I'm sorry to say that the sisters who traveled with us from the city are, in fact, not real sisters. They are imposters."

The king leans forward in his chair. "Who on earth are they, then?"

"I'm sure your majesty is familiar with the term zealots?" says Orlov.

The king rolls his eyes. "Are you telling me they walked out of prison dressed in nun's outfits?"

"I believe they took a detour up here to collect the habits."

"So, where are the real sisters?" asks the king. "Are they safe?"

"They are safe, for now, and currently staying at the prison, wearing prison clothes. All except two, who are waiting outside."

The King eyes Orlov with a curious expression. "So, the prisoners are dressed as nuns and the nuns are dressed as prisoners?" he says.

"Yes, your majesty," says Orlov.

The king runs both his hands down his face. "And now you want to persuade me to move to the prison?"

"There's something else," says Orlov. "Four members of the People's Party arrived here this afternoon. They are currently in the chapel, where they are holding two of the zealots."

The king frowns. "My team here can handle that, if necessary."

"Yes, your majesty," says Orlov. "I just wanted to make you aware that, well, now the rest of the platoon has left, I believe the zealots are planning something. And I know for sure that the People's Party are. If I may say so, I believe you would be safer at the prison with the real sisters."

The king swigs the remainder of his slivovitz in one go. "It's not quite so attractive a location."

"I understand," says Orlov.

The king waves at someone hovering out of Orlov's sight. A soldier steps into the living room.

"You heard all that?" says the king.

"I did, your majesty," says the soldier.

"What do you say?" asks the king.

"We can keep you safe here, your majesty," replies the soldier.

The king appears concerned. "I'm quite sure you could handle four members of the People's Party. But what of these imposters? If the minister is correct, a dozen armed zealots could arrive here at any moment. That would be a problem, would it not?"

The soldier appears reluctant to accept the point. "Well, your majesty, that would perhaps be a little more," he hesitates, "lively."

The king nods to acknowledge the point. "The plan was to stay with the Sisters of Our Lady of Perpetual Sorrow. Everyone agreed that is the safest place in the kingdom. It seems we have failed to achieve that so far, but now another opportunity has presented itself. Could we move safely to the prison, tonight?"

The soldier seems a little taken aback. "May I speak frankly?"

"I would prefer it," says the king.

The soldier frowns. "If your majesty prefers to move to the prison, of course we will facilitate that. But the journey would be safer if we had several nuns, instead of just one."

"The minister has brought two nuns with him," says the king, as though warming to the idea. He turns to Orlov. "Would these sisters be prepared to accompany me on my journey down the mountain?"

"Just one moment," says Orlov. He sets his glass down and approaches the front door. The soldier opens the door and locks it again behind him.

Out in the starry, moonlit night, Sisters Sofia and Petra are pacing in an agitated fashion and clapping their hands together against the cold.

"What news?" says Sofia.

Orlov explains. One minute later, the two sisters are being introduced to the monarch by the fire.

"I'm terribly sorry to hear how you were treated," says the king. "We will rectify the situation just as soon as this wretched trouble is over."

"Thank you, your majesty," say the two nuns, almost in unison.

"Unless anyone has a better idea, I had better don my habit," says the king, cheerfully, stepping toward the bedroom at the back of the little house.

Orlov waits with the two sisters by the fire, saying nothing.

Two minutes later, Sister Karla emerges. Apparently unsatisfied, Sister Sofia asks politely for permission and then adjusts the king's headdress so that it covers more of his face.

The king has a quiet word with one of the soldiers that no one else can hear, then he turns to Orlov. "Will you accompany us, Minister?"

"Thank you, your majesty," says Orlov. "I wish I could. But I have other business to attend to here."

"Very well," says the king, "if you're sure."

He nods to one of the soldiers, who leads the way to the back door of the guest house.

The group falls into formation; two soldiers in the lead, followed by three nuns, followed by two soldiers at the rear.

Orlov follows them to the back door and sees in the moonlight a precarious, winding path looping down the mountain in a trajectory that steers well clear of the front gate of the convent. Presumably it meets the main path to the prison somewhere down below.

He stands at the door and watches the party of seven pick its way slowly down the path until they disappear into the night.

CHAPTER SIXTEEN

In which our hero finds himself in mortal danger once again

Citizen Orlov exits through the front door of the guest house, now gripped with the need to invent a story that will placate Citizen Vanev. He picks his way slowly and carefully along the path toward the chapel, trying out different stories in his head. By far the safest story, he concludes, would be to say that they found the guest house empty; if the king had ever been there, he must have left earlier when shots were fired. It's not unreasonable to assume that the soldiers might have heard the shots and decided to move the king immediately.

On the other hand—and Orlov decides it might be best to focus on this point—he cannot confirm that the king was actually there in the first place. It is perhaps best to say that he looked for evidence that the king had stayed at the guest house, but found none. Having said that, he cannot immediately think of anything that would constitute such evidence. Had the king stayed at the guest house earlier and then moved on to another location, he would be unlikely to leave any telltale signs of having been there.

Orlov notices an improvement in his ability to ponder such things while also traversing the treacherous path. He reminds himself not to be complacent; one wrong step and he will plunge a thousand feet to a grisly death.

As the chapel comes into view, Orlov has second thoughts about whether it is wise to return to Vanev and his comrades. He could, of course, have traveled with the king and the nuns down to the prison. But then he would have firmly declared allegiance to a monarchy he does not really believe in. He does not believe in any of the sides in this conflict.

In fact, he is not sure he fully understands how many sides there are or what they stand for. If he had chosen to disappear while Vanev was waiting for him—after taking a treacherous journey up from the city in response to his message—he is not sure his old friend would ever speak to him again. And that would be the end of his employment as well as his oldest and dearest friendship. On thinking through the options, he concludes that returning to see Vanev with an embroidered story is not just the best option, it is the only option available.

Feeling a little more comfortable that he has made the right choice, Orlov stops just short of the chapel and leans against the rock face to catch his breath and rest his sore knee. It has been a long and tiring day, full of intrigue and not a little confusion. He is grateful that Sisters Sofia and Petra were prepared to contribute in such a brave manner; their courage may just have saved the life of the king. And he is grateful for the loyalty of Citizen Vanev; even if Orlov does not share his political leanings, he thinks how much worse today might have been, had Vanev and his comrades not arrived to intervene. For a second, this realization causes Orlov to feel a little guilty that he is about to tell his friend an invented story; he takes no pleasure in it, but neither can he think of an alternative course of action.

Wondering what might have become of Zelle and Agnes—and whether their fate might be connected to the awful scream—Orlov treads carefully to the door of the chapel. He takes a deep breath before stepping inside.

Something is not right. On the floor in the middle of the vestibule, face down and with their hands tied behind their backs with items of clothing, are Comrades Vanev, Weisz, and Nemeth. Standing above them, with a pistol trained down at her captives, is Sister Agnes. There is no sign of Comrade Rozum.

Instinctively, Orlov takes a step backwards, but stops when a pistol barrel emerges from the darkness and presses against his temple.

"So glad the Minister of Security could join us," says Zelle, emerging from behind the door.

Orlov raises his hands. Zelle frisks him and quickly concludes that he has no weapon.

Continuing to stare down at the three captives, Orlov barks, "Where is Rozum?"

Zelle ignores this. "I trust you had a productive meeting with Sister Karla," she says.

Orlov thinks quickly. The story he invented was intended for Vanev. But now the circumstances are rather different. Nevertheless, it seems best to stick to the same story.

"The guest house was empty," he says.

Zelle steps in so close that he can smell her cologne. She presses the pistol more firmly into his temple. "I do not believe you, Minister."

Orlov strains to remain calm, staring down at a prostrate Vanev. "Where is Rozum?" he says again, now in a whisper.

"Where are the two nuns?" hisses Zelle.

He had not expected this question, so must think quickly. "They stayed at the guest house. They were afraid to return here."

"Once again, I do not believe you," says Zelle. She turns to Agnes. "The Minister and I will be taking a walk."

Agnes nods. "Everything is under control here," she says, continuing to train her pistol down at the three captives.

Without another word, Zelle grabs Orlov by the shoulder and pushes him through the door so hard that he thinks he might topple off the path and over the edge. He steadies himself with the spindly branch of a little tree.

"Be careful, Minister," says Zelle, shoving her pistol into his back to encourage him to turn left toward the guest house. "Unless you want to share the fate of Comrade Rozum."

Orlov feels his blood boil. He can scarcely believe that even Zelle would do such a thing. He forces himself to suppress his anger in favor of focusing on making this treacherous walk once again. It is now even darker and colder than before, and it must by now be the early hours of the morning. Orlov senses himself becoming tired and forces himself to focus on stepping carefully, a task made no easier by the pressure of Zelle's gun in his back. He is determined to discover the fate of Rozum, but first he must navigate the immediate danger. He knows from previous experience that appearing to go along with Zelle is safer than confronting her.

As he picks his way carefully back to the guest house, with Zelle right behind him and her gun never far from his back, he wonders how she will react when she discovers the truth. Zelle must have considered the possibility that the king would escape, even if she is not aware that the guest house has a back door. That much is certain. Nevertheless, he decides it would be best to stick to his story: when he arrived, there was no sign of the king. Perhaps he had never been here. Could Zelle even be sure that Sister Karla was really the king? Is it not possible that the zealots had been fooled by the military into accepting a decoy while the real king fled the country with his family? That argument, in particular, is rather persuasive, and he determines to use it as a retort, in the highly likely event that Zelle becomes angry and argumentative when she discovers that the king is missing.

Now becoming more familiar with the path, Orlov makes progress as quickly as he feels is safe.

They arrive in the weak glow of the guest house. Saying nothing, Zelle waves her pistol to indicate that Orlov should open the door. He obliges, and they step inside.

Obviously becoming agitated, Zelle marches Orlov around the little house at gunpoint, opening every door and searching the bedroom and kitchen before discovering the back door. She opens it and stops to contemplate the path that runs down the mountainside. She steps outside onto the path briefly, as though checking whether anyone is out there.

Seeing nothing, Zelle marches Orlov to the fireplace; it is obvious to anyone that this fire was still burning just a short time ago.

She backs him up against the fire such that he can feel its glow against his habit.

"So, the Minister of Security warned the monarch to leave."

"There was no one here," says Orlov defiantly.

"And yet the fireplace is still warm," says Zelle.

"Must have been the sisters," says Orlov.

Zelle scoffs. "They lit a fire and then immediately left through the back door?"

Orlov is unsure what to say. "It seems so."

Zelle's face transforms in an instant from scorn to anger. She grabs him by the shoulder and spins him toward the front door.

"Move," she barks.

Orlov complies. He senses himself stiffen as he contemplates his fate.

Once outside, Zelle thrusts the pistol into his back once again. "Minister, I have had my fill of you."

Unsure what to say, he begins to walk along the path.

"This way," barks Zelle, pushing him left, across the path and into a gap between two small trees, beyond which is nothing at all besides the ravine, whose floor lies some one thousand feet below.

Alarmed, Orlov turns back to face Zelle, holding onto a branch with his back to the ravine. "Please," he says.

There is a strange look on Zelle's face, a look he has never seen before. It might be pity, or disgust.

"It has been a pleasure to know you, Minister," says Zelle, quietly.

She pushes him over the edge.

PART FOUR

Escape from Mount Zhotrykaw

CHAPTER SEVENTEEN

In which our hero falls from a great height

Citizen Orlov clenches everything that can be clenched.

He plunges face up, arms and legs flailing above him.

Zelle and the guest house are there for one, two seconds, then gone.

He closes his eyes.

He feels sick to his stomach.

He braces for impact.

Much sooner than expected, something smacks Orlov in the right arm, causing him to spin. Instinctively, he tries to shield his head with his arms.

Now face down, he hits something else, slowing his movement.

Then something else.

He grabs it. It is the branch of a tree.

He falls farther. Forced to give up the first branch, he grabs another.

The next branch smacks him in the face.

He grabs it.

Orlov has never been so thankful to be scratched and slapped in the face.

Each branch brings more slaps to the head, arms, stomach, but also slower movement.

Finally, he grabs a big, fat branch with both arms, determined to hold on.

He falls again, spinning.

This time, he hits something solid: undergrowth.

Something sharp is sticking into his back; he rolls over.

Everything stops dead. He feels pain everywhere. First, it feels like scratches to his face.

But slowly something much worse emerges: deep muscular pain in his arms, legs, and back, as though an angry mob has beaten him with sticks.

Lying completely still, not daring to move, Orlov surveys the various pains across his body, trying to discern how badly he is injured.

More worrying than his aches and pains is the situation regarding his right arm and shoulder: he cannot feel either of them. Still prostrate in the undergrowth, he attempts to move his right arm a little, but has no idea if this has been successful, since he feels nothing.

Unsure of the situation on his right side, he rolls over gingerly on his left side and slowly deploys his left arm in an attempt to sit up. This proves painful, so he lies back in the undergrowth for a while, wondering where he is.

Very little moonlight has penetrated this strange forest, so it is difficult to see much of anything. He wonders if it would be safe to walk anywhere in the darkness, even if he could do so, given the possibility that one might at any moment encounter the edge of a cliff. It might be better to stay put for a while, at least until his aches and pains have eased a little.

CITIZEN ORLOV IS woken by a frigid wind swirling into his face. Early morning daylight seeps through the trees in an eerie, mottled pattern. Feeling damp, he half sits up; the dew of the undergrowth has seeped into his habit. Only now, he sees that the habit is filthy and torn to shreds following his unceremonious arrival through the tops of the trees that now stand majestically above him, reaching proudly into the sky as though nothing unusual has happened.

Realizing that his right arm is still refusing to respond to his commands, Orlov uses his left hand to tear the covering from his head and fashions a simple sling to tie his right arm to his side until he can find someone medical to examine it.

He gets to his feet slowly, using a nearby tree to steady himself, his right knee still complaining from its run-in with Sister Agnes. Everything is painful but, with the exception of his right arm, everything else appears to be working.

Orlov concludes that the strange little forest into which he has fallen is on a shelf. No doubt there is a more technical name for it than that. His concern, however, is not what this feature is called, but how to escape from it. He pauses to acknowledge his gratefulness for landing here versus the bottom of the ravine many hundreds of feet below. But this temporary blessing will be short lived if he cannot find a way to leave the shelf and return to civilization.

The thought of being too near the edge makes him feel queasy, so Orlov gets up gingerly and begins to trudge back toward the mountain, wondering if there might just be—by some stroke of good fortune—a navigable path up to the convent or, better still, to the mountain path beneath it.

He wonders if he is the first person ever to stand on this shelf. Since there is nothing here except trees, he can think of no reason why anyone would want to visit this place. Moreover, he can see no way a person could arrive here, aside from the rather unfortunate route which he himself took last night. The reverse of that, of course, is that there might be no way for a person to leave again. He tries to suppress a feeling of panic and instead continues exploring.

As he trudges through dense trees, the shelf begins to fold itself into the mountain until eventually a split opens up, the vegetation thins out, and a roof of sharp, angular rock appears above his head.

He pauses to consider the options. Turning back to where he landed, the light is better and the trees are more plentiful, but it offers no obvious way out. The dark, rocky tunnel opening up ahead of him is foreboding in comparison, but at least it does not appear to involve a sheer drop to certain death. That seems worth investigating.

He determines to continue into the tunnel for as long as there is light. If it becomes completely dark, he will simply retrace his steps and return to the shelf while considering his next move.

With that decision firmly fixed in his mind, Orlov picks his way carefully over huge boulders as the undergrowth gradually disappears, replaced by smooth, damp rocks. Now the roof begins to close in over his head and it becomes wetter underfoot. Soon he senses that water is running down the walls and through the floor of this gradually closing tunnel.

He concludes that water running down off the mountain—perhaps including melting snow—has formed this tunnel. That offers a glimmer of hope.

After all, the water must run somewhere. There is no guarantee the tunnel is navigable by a person, but at the moment it is perhaps three times Orlov's height, which is a promising start.

Now he is effectively wading in a stream, and the tunnel turns to the right, into the heart of the mountain. As it does so, the light fades alarmingly quickly and the temperature drops. Soon, he will not be able to see his hand in front of his face.

Pressing on carefully, he hopes to see something new up ahead; perhaps a glimmer of light from another source, some evidence that the tunnel leads somewhere. With each step, however, the conditions become darker and colder, with no signs of hope. He takes slow, exaggerated steps to avoid tripping over rocks that he can now scarcely see.

After several minutes of worsening conditions, Orlov reluctantly admits to himself that the tunnel is now entirely dark.

Without warning, his footing gives way and he plunges down into frigid water. He thrusts his face upward and gulps the air. Still in almost total darkness, he is pulled along by the flow of this stream, now rapidly becoming a river.

He thrusts his good hand upward to get a sense of the height of the tunnel. He can touch the top at a stretch. That is fine for now, but what happens if the tunnel narrows so much that he cannot pass through? This does not bear thinking about since there is no way that he can now retrace his steps back to the shelf. Whatever happens now, he must keep moving forward.

For several minutes, Orlov allows himself to be carried by this strange, dark river, constantly waving his good arm up and to the side to ensure the tunnel remains wide enough for him to pass. He shudders in response to the frigid water.

Soon, the water level begins to drop, and he can kick the rocks on the river bed. Without warning, the water dissipates, and Orlov is unceremoniously dumped onto slimy, damp rocks. Sodden and weary, he drags himself back onto his feet, shakes some of the water out of his bedraggled habit, and trudges on along the clammy tunnel.

Only now, he realizes that the river has taken one of his shoes. A quick search behind him reveals nothing. Given his now uneven gait, he takes off his remaining shoe and flings it away in frustration.

Perhaps because he is tired and damp, Orlov wonders what he has done to deserve this. All he has done at every turn is what he thought was best for his beloved country. Caught in the middle between the zealots and the People's Party, the only reasonable course of action was to give the king the chance to escape. Any of the other options would have been unthinkable to an ordinary citizen, regardless of their views on the monarchy. And yet, in exchange for choosing the most peaceful option, he very nearly died by falling from the mountain and might very well still die if he cannot soon work out how to escape from inside it. Orlov has been alive long enough to know that life is not fair, but in this case it seems an unnatural degree of unfairness has arrived at his door.

Orlov continues to pick his way along the dark tunnel, using his good arm to keep a consistent distance from the wall.

Good news and bad news arrive at the same time. The good news is that a dim light appears far up ahead, illuminating the damp walls of the tunnel in an eerie glow. The bad news is that this new light is accompanied by a foul smell that soon reveals itself to be excrement. On balance, Orlov considers these dual developments to be positive: he is prepared to tolerate a foul stench in exchange for being able to see where he is going. More importantly, both these developments suggest he is about to arrive somewhere, and that offers the promise of leaving the bowels of the mountain and emerging back into civilization.

A sound up ahead causes him to stop dead. A cough. And then another. In the dim light, Orlov can see no one nearby. He tenses. Now he can hear footsteps approaching slowly.

"Hello?" says Orlov.

The only response is more coughing, followed by slow, shuffling footsteps.

Emerging from the darkness appears a wizened, bearded old man wearing the rough clothes of a mountain shepherd and carrying a huge staff. He appears not to notice Orlov until almost walking into him.

Orlov takes a step back. “Hello,” he says.

Only now, the man appears to notice Orlov, stopping to peer at him. He is roughly Orlov’s height but is bent over with age and so must look up to see Orlov’s face.

“Is this the way out?’ says Orlov, gesturing in the direction from which the man has apparently arrived.

“Are you a shepherd?” asks the man in a gruff, rasping voice.

“I’m a fishmonger,” says Orlov.

Without warning, the man swings his staff out to his side with surprising speed and then drives it hard into Orlov’s injured knee. Orlov cries out in pain and crumples to the ground.

“Shepherds only in the tunnel,” says the old man, as though this should be well known to everyone, and continues on his way.

Still crouching, Orlov sucks in a few deep breaths before turning to the shepherd. “Is the way out?” he says, pointing in the direction from which the shepherd had come.

The old man continues to shuffle away, mumbling to himself, until he has disappeared into darkness.

Orlov waits for the pain in his knee to subside before walking on again. Soon, the light grows brighter, the stench grows fouler, and the rocky, uneven tunnel gives way to a round, man-made tunnel. When he finds that he is wading through a hideous sludge, Orlov realizes that he has arrived in a sewerage system. The smell quickly becomes unbearable; he removes his makeshift sling and uses it to cover his nose and mouth.

His hopes pick up when he sees a rusty, iron ladder up ahead. It transpires that this ladder leads up to the source of light, a wide opening in the roof of the tunnel. Dragging himself up with his good hand, Orlov climbs slowly and cautiously up the ladder. He is mightily relieved to leave the tunnel, rolling from the opening onto rocks, gasping for fresh air and looking up from his prone position to see if he can determine where he is.

After hours inside the mountain, the daylight is blinding. He shields his eyes with his good arm and lies for a while on his back, catching his breath and enjoying the relative warmth of a weak sun.

Rising up above Orlov is a dark, forbidding building. He sits up and surveys the scene. It takes him a few moments to realize that he has emerged behind Prison Zhotrykaw. To his right he can see the fenced exercise yard. He is sitting in some sort of service yard that contains maintenance equipment and tools.

He feels a sense of hope. Perhaps he can stay for a while with the Sisters of Our Lady of Perpetual Sorrow. If the king can keep himself safe by hiding among the sisters at the prison, why should Orlov not do likewise? He looks down at his bedraggled, ripped, filthy habit and determines to exchange it for prison overalls.

He drags himself to his feet, replaces the makeshift sling around his injured arm, and makes his way to the door of the maintenance room. Having never been in this part of the building before, it takes a while to orient himself.

He trails along corridors of cells, amazed that almost every door has been left wide open. But perhaps that is to be expected; after all, on coronation day, the guards walked out and apparently encouraged the whole company of prisoners to follow them, if the rumors are to be believed.

Eventually, Orlov arrives at a familiar spot: the door to the dining hall. He wonders if the sisters are here, cooking or cleaning up after a meal, but there is silence. The dining hall is empty, and so are the kitchen and the store room. Worse still, most of the food has gone. A few sacks of potatoes remain, but little else.

He walks on through long cell blocks and is delighted to stumble across the laundry room, where he abandons what remains of his bedraggled habit and instead dons gray prison overalls. The closest fit he can find is still too large, making him look like a convicted circus clown. But it is a relief to wear something clean and dry, and not stinking of sewage. Sadly, there is no sign of any shoes, and so he continues barefoot, stepping carefully to avoid hazards.

Searching through the cell blocks and arriving at the reception area at the front of the building, there is no sign of the sisters or the king or anyone else. Sadly, Orlov reaches the conclusion that they have all moved on, together or otherwise, and that they have taken most of the food with them. He does not wish to stay here on his own, and in any case cannot do so without food supplies. He is tired and hungry already. Since he has no intention of returning to the convent, the only option available to him—despite the dangers—is to attempt to travel down the mountain alone.

Treading very carefully in his bare feet, Orlov tiptoes outside and walks around to the vehicle yard, where his suspicions are realized. Several of the vehicles that stood here on his last visit have now gone, leaving just two prisoner transport trucks; cages on wheels. They look ancient and dilapidated. It's easy to see why these vehicles might have been rejected by the sisters and the king. He steps up into the nearest one and, with some difficulty, persuades it to start. It is uncomfortable to drive in bare feet, but Orlov manages to maneuver slowly around the side of the prison and out onto the mountain road. He checks both ways for signs of danger and, seeing no one, turns right to head down the mountain.

The road is uneven and frequently Orlov needs to slow the truck down to avoid rocks. Occasionally, he stops and gets out to push larger rocks out of the way before continuing. It is slow and exhausting work, especially with an injured arm, and much trickier barefoot than it would have been if he could wear his heavy work boots that are—or were—in his humble little apartment in the city. This reminds him of the broken window and the fact that an unidentified collection of his belongings were strewn on the street underneath, where they have by now presumably been stolen or ruined by the rain. He wonders what state his apartment is in and whether anyone has at least boarded up the window to prevent weather damage. He longs to be able to go back there without incurring the wrath of his neighbors, but first there is the small matter of a civil war to be settled.

Although Orlov is a little downhearted when remembering the situation at his home, he determines to remain upbeat as much as possible. After all, he might have been killed when Zelle pushed him off the cliff last night, and he might just as easily have died if he had not been able to find his way out of the mountain today. So, he has a good deal to be thankful for.

Just as he is coming to this conclusion, the truck begins to make a strange grating noise, as though the engine is complaining about something. This is followed by spluttering, in which the vehicle lurches forward and then stops several times. Finally, it comes to a halt.

It seems the truck has run out of gasoline, less than a half hour after leaving the prison. Orlov attempts to persuade it to glide down the hill unaided, given the steep gradient, but it quickly becomes clear that the ground is much too rough to allow this.

Dejected, Orlov steps down from the truck and sits on a rock. He rests his head in his hands and sighs heavily. He is three-quarters the way up the highest mountain in the kingdom with no transport and no shoes.

CHAPTER EIGHTEEN

In which our hero is reacquainted with an old friend

Citizen Orlov sits on his rock for a long while and considers his options. He searches for his pocket watch and realizes that he has parted with it somewhere along his journey, although he does not know where. From the position of the sun, he guesses that it is the middle of the afternoon, which means he spent half a day walking through the mountain. No wonder he is tired and hungry.

Since he is much nearer the top of the mountain than the bottom, he determines to walk back up to the prison where there is one vehicle remaining. Perhaps he simply chose the wrong truck. He will drive the other truck and hope it has more gasoline. Better still, he will check in the vehicle yard to see if there are any canisters with supplies of gasoline. If so, he could simply walk back down to this vehicle and fill it up before continuing. But that, of course, would involve walking twice as far without shoes.

With these options racing through his mind, Orlov stands up gingerly and begins to walk back up the road. Instantly, he finds it is a much more difficult and painful process than he had imagined. He dances and winces like someone walking on proverbial hot coals. A piece of flint stabs the sole of his foot. He screams and topples over, landing awkwardly on his injured arm. His head stops just short of colliding with a rock. He grimaces and ejects an expletive into the cool afternoon air.

Concerned about his bad arm, Orlov lies for a while and waits for the pain to subside. At least some feeling has returned to his arm; perhaps blinding pain is better than no feeling at all.

Against his better nature, he is rapidly becoming downhearted. Nothing seems to be going his way. From his prone position he looks down the road at the truck and sees that he has only climbed a matter of one hundred yards above it. At this rate, it will take him until nightfall to return to the prison. A night at the prison with nothing to eat besides potatoes is not an attractive plan.

Still prone, Orlov is thinking about boiling potatoes in the prison kitchen when he hears a noise above him. Straining to look up, he sees the other truck trundling slowly toward him. It is too far away to see who is driving it.

Orlov thinks quickly. This could be very good or very bad.

He springs up, adrenaline kicking in, and sets off back down the hill toward his own truck, now hobbling twice as fast as before.

He reaches his truck while the other truck is still some distance above him. Crouching down at the front of his truck, he hides behind the hood, peering out furtively to see if he can make out who is driving the other vehicle.

Orlov breathes heavily, wondering what fate has in store for him. The other truck trundles painfully slowly over the rough terrain.

Orlov holds his breath and hopes for the best.

Eventually, the truck draws close enough for Orlov to conclude that its driver is a very large person. This is good news, potentially.

Soon after, he can see enough to suggest that this large driver has a beard. Finally, he is sure that the driver is Vanev and that Weisz and Nemeth are in the cab beside him.

Orlov breathes a sigh of relief. But he cannot see if anyone else is in the truck behind the three comrades, so he stays out of sight for now, until they draw closer.

While waiting for the truck to reach him, Orlov wonders what mood the comrades will be in. He wonders how they escaped from Zelle and Agnes. He wonders whether they will be angry at him for letting the king escape. He wonders how far away the king and the sisters are, and whether it is far enough to keep them from danger. These are all good and important questions, but they are the details of a civil war that Orlov does not care for and does not believe in. He simply wants it to be over. He also longs for a pair of shoes.

The second truck stops just behind the first truck. All three comrades climb down, in an urgent, frantic manner.

Seeing no one else with them, Orlov stands up, raising his good arm in a half gesture of surrender.

"Comrades," he says, "it's me. Comrade Orlov."

"You again," spits Weisz, stepping toward him menacingly. "It's always you."

Orlov does not know what to say, so says nothing.

Weisz continues, "What happened to the king?"

Vanev puts his considerable frame between Weisz and Orlov. "That's enough," he says. "We don't have time for this." Turning to Orlov, Vanev says, "Comrade, help us."

For a moment, Orlov is unsure what Vanev intends. The three comrades stand on the mountain side of the first truck and begin, without speaking, to push it off the road. Orlov quickly joins in. He puts his shoulder into it and, with a burst of exertion from all four men, the truck slowly begins to tip. It takes several seconds for it to reach the point of no return and then, as the comrades take a step back, the mass of the truck takes on its own momentum, toppling it with surprising speed and force off the road and down the steep mountainside.

It crashes into pieces on rocks below them. Vanev grabs Orlov to stop him from following it over the edge.

Vanev looks urgently up the mountain and then back at Weisz and Nemeth. "You two take the cab," he says, staring at Orlov's bare feet and bundling him into the cage at the back.

The second truck continues on its way down the mountain road, with Nemeth driving and Weisz beside him in the cab. Vanev and Orlov hang onto the sides of the cage.

Orlov breathes a huge sigh of relief. "Citizen, I have never been more pleased to see you."

"We are not out of the woods yet," says Vanev. "The zealots are pursuing us." He glances back up the mountain.

"But this is the last truck," says Orlov.

Vanev grimaces. "I do not think that will deter your friend, Agent Zelle."

Orlov senses there is something behind this remark. "What happened?"

Vanev hesitates. "Let us just say that Sister Agnes met the same fate as poor Comrade Rozum."

Orlov holds his head in his hands. "Oh dear," he says.

"An eye for an eye," says Vanev grimly.

Orlov looks up at him. "If it is any comfort, comrade, you should know that Zelle did the same to me."

"You mean she *tried* to do the same?" says Vanev.

For much of the rest of the journey down the mountain, Orlov tells Vanev the story of what happened with Zelle, how he survived it, and how he found himself back at the prison. He is about to mention meeting the shepherd, but decides against it. Vanev listens in horror, while keeping an eye on the road above them, as though he expects Zelle, Molnar, and their fellow zealots to appear at any moment, sprinting down the mountain with pistols firing.

By the time the road begins to level out at the foothills of Mount Zhotrykaw, the light is fading. Orlov is mightily relieved to see civilization again, the lights of small villages now coming into view as the truck turns and heads toward the city. But he is surprised to hear almost a total silence; no gunshots, no sirens, no emergency vehicles. No sounds at all, in fact, to indicate that a civil war is still raging.

He turns to Vanev. "When I was at Hotel Melikov, they said their ammunition would last only two more days. Do you think they've run out?'

Vanev looks around at the quiet village through which they're passing. "Maybe, but we need to be cautious. If the one soldier pointing his rifle at your head has bullets, it doesn't much matter whether the rest of the army has run out."

Orlov considers this. "I see what you mean," he says.

Vanev stares out into the night for a while, as though trying to sense the level of danger. "Maybe they ran out today, maybe it will be tomorrow. They're not going to announce it."

"What about *our* supplies?" asks Orlov, realizing only after he's spoken that he has never before sounded so partisan.

Vanev, apparently noticing this, raises his eyebrows. "The situation was bad before we left the city. Now it will be worse. Maybe we have run out already. We'll find out soon enough, if we can make it back to the hotel."

"Supposing both sides in a civil war run out of ammunition," says Orlov. "Who wins?"

Vanev considers this. "Whoever finds ammunition first," he says.

Orlov is about to ask another question, but he is interrupted by Weisz knocking on the back of the cab to attract their attention.

Weisz turns to talk to Vanev through the cage. "Checkpoint," he says.

The truck slows to a crawl. The lights of a small village are flickering up ahead, illuminating a long building and barriers across the road. As they draw nearer, it becomes clear that several armed guards are patrolling in front of the barriers. In contrast to the checkpoint where the ministers and fake nuns were stopped on their way up the mountain, this checkpoint is much larger, more organized and attached to a regional police station. It seems clear that this checkpoint is operated by the army.

Orlov turns to Vanev, whispering to him since they are now drawing near to the barriers. "Do you think they have bullets?" he asks.

"Do you want to be the one who guesses?" says Vanev.

Since none of the comrades are now armed—having had their guns disposed of by zealots—the idea of trying to guess who has bullets left and who does not is an unattractive proposition. Orlov sits quietly and listens on carefully as Nemeth stops the truck and leans out to talk to a soldier now approaching him.

The soldier trains his rifle on Nemeth, who raises his hands.

"We are unarmed," says Nemeth.

"Where have you been?" says the soldier.

"We passed this way just yesterday," says Nemeth. "We were escorting two sisters up to the convent."

The soldier is joined by another soldier, who trains his rifle on Weisz. Weisz does not raise his hands.

The first soldier speaks to Nemeth again. "Who are you? The Pope?"

Nemeth hesitates. "Just doing our civic duty," he says.

The second soldier barks at Weisz. "Raise your hands."

Weisz stays completely still.

Vanev raises his hands, nods to Orlov to do the same, and hisses at Weisz, "Raise your hands."

Orlov grimaces as he tries to keep his injured arm aloft. One of the soldiers eyes his prison uniform suspiciously, but says nothing.

"We are unarmed," says Nemeth, again.

Weisz stares at the second soldier, impassive and still not moving.

Keeping his gun trained on Weisz, the second soldier moves around to the passenger door, where two other soldiers are standing. "Out of the vehicle," he barks. "Everyone."

Keeping his hands raised, Vanev sighs heavily and climbs down onto the road. Orlov follows him. Nemeth climbs down from the cab, hands still raised. Now the three comrades are standing at the side of the road in a line, arms raised, while Weisz remains dead still in the cab.

"Everyone," repeats the second soldier.

Weisz does not move.

The second soldier fires a single shot into the air.

Weisz does not flinch, but slowly raises his hands and climbs down from the cab, where he is met by three soldiers who push him with the barrels of their rifles toward the other comrades.

It is clear to Orlov that Vanev is furious with Weisz.

Vanev whispers fiercely at Weisz, "Comrade, cool your head."

Weisz ignores this and simply stares straight ahead.

Orlov keeps his hand aloft and hopes the atmosphere will soon become calmer.

The first soldier waves his rifle toward the police station. "That way," he says. He glances down at Orlov's shoeless feet but makes no comment about them.

Hands still raised, Vanev begins to walk, but also complains, "We are simply returning home to the city."

"Not tonight," says the first soldier, marching them abruptly through the dark reception area of the police station and into the holding cells. It smells as though someone has died in here. A dark corridor leads to a half dozen adjacent, empty cells, separated by heavy bars. Two soldiers quickly frisk each prisoner for weapons and, finding none, push them into a cell and lock the door.

As the soldiers start to leave, Vanev speaks, now adopting a quiet, pleading voice. "Officers, we have traveled all day without food. There is no reason to detain us here but, if you must, please bring us something to eat."

One of the soldiers grunts unintelligibly as they leave.

The four prisoners sit quietly in their cells. The atmosphere is very much downhearted. Orlov senses that Vanev is too weary to argue with Weisz.

To everyone's surprise, a soldier returns with a small loaf of bread. It is round, with a heavy crust, as is the tradition in the north of the kingdom. In fact, it is precisely the sort of loaf that is sold—to the tune of dozens every day—by the baker whose stall stands in the market at the Grand Plaza almost exactly opposite the fish stall manned by Citizens Vanev and Orlov. Sometimes, on a quiet morning, before the customers begin to gather in crowds, Orlov likes to take a walk across the square to say good morning to the baker and to enjoy the smell of his freshly-baked loaves as he sets them out on his stall. Orlov is far from the only market vendor who makes a habit of this; it is true to say that, on some mornings, the baker attracts quite a crowd. Naturally, the baker does not object to this, and he offers a generous discount to any fellow market trader who buys a loaf before lunchtime. For this reason, Orlov has for many years adopted the tradition of walking to work with a half crown in his pocket. He buys a loaf as early as possible—before the crowds arrive—and stores it in the pocket of his great coat, to be enjoyed later with sausage and boiled cabbage.

Saying nothing, the soldier thrusts the loaf through the bars of Vanev's cell, where it falls on the filthy floor. As the soldier leaves again, Vanev scoops up the loaf, makes a token effort to clean it, then divides it carefully into four pieces, which he shares by passing them through the bars along the line of cells.

The four prisoners eat their bread quietly in their cells. Orlov is exhausted and relieved to eat something. It is frustrating to be imprisoned for no reason but, since he began the day genuinely concerned for his life, he concludes that things are not as bad as they were.

Vanev breaks the silence. He speaks wearily, looking down at what remains of his bread. "When a soldier with a rifle tells you to raise your hands, you raise your hands," he says.

There is a pause before Weisz replies. "I wanted to see if they had bullets."

"And now we know," says Vanev.

CHAPTER NINETEEN

In which our hero signs on the dotted line

Citizen Orlov wakes very early on a hard bench, still dressed in prison overalls. It takes him a few moments to remember that he has spent the night in the holding cells at the regional police station. Looking along the line of cells, it appears that the three comrades are still asleep. There is no noise aside from the heavy, irregular snoring of Citizen Vanev.

Unable to get back to sleep, Orlov looks up at the crumbling ceiling and thinks about Agent Zelle. He wonders where she is, and how long it will take her to track down the three comrades. In Orlov's experience, Zelle is both ingenious and ruthless. She is bound to find them soon enough. She will, no doubt, be under the impression that Orlov is dead. She will discover eventually that he is still alive but, for now, he likes the rare experience of having an advantage over her. He will be safer if he can remain dead—as far as Zelle is concerned—until the troubles are over. What happens after that is anyone's guess. For now, given that Zelle has a pressing reason to find the three comrades, it might be best for Orlov to separate himself from them as soon as possible. He determines to do so, once they are released from the cells.

Eventually, the three comrades begin to stir and slowly they wake up.

While all four prisoners are still lying on their beds, Weisz speaks suddenly and loudly. "So, where is the king?"

Orlov assumes this question is directed at him but, since he doesn't know the answer, he stays quiet.

"Comrade," says Vanev, with the tone of a disgruntled schoolteacher.

Now Nemeth joins in, in support of Weisz, directing his remark at Vanev. "He was supposed to bring the king through the chapel."

"I will remind you, comrades," says Vanev, "that we were not in a position to do anything about it, at the time."

"That could have changed in an instant," barks Weisz.

Vanev sighs. "I suppose it could."

Orlov notes that the three comrades are talking about him as though he is not there. Some people might be offended by this, but Orlov does not mind it. In fact, he much prefers it to direct confrontation, and so he says nothing, continuing to lie quietly on his bed, staring at the ceiling. The conversation continues in the same manner for some time, the three comrades revisiting what they could have done differently, given that they were so close to the king, how they would have handled it if His Majesty had appeared in the chapel, and what they did to escape captivity, including the violent end of Sister Agnes. Although Orlov is not a violent person, nevertheless he finds it fascinating to hear the tale of how the three comrades distracted Agnes and escaped outside to the cliff face where, pursued by the two women, they evaded Zelle by pushing Agnes to her death.

Just as Orlov believes that this conversation is drawing to a close, Weisz stands up from his bed, approaches the bars of his cell, and looks directly at Orlov. "He still hasn't told us where the king is," he says.

All three comrades are now staring at Orlov. Unsure how to answer, he hesitates.

He is still hesitating when, without warning, the cell block door swings open and bangs into the wall. Three soldiers bundle into the cell block at speed, talking loudly between themselves.

Orlov jumps, but is grateful for the interruption.

It is immediately clear that these are not the same soldiers who were on duty last night. Judging by his manner and uniform, the leading soldier is senior to the others and senior to the soldiers who incarcerated them last night.

The senior soldier speaks loudly to his underlings. "Why do we have prisoners in here?"

The other two soldiers look at each other. One of them has a clipboard. He consults it briefly before replying hesitantly, "Insubordination at the checkpoint."

The senior soldier frowns and now addresses the prisoners. "Good morning, citizens. I trust you slept peacefully." There is no reaction. He continues, "Please explain your insubordination on arrival at our checkpoint."

Vanev stands up slowly from his bed, straightening his hair and beard. "Good morning, officer," he says. "A simple misunderstanding, nothing more."

The senior officer looks Vanev up and down dispassionately. "Who are you, Citizen, and where are you going?"

Without missing a beat, Vanev says, "Citizen Vodnik, fish delivery service. As we told your colleagues last night, officer, we are simply returning home to the city after escorting two of the Sisters of Our Lady of Perpetual Sorrow back to the convent. They were afraid to travel alone, in the circumstances."

The officer seems skeptical. He frowns at Vanev as he continues.

"Is it customary in the fish delivery business to undertake dangerous journeys for the purpose of escorting nuns?"

"Not customary, officer," says Vanev, calmly. "We were simply attempting to be good citizens."

Without responding to Vanev, the officer swivels to take a closer look at the three other prisoners. Orlov wonders if Weisz and Nemeth will follow Vanev's lead in giving a false name. He wonders if he himself should do likewise. He tries to think of a suitable name. He notices that Vanev chose the name of a real person (Vodnik delivers their supply of fish each morning the market is open). Perhaps this is because Vanev is concerned they might check government records for the names. Orlov hopes that Weisz and Nemeth are invited to speak first. That would provide the opportunity to note if they follow Vanev's lead and, if so, Orlov will have a little more time to prepare his own response.

The officer looks Weisz and Nemeth up and down briefly before turning to Orlov. He stops and a curious look appears on his face. Orlov is not immediately able to interpret it. The officer steps in a little closer to the bars and beckons Orlov to do the same.

Orlov stands up a little straighter, steps toward the bars, and flattens what remains of his hair.

The officer speaks quietly, so that no one else can hear. He is a serious fellow with a heavily lined face, a well pressed uniform, and a pungent cologne. "Are you not, in fact, Minister Orlov, Minister of Security?"

Surprised to be recognized, Orlov flashes a glance at the three comrades before turning back to the officer. "I am," he whispers.

Now the officer glances at the other prisoners before speaking again. "I am very sorry for this misunderstanding. Please follow me."

The officer waves impatiently at his underlings. They open the door to Orlov's cell and whisk him out of the holding room, through the reception area, and into a small office. The officer sends the underlings away, invites Orlov to take a seat, and pours coffee for them both. It is the best and strongest coffee Orlov has tasted in days.

"I am Colonel Laszlo," he says. "My apologies once again, Minister. The night shift can be a little over zealous. I will take the appropriate disciplinary action."

Orlov is pleasantly surprised by this sudden change in circumstances. He sinks his coffee and asks for another one. "A simple misunderstanding," he says.

"Why the prison uniform, Minister?" asks Laszlo, sipping his coffee.

Orlov sighs. "In a civil war, I suppose one must use whatever is available."

Laszlo nods sagely and glances down at Orlov's feet. "And what happened to your shoes ?"

"I'm afraid they are at the top of the mountain," says Orlov.

"One moment," says Laszlo. He summons one of his underlings and instructs him to locate some boots.

While pouring more coffee, Laszlo adopts a concerned tone. "May I ask you about the other prisoners? Are they known to you? Did they threaten you?"

Orlov takes a long sip of coffee to buy some time. He has a welcome but unexpected opportunity to separate himself from the comrades and perhaps to get a military escort back to the city. But, in those circumstances, where would he go? He is not yet ready to risk returning to his own apartment block, and he has no intention of going back to Hotel Melikov to stay with the likes of General Varga and his cronies. He could visit his mother for a while, certainly, but her address is known to Agent Zelle and, if she or her zealot friends turned up there, Orlov would be a sitting duck. He would have absolutely no protection and, worse than that, he might also put his mother in danger. It quickly becomes clear that he has, in reality, only one option: he must return to Hotel Milekov and take his chances with the People's Party. His safety there largely depends on the presence of Comrade Vanev, that much is certain. On the other hand, he feels much less safe whenever Comrade Weisz is nearby, not just because of his aggressive attitude but also because he once—not too long ago—attempted to push Orlov into one of Mount Zhotrykaw's ravines and would have succeeded without Vanev's intervention. Orlov takes all these factors into account when crafting his reply.

"May I speak frankly?" he says.

"Please do," says Laszlo.

"The very large man in the cell next to mine, Citizen"—he is about to say Vanev, but catches himself just in time—"Vodnik, is a former colleague of mine in the fish business. We were escorting the two nuns, just as he said. However, the situation with the other two is a little different."

"I see," says Laszlo eagerly, setting down his coffee and leaning forward in his chair.

Orlov continues, telling himself that a white lie is permitted in times of war. "They forced their way onto our vehicle as we returned down the mountain. They threatened us with violence and told us to drive them back to the city. It was their aggressive attitude toward your troops last night that caused us to be detained here." He is pleased that, because the last part is true, this story is only partially a lie.

Laszlo is hanging on Orlov's every word. "And who are they?" he asks.

Orlov frowns. "I wouldn't like to speculate," he says.

Laszlo gestures with open hands. "Please, be my guest. Just between us."

"I fear," says Orlov, conspiratorially, "that they may be members of the People's Party."

Laszlo sits back in his chair. "I knew it," he says. "Revolutionaries."

Orlov nods gravely. "I'm afraid so."

"Well," says Laszlo, "you have done me a favor. Two members of the People's Party delivered to the cells without me needing to lift a finger. My general will be most pleased."

"Would that be General Varga, by any chance?" asks Orlov.

"Yes, General Varga," says Laszlo. "A most impressive soldier."

"Very much so," agrees Orlov.

Laszlo stands and claps his hands together, as though pleased with the business that he and Orlov have conducted. "Minister, my apologies once again for this error. It has been my pleasure to meet you. If acceptable to you, I will have Citizen Vodnik released, and then two of my best men will drive you to the city in one of our armored cars, just as soon as we have located some footwear. You will be quite safe." He offers his hand.

Orlov sets down his coffee cup, stands up, and shakes the colonel's hand. "Very kind," he says. "Thank you."

Laszlo leads Orlov back out to the reception area and offers him a chair. "Just a few moments, please," he says.

Orlov sits in one of the visitor chairs by the window, from where he can see the checkpoint outside. As has been the case everywhere since the troubles started, the street is very quiet. Several soldiers pace up and down at either side of the barrier, rifles held prominently forward, searching for trouble. But in reality there are few vehicles passing by and very little trouble to be quashed. It occurs to Orlov that the ordinary citizens of his beloved nation are very wise; almost everyone has locked themselves into their homes and is likely to stay there until peace is declared. Given his expectation that Comrade Vanev will be released at any moment, and that he will have some questions about why the others have not, Orlov thinks quickly about what he will say in reply.

A soldier appears and presents Orlov with a pair of army-issue boots. They are several sizes too big, but nevertheless Orlov thanks the soldier profusely and pulls on the boots with some relief.

He is still tying up his laces when Colonel Laszlo emerges from the cell block with Vanev, who is wearing a bemused expression. The colonel asks Vanev to take a seat near Orlov for a few moments while the necessary paperwork is completed.

The colonel stands at the front desk, talking quietly to one of his subordinates, while Vanev settles heavily in the chair next to Orlov. They are far enough from the front desk to be able to whisper privately.

"What is going on?" asks Vanev. "What about Weisz and Nemeth?"

Orlov looks over at the colonel and then back at Vanev. "He suspects they are members of the People's Party. He wants to report the capture of two of its members to his general."

"But you tried to persuade him otherwise," says Vanev, turning his question into a statement.

Orlov shrugs. "I couldn't say we're all fishmongers. Everyone knows ours is the only stall in the Grand Plaza. How many fishmongers can there be?"

Vanev sighs, exasperated. "You could have said they are neighbors. Or friends. Or drinking companions from Tavern Kreminic."

Orlov decides it might be better to be a little more truthful. "You will remember, Comrade, that it was only a short time ago when you were forced to lay Weisz out cold to prevent him from throwing me off the mountain."

Vanev buries his head in his hands. "He has still not forgiven me," he says.

"And I have not forgiven him," says Orlov.

Now Vanev leans in closer so he can whisper to Orlov. "I am their deputy leader. I can't leave them here."

"You may blame me," says Orlov.

While they are talking, Orlov notices a vehicle pull up and stop at the checkpoint. It is a large, camouflaged truck of the sort used by the army to transport troops and equipment. A soldier steps down from the cab, speaks briefly to one of his colleagues at the checkpoint, then steps into the police station. He is carrying a clipboard. He approaches Colonel Laszlo, salutes him, and speaks to him for a few moments.

They are speaking too quietly for Orlov to hear the details, but it seems from their expressions that they are discussing a matter of some importance.

Laszlo walks over to Orlov and beckons the newly arrived soldier to follow him. Orlov and Vanev remain seated in their chairs, wondering who this soldier is and what he wants. Orlov's first thought is that this might be the vehicle and driver designated to take them back to the capital, but the reality turns out to be rather different.

"If you would excuse me, Minister," says the colonel, "I think your presence here this morning might be rather fortuitous." Unsure what this means, Orlov attempts a smile but says nothing. Laszlo continues, "This soldier is on his way to the border to collect a new shipment of ammunition." He glances at Vanev and back at Orlov. "If I may speak frankly, Minister."

"Please do," says Orlov. "Citizen Vodnik is a good and patriotic citizen."

Laszlo smiles reverentially at Vanev before turning back to Orlov. He continues, "This is the only supply of ammunition that we have been able to locate within a few days of the border. Since all domestic supplies are exhausted, it is our only hope of quickly overpowering the enemy. Nevertheless, there is still bureaucracy to be completed. Corporal." He turns to invite the soldier to speak.

To Orlov's surprise, the young corporal thrusts his clipboard toward Orlov, who takes it, hesitantly. "This is a requisition form," says the corporal. "Given the value of the shipment, it must be signed by a general." He glances at Laszlo.

"I don't have sufficient rank," says Laszlo, apologetically.

The corporal continues, "In the absence of a general, the form may be signed by the Minister of Security or the Minister of Intelligence. If you could oblige, sir." He holds out a pen.

Laszlo, Vanev, and the young corporal all stare at Orlov expectantly. Orlov can sense Vanev shift uneasily in his chair. Orlov desperately wants a few moments to discuss this with Vanev, but of course he cannot do so. Since the colonel believes his companion is Citizen Vodnik the fish delivery driver, there is absolutely no reason to discuss such matters with him.

Orlov cannot resist the briefest of glances at Vanev before smiling up at the two military men. "Of course," he says, "I am pleased to assist."

Orlov senses sweat breaking out on his brow as he grips the pen and begins to read the form. He is very aware of three sets of eyes monitoring him, and he finds this an unpleasant experience. So unpleasant, in fact, that it is difficult to focus on the details of the requisition form.

The corporal hops anxiously from one foot to another. "If you don't mind signing on the line at the bottom, Minister, I will be on my way."

Orlov pauses and looks up at the corporal. "I never sign anything without reading every word," he says.

The colonel intervenes, speaking to his corporal. "Give the Minister a little time, soldier," he says.

"Yes, sir. Sorry, sir," says the corporal.

With the three men still watching his every move, Orlov tries to focus on the form. Most of the page is taken up with a long list of munitions, including their names, quantities, and prices. The detail of this list means nothing to Orlov, but one does not need to be a military expert to know that this is a very large shipment. At the foot of the form, he notices three things. Firstly, there is a paragraph of legal jargon which Orlov cannot follow. Secondly, there is a dotted line for a signature. Thirdly, and most intriguingly, the line just above the signature line begins with the typed word *Destination*. Next to *Destination*, someone has written in ink the words *Hotel Melikov*. Orlov imagines General Varga breathing his terrible breath over everyone and holding court in the ballroom of the hotel, waiting for his ammunition to arrive.

Orlov glances up briefly at the three men before signing. He smiles, as if to indicate that all is in order. But in reality he is checking that Colonel Laszlo—who is standing slightly farther away than the corporal—will not be able to see what he writes.

Citizen Orlov pulls the clipboard a little closer and signs the form. He puts a line through *Melikov* and writes *Milekov* in its place. Turning the clipboard such that the colonel cannot see it, he hands it back to the corporal.

Obviously relieved, the corporal takes the clipboard with his left hand, salutes Orlov with his right hand, and turns to leave.

Orlov holds his breath as Colonel Laszlo prevents the corporal from leaving. Laszlo grabs the corporal's shoulder, and Orlov is convinced that the colonel is about to inspect the form. But he simply rotates the corporal so that he is looking at Orlov again.

"I think you are forgetting something, Corporal," says Laszlo.

The corporal barks at Orlov. "Thank you, Minister."

PART FIVE

The Battle of Hotel Melikov

CHAPTER TWENTY

In which our hero receives a delivery

Citizens Orlov and Vanev, fishmongers, find themselves in the rear of an armored car rolling slowly through villages and the agricultural lands between, en route to their nation's capital, in the middle of a civil war which has descended into near silence. In lieu of windows, the rear of the vehicle has two small viewing holes covered by metal plates. Orlov lifts the plate next to his head and watches his beloved nation roll past. Occasionally, he sees a building burnt out by an explosion or pocked with gunfire. Passing through a small, provincial town, the town hall is still smoldering, thin smoke rising from its charred roof. But Orlov sees no one, not even farmers. And he hears nothing aside from birdsong and the occasional bleating of sheep in the fields. It is as though the whole kingdom is holding its breath, waiting to see what happens next.

Uncharacteristically, Citizen Vanev is very quiet. He says nothing and glowers straight ahead, looking at nothing in particular. Orlov has no doubt that Vanev is furious with him for signing the requisition form so willingly, and—were that the end of the story—he could understand it. Vanev and his comrades have given everything they have to their cause, now including the life of Comrade Rozum. There have probably been many other deaths during the past few days, some of which may not yet be accounted for. Vanev has scarcely mentioned Rozum since their descent from the mountain, but no doubt what happened is weighing heavily on his mind. In all those circumstances, it seems natural that Vanev would be furious about Orlov's apparent willingness to help the government get its hands on the only supplies of ammunition for miles around.

Orlov longs to be able to tell Vanev about the details of the form; what he crossed out and what he wrote in its place. But he is not currently in a position to do so. The cabin of the armored car is very cramped, and the two soldiers in the front are just a few feet away. It would be impossible even to whisper something such that Vanev could hear it while being sure that the soldiers could not. As a result, Orlov sits quietly, looking out through the viewing hole, waiting for the opportunity to speak to Vanev in private.

Occasionally, he glances over at Vanev, hoping to catch his eye; perhaps he will be able to convey simply by the expression on his face that he has a secret Vanev needs to hear, although he is unsure precisely how one would suggest that with a facial expression. In any case, Vanev does not meet his eye—perhaps deliberately—and so Orlov has no choice but to endure the entire journey in frustrated silence.

As the armored car eventually trundles slowly into the capital in broad daylight, Orlov sees for the first time the full extent of the destruction wrought by several days of fighting. Much of the government sector is damaged; some buildings are blackened by fire, others are pocked with bullet holes. At the grand front entrances of government ministries, doors hang open or—in some cases—have been removed completely. The armored car is forced to snake around abandoned, burned-out vehicles still sitting immobile in the street. Orlov believes he can spot the overturned vehicle in which he left the coronation and in which poor Minister Boch breathed his last breath. He notices that graffiti has appeared on many of the walls. Across the front of the Ministry of Justice is painted in huge, red letters the word *REPUBLIC.*

The soldier behind the steering wheel turns suddenly to Orlov and says, "Where shall we leave you, Minister?"

Orlov thinks quickly. He does not want the vehicle to drive up into the Grand Plaza, for fear of being seen by someone at Hotel Melikov—General Varga or Citizen Galin, perhaps. Neither does he want to do anything to give away the significance of Hotel Milekov in terms of its current role as the temporary headquarters of the People's Party. He wants to be able to walk to Hotel Milekov from a sufficient distance such that he and Vanev will have time to talk and will be able to lose themselves along the alley that runs behind it, without fear of being watched by the soldiers.

"Please let us out at the bridge," says Orlov.

Now Vanev speaks for the first time since they left the police station. "We will go our separate ways from there," he adds.

"It would be safer if I took you all the way home," says the driver.

Orlov waves this away. "No need," he says.

The armored car shudders to a halt at the foot of the bridge on the government side. The two fishmongers climb out, thank the soldiers for their assistance, and stand at the side of a deserted road waiting for the vehicle to get a suitable distance away before speaking.

Vanev strides onto the bridge. "I cannot believe what I just witnessed," he spits.

Orlov rushes after him. "Citizen, please, you don't understand."

Vanev keeps walking, looking straight ahead. "I understand that you signed away the one advantage available to either side," he says.

Orlov is struggling to keep pace and is still behind Vanev when he says, "And ensured it would be delivered to you."

Vanev stops and turns back to look at Orlov for the first time. "What?"

"The ammunition must be delivered somewhere," says Orlov.

"Of course," says Vanev. "The military base, I expect."

"No," says Orlov. "The form was made out for delivery to Hotel Melikov. I changed Melikov to Milekov."

Now Vanev grabs him firmly by the shoulders, the anger on his face giving way to a glimmer of hope. "They're delivering to Milekov?"

Orlov shrugs. "That's what the form says."

"When?" says Vanev.

"How long does it take to drive to the southern border and back?" asks Orlov.

It is as though a switch is thrown in Vanev's head. His bad mood lifts instantly in favor of an urgent focus on action. Still grasping Orlov's shoulders, he ignores the question and says, "Quickly. We will take the alley and stay in the shadows."

The two fishmongers rush over the bridge and, instead of heading up the hill directly into the Grand Plaza, they take a dark side street, and then another, until they turn into the alley that runs up the eastern edge of the square to the rear entrance of Hotel Milekov.

Clambering over temporary barriers built from sandbags, Vanev raps hard on the delivery door in a curious pattern that Orlov assumes is a code. The door is opened immediately by a young, bearded man whom Orlov does not recognize. He is holding a rifle. Looking up and down the alley, the man ushers the two fishmongers inside and locks the door behind them.

The man speaks urgently to Vanev. "They're all in the ballroom."

Vanev says, "Thank you, Comrade," and beckons Orlov to follow him up the stairs.

Vanev stops outside the ballroom doors and turns to Orlov. "Let me do the talking," he says.

As they step through the door into a meeting of some thirty or forty comrades, it occurs to Orlov that he is entirely in Vanev's hands in terms of what is discussed regarding the king's escape. Vanev has not asked him precisely what happened, but no doubt he has an idea. If he chose to do so, Vanev could now expose Orlov in front of the entire leadership of the People's Party as being the person responsible for thwarting their mission to kidnap the monarch. If he chooses to do so, Orlov will have to face the consequences. If not, Orlov will owe him a debt of gratitude.

In the absence of furniture, the comrades stand in a loose huddle in the middle of the ballroom, illuminated only by the natural light through the windows. Apparently, they are in the middle of a meeting when the two fishmongers burst in.

Comrade Volf raises a hand to silence the conversation. He speaks to Vanev. "Comrade, I am relieved to see you."

"Likewise, Comrade," says Vanev, as he joins the gathering with Orlov at his side.

"What of the others?" asks Volf.

Vanev hangs his head. He looks up again and casts his gaze around the group before replying. "Comrades, I am sorry to report that Comrade Rozum did not make it back from the mountain. He was murdered by zealots attempting to thwart our operation. Comrades Weisz and Nemeth are safe but detained at a checkpoint. Comrade Orlov here rescued me from the same checkpoint. Unfortunately, our mission was unsuccessful. The monarch was on the mountain for a time, but escaped before we could reach him."

Volf looks pained, like a man who has seen enough suffering for several lifetimes and does not wish to add to it. "Comrades," he whispers, "let us observe a moment's silence in memory of Comrade Rozum."

The room falls silent. Everyone looks down at the floor.

After a few seconds, Volf says, "Thank you, comrades." He looks at Vanev. "Where is the king now?"

"We don't know," says Vanev.

Orlov notices that several of the comrades are regarding him with suspicious expressions.

Volf glances at Orlov and back at Vanev. "So, the Minister of Security rescued you from the checkpoint but not the others?" This is followed by murmurs around the group.

Vanev holds up both his hands to ask for calm. "Please, comrades. My colleague here did his best to use his position as a former minister for our benefit. Comrade Weisz acted aggressively toward the soldiers; his incarceration is his own fault. If you could simmer down, please, I have some much more significant news about the way Comrade Orlov has used his influence this morning."

Volf holds up a single finger and the group falls silent.

Vanev continues, "The army has located a shipment of munitions at the southern border. They are on the way to collect it as we speak." Gasps break out around the group. Vanev talks over them. "Comrade Orlov instructed them to deliver it here. Before he intervened, the shipment was destined for Hotel Melikov."

There is a moment of silence while the comrades take this in. They glance at each other and back at Vanev.

Volf speaks up. "Are you confident this will happen?"

Vanev looks at Orlov, who now speaks to the group for the first time. "I believe so, yes."

A comrade Orlov does not recognize says, "What if they drive into the square, to the front of the hotel? The troops guarding the front of Melikov will see it and intercept it."

Volf looks at Vanev. "I fear that is right, Comrade."

Vanev thinks for a moment. "I believe we can prevent that. I need two volunteers, plus Comrade Orlov. Everyone else must remain out of sight."

Everyone looks at Volf, who waves his hand to indicate assent. "Very well," he says.

FOR THE REST of the morning, the two fishmongers sit in a huddle in the kitchens at the back of Hotel Milekov with Comrades Dinev and Smid, machine operatives from the Krupnik glassworks who are also members of the security subcommittee of the People's Party, of which Orlov was briefly the leader. They are both heavy set men with no-nonsense attitudes and an impressive array of tattoos. More importantly for the current operation, they are absolutely fearless.

Comrade Vanev asks for opinions about the direction from which the delivery truck is likely to arrive.

Comrade Smid speaks up first. "Through the government sector," he says with confidence. "If they're coming from the south, it's the obvious route. They'll turn off the main road, cross the government sector, then go over the bridge into the square."

"And the troops across the square will see them immediately," says Dinev.

"Not if they can't turn into the square," says Vanev.

"Go on," says Smid.

"Imagine you're driving a large vehicle, a truck, over the bridge," says Vanev. "The left turn up the hill toward the square is tight." The others nod in agreement. Vanev continues, "It would take only a small obstacle there to cause you to turn right instead. The city is full of abandoned vehicles. If we can move one into the right spot without being seen, that should be enough to block the turn."

It is decided that they will go on a reconnaissance mission to find the nearest vehicle that might be moved into the agreed location at the end of the bridge. The four men step out through the back door and into the alley.

Vanev looks at Orlov. "Comrade, you are technically still a minister of the government . . ."

Orlov cuts him off. "Comrade, I have made my bed. Now I will lie in it."

Vanev slaps him on the shoulder, but says nothing.

As they stride along the alley with the urgency of a military operation, Orlov wonders if now, finally, he has made a choice about where he stands. He wonders if the People's Party will finally accept him as one of them. He wonders, most of all, what will happen when the munitions arrive.

Since it is the middle of the day and a weak sun has risen as high as it is going to rise, the four comrades stay in the shadows of the buildings, looking around anxiously for any soldiers who might spot them and whose inevitable interrogation could bring an end to their plans before they have begun.

On reaching the end of the alley, Vanev leads them into a side street and then another, and soon they find a burned-out postal van, abandoned and rendering the street impassable.

None of the residents of this street has chosen to be outside long enough to move the vehicle out of the way. The comrades rock the van back and forth to gauge its weight and determine that they could push it into position.

Before doing so, however, they walk back to the alley and carefully round the corner until they can see the chosen location at the end of the bridge.

Vanev holds up a hand to indicate that the others should go no farther. He looks around the corner into the Grand Plaza and then turns back to speak to his comrades.

"We can't do it now," he whispers. "There is a clear line of sight from Hotel Melikov and four troops patrolling."

"Let's do it after dark," says Smid.

"And hope we get there before the truck arrives," says Dinev.

"We need a sign, right here," says Vanev, pointing at a spot on the opposite side of the alley, in front of a corner hardware emporium.

As they walk back along the alley to the delivery entrance of Hotel Milekov, Orlov is racked with worry about what happens if the truck arrives before dark, but there is nothing that can be done about it. He sets off up to the top floor of the hotel, finds the painter's equipment, and fashions a large sign reading *HOTEL MILEKOV DELIVERIES*.

A SENSE OF nervous anticipation settles on the group of comrades hiding out in Hotel Milekov. They pace silently around the grand halls, nodding politely to acknowledge each other, saying nothing. For much of the afternoon, Volf and Vanev are huddled in the ballroom with a small group of comrades. Imagining that they are planning what to do with the munitions, Orlov is relieved to be excluded from this meeting. In truth, he still feels conflicted. Although circumstances have caused him finally to throw in his lot with the People's Party, nevertheless he could not imagine being directly involved in an attack on General Varga, Citizen Galin, and the other remaining members of the government, whose meetings he attended just a few days ago. He might now be sure that he wants the comrades to prevail, and to usher in a new era for the nation, but that is not the same thing as taking up arms against people that he knows personally. It would be better if any further fighting occurs between strangers.

After all, Orlov is the only person with a claim to be a member of both camps. He is perhaps the only person in the whole kingdom who could walk into either of these hotels safely. But now he has made a choice.

As soon as darkness falls, Orlov meets again with Vanev, Dinev, and Smid in the kitchens. Rushing along the dark alley, they fix the sign in place against the wall of the hardware emporium, then dash around the corner to the abandoned postal van. With each man at a corner, they heave the decrepit vehicle into motion, rolling it slowly along the cobbled street, around the corner into the alley, and right up to the threshold of the Grand Plaza.

Vanev raises a hand to stop them. He peers cautiously around the corner to gauge whether they can be seen by the troops in front of Hotel Melikov. Apparently satisfied, Vanev waves them forward. Now moving very slowly, and attempting to be as close to silent as possible, the comrades wheel the van into the chosen position near the bridge. Without speaking, they gather at the side of the vehicle and begin to push it over onto its side. As soon as they have created some momentum, Comrades Dinev and Smid rush around to the other side and use their considerable bulk to slow the descent, resting the van carefully on the cobbles.

The four comrades are about to congratulate themselves on their achievement when the bright beam of a headlight flashes above them. They turn to see a truck mounting the bridge from the government sector. It is not possible to see the truck clearly, but from the power of the headlamps, this could certainly be the military delivery truck that Orlov saw outside the police station this morning.

Saying nothing, Vanev waves vigorously to indicate that they should hurry back to the hotel.

With a matter of seconds before the truck emerges from the bridge, the four comrades—all much heavier and slower than they once were—attempt to run back to Hotel Milekov.

Orlov is pleasantly surprised to find that he is the least slow of the group. He stops in the middle of the alley to catch his breath and turns to see the other three comrades behind him. The beam of light from the truck swings to the right, illuminating the makeshift sign.

Orlov waves at the others to hurry, then resumes his dash back to the hotel.

The comrades gather, out of breath, at the delivery entrance. The truck has now arrived in the alley, trundling slowly over the cobbles toward them.

Vanev slaps Orlov on the shoulder. “Good luck, Comrade,” he says, and then disappears inside with Dinev and Smid.

Orlov waits outside the delivery entrance, the armed guard remaining out of sight on the other side of the door.

The guard whispers to Orlov through the door, “Just knock, Comrade, if you need me.”

“I will,” says Orlov, now wrapping his arms around himself against the cold.

The truck makes painfully slow progress along the alley, perhaps because there is very little clearance on each side and the driver is being careful to stay in the dead center.

Eventually, with its engine still running, the truck stops right in front of Orlov. A uniformed soldier jumps down from the cab carrying a clipboard. Orlov is relieved to see that this is the same young corporal whose requisition form he signed this morning.

The corporal salutes. “Good evening, Minister,” he says. “Everything is in order.”

“Thank you,” says Orlov.

The corporal looks up at the hotel. “Everything inside, is it, sir?”

“No, no,” says Orlov. “Please unload it here in the alley. We’ll take it from there.”

“Very good, Minister,” says the corporal. He thrusts the clipboard and a pen at Orlov. “One more thing, sir. More paperwork, if you please.”

“Of course,” says Orlov, and he signs the form.

CHAPTER TWENTY-ONE

In which our hero stands on a roof

From the moment the truck leaves the alley until the early hours of the morning, the entire company of People's Party comrades holed up at Hotel Milekov works diligently but silently to move the munitions indoors, store them in different rooms according to type, and distribute them as appropriate according to a plan of which Orlov is not aware but which seems to be well understood by many of the comrades. Someone has rigged up a telephone in one of the ground floor offices, and one of the comrades sits in there for hours making calls. Orlov notices that, from about two o'clock in the morning, new comrades begin to arrive—always through the rear entrance—and dutifully go about collecting weapons. Those arriving with their own weapons collect new ammunition. Once fully armed, they file quietly into the darkened ballroom where they sit against the wall, snoozing or playing cards. Speaking and smoking are both forbidden. Some comrades while away the hours polishing their rifles meticulously. Others silently practice loading and reloading. There is a good deal of whispering about plans and tactics. The atmosphere is tense but also collegiate; it is impossible to miss the sense that everyone is working together, content to play a small part for the good of the whole group. Although Orlov is becoming deeply nervous about what will happen next, nevertheless he cannot deny enjoying this camaraderie. It is a far cry from the egotistical bickering of the generals and government ministers.

At one point, Orlov hears something of a commotion in one of the bedrooms. Since most of the operation is taking place in total silence, some enthusiastic whispering and back-slapping from this bedroom are enough to be heard and attract a crowd. On investigating, Orlov finds a half dozen comrades opening up large boxes to reveal three rocket launchers, each resting on a gray metal bipod and equipped with a rocket. Orlov last saw this weapon years ago, during national service. One of the comrades opening the boxes is apparently agitated by the commotion; he implores everyone to keep calm before sending one of the other comrades to fetch Volf and Vanev. The leader and deputy leader soon arrive to admire the rockets.

Volf whispers something into Vanev's ear before addressing the whole room. "Very good, comrades, very good. We will switch to Plan B. Take these weapons up to the roof, please. But do not put them into position yet. Keep them out of sight, and be absolutely silent."

Orlov finds himself among the small group of six climbing up the stairs to the roof, each comrade holding either a rocket or a launcher. Once out on the flat section of the hotel roof, they silently reassemble the rockets with their launchers, but leave the completed weapons in the middle of the roof, such that there is no chance of them being seen from the street below or the buildings opposite. Standing in the chill early hours of a mostly cloudy night, Orlov admires the careful attention to detail of these serious, diligent comrades.

Once back inside, it transpires that everyone is gathering in the ballroom, and Orlov dutifully follows along. He sees that the company has now swelled to perhaps sixty or seventy people, most of them carrying at least a rifle. They all listen intently as Comrade Volf stands in the center of the room, speaking just above a whisper. Orlov notes that it is a little after three o'clock in the morning.

"Comrades, we are almost ready," says Volf solemnly, his pained, raspy voice even thinner than usual. "We are indebted to Comrades Vanev and Orlov for ensuring the shipment was routed here instead of Hotel Melikov. That piece of cunning might prove to be decisive. Since the shipment included three rockets, we will use Plan B. That means the operation will begin on the roof. Comrades Smid and Dinev will fire the starting gun, so to speak, on my command, not before. Comrades, you will need to choose a third man, please."

Dinev glances at Smid and says, "We would be pleased to have Comrade Orlov."

Orlov raises a finger and begins to say, "Comrades, my arm is injured," but Volf speaks over him.

"Very good," says Volf. "Comrades Dinev, Smid, and Orlov will be on the roof. Everyone else, you have been allotted a team leader. Follow your leader's instructions at all times. That will increase your chances of arriving back here alive. And remember, comrades, that we do not know which of our enemies have ammunition left and which do not. So, expect the worst and protect yourselves."

Disturbed that he has been assigned to rocket-launching duties, Orlov tries to catch Vanev's eye, but Vanev's attention is focused on Comrade Volf. Orlov determines that, as soon as the meeting breaks up, he will speak to Vanev and excuse himself.

Volf looks around to locate Comrade Dankova, the bespectacled administrator. The slight, serious woman nods and steps forward into the middle of the room. Orlov notes that Dankova, like himself, is wearing the gray overalls of Prison Zhotrykaw. He remembers that she had been detained following the murder of the old king and must have traveled here directly from the prison when the revolution started.

Volf continues, "Comrades, ordinarily we would join in singing "The Red Flag" at this time, but of course operational security will not allow it. I have asked Comrade Dankova to do the honors."

Dankova opens her mouth and begins to sing very quietly. Even at such a low volume, she has a sweet, precise singing voice. Using the traditional melody—"O Tannenbaum"—she delivers the first verse and chorus of the party's official song.

The people's flag is deepest red,
It shrouded oft our martyred dead,
And ere their limbs grew stiff and cold,
Their hearts' blood dyed its every fold.
Then raise the scarlet standard high.
Beneath its shade we'll live and die,
Though cowards flinch and traitors sneer,
We'll keep the red flag flying here.

For a second, it appears that comrades might break out into spontaneous applause.

Volf lifts a finger to prevent this. The room falls silent. "Comrades, take your positions, please. Wait for my signal."

The entire company shuffles out of the ballroom, rifles on shoulders. Most of them head down the stairs to leave through the delivery entrance. Orlov hangs back at the top of the stairs with Comrades Dinev and Smid, waiting for Vanev to emerge. He notices the solemn, almost religious, mood that settles over the group as they file out, heads bowed, entirely focused on the task at hand, knowing that it could be a decisive moment in the story of the nation. Orlov has never particularly cared for these comrades in the past, because of their constant arguing, their petty rules, their insistence on voting on every little decision, their suspicion of outsiders, and so on. But here, at a moment of crisis, a moment of supreme importance, he cannot help but admire them. They are serious, focused, committed, and passionate. While he does not always find their political views to his liking, it is clear to him now that they honestly believe they are acting in the best interests of the whole country. Time will tell whether that is so.

Once most of the company has dispersed, the senior leadership of the People's Party emerges from the ballroom. It appears that Comrade Volf and a few others plan to remain in the hotel, but most are heading outside.

Comrade Vanev, a rifle over his shoulder, marches from the ballroom in Orlov's direction.

Here is Orlov's chance. He raises a hand to catch Vanev's attention. But his old friend is moving too quickly and clearly his attention is elsewhere.

Vanev slaps Orlov on the back as he passes. "Good luck, Comrade," says Vanev, and he disappears down the staircase.

Orlov begins to say, "Comrade, just a moment," but his chance has already passed.

Comrades Dinev and Smid lead Orlov up the stairs. They stop before opening the door to the roof.

Dinev speaks to Orlov. "Have you used one of these weapons before, Comrade?"

"I'm really not sure I'm the best person for this," says Orlov.

Dinev waves this away. "Don't worry, Comrade. Just follow us."

The realization settles on Orlov that, with all the other comrades dispersed to their positions, he will have to assist with the rocket launching, or else he will need to explain why he is choosing not to contribute at all. He does not want to have that conversation now, not least because he has nowhere else to go. Although the thought of firing rockets at his former colleagues fills him with dread, it might just be the least terrible option available.

"Our target is the front doors of Hotel Melikov," says Smid. "Any questions?"

Orlov thinks. "Is it our intention to kill the troops guarding the front of the hotel?"

"We're going to blow the doors off," says Smid. "If the soldiers are nearby, so be it."

Orlov nods to indicate that he understands.

Smid continues, "These weapons are normally fired lying down. Given the angle, we will need to stand briefly, then fire, then drop. Understood?"

"Understood," says Orlov.

Dinev grips the door handle. "No talking once we are outside," he says.

They step out noiselessly into the cold night air. Orlov follows the two comrades as they each pick up a rocket launcher and gingerly move it to the front of the roof until the three weapons are in a neat line just a few feet apart, all pointing across the square toward the grand front entrance of Hotel Melikov. Dinev waves to indicate they should all lie down. Each man lies next to his weapon and waits.

Citizen Orlov, fishmonger, Minister of Security, double agent, and member of the People's Party, lies on his back and looks up at the stars visible between rushing gray clouds. It occurs to him that he is lying above the front door of the hotel and therefore immediately above the makeshift bed where he slept the night he first stepped into Hotel Milekov after escaping from his neighbors. On that evening, the revolution had just begun and there was still a sense that ordinary citizens had not fully accepted that it was really happening. He remembers the shock on the faces of his neighbors as they sat around the wireless listening to the news reports. Tonight, he has a sense that perhaps this is the end, or the beginning of the end, at least. After all, how can there be a war in which only one side has ammunition? Surely such a war ends very quickly.

The door onto the roof opens and a comrade pokes his head out. Once he has caught their attention, he raises two thumbs high in the air, saying nothing. Comrade Dinev salutes him and jumps up. Smid follows suit.

Orlov's heart is suddenly racing. He stands and looks across at the others. They are standing up straight, gripping the end of the launcher mechanism like a rifle and pointing the rocket down at the front door of Hotel Melikov. Orlov attempts to do the same, glancing at Smid and back at his own launcher several times to check that he is holding it correctly. He squints down at the target. He grimaces as he attempts to ignore the pain shooting through his right arm, exacerbated by the need to grip the weapon tightly.

Dinev looks across, sees the other two in position, and nods.

As he nods, he pulls his trigger. The rocket fizzes out of the launcher. Orlov flinches.

A fraction of a second later, Smid pulls his own trigger.

Dinev's rocket, too low, explodes just short of the hotel steps.

The four soldiers on guard scatter.

Orlov's hand is still on his trigger.

Smid's rocket curves in an arc to the left and skids, unexploded, to a halt at the southern edge of the square.

The four soldiers climb back to their feet and begin to fire aimlessly into the darkness.

Instinctively, Orlov ducks slightly at the sound of gunfire. He pops back up again to correct his aim.

"Now," hisses Dinev.

The next second seems to Orlov to last an eternity.

He grimaces as he takes aim.

He takes a deep breath.

He squeezes the trigger.

His rocket fizzes out, spinning. It hits the steps just below the front door of Hotel Melikov.

Nothing.

The soldiers guarding the hotel scatter again, flinging themselves away from the door and down the steps.

Orlov looks across at Dinev and then at Smid. All three men look down anxiously, waiting for the third rocket to detonate, but it does nothing.

Gunfire rings out from the soldiers down below. The three comrades drop down onto the roof, breathing heavily.

Another comrade opens the door onto the roof and silently raises his arms in anguished confusion.

Dinev whispers to him, "Failed to detonate. Failed to detonate."

More gunfire from across the square.

The comrade disappears again and returns to the roof momentarily with Volf and Vanev. They huddle near the door and summon the three rocket operators to join them.

Comrade Volf has never looked so angry. The veins on his forehead are close to exploding. "What the hell is going on?"

"Sorry, Comrade," says Smid. "Two rockets missed the target. The third was accurate but failed to detonate. It's still sitting right in front of the target."

Volf glances around the group. "It must be detonated. Now."

"Shoot it," says Vanev, urgently.

Dinev dashes over to the edge of the roof, lies flat on his belly, peers over at Hotel Melikov, and rushes back to join the impromptu gathering. "It could work. But not from here. We're too far away to hit the detonator. The shooter needs to be nearer."

"We need to be quick," says Smid. "Before they try to move it."

All eyes are suddenly on Orlov. He has no idea why, but being the center of attention at a moment such as this makes him exceedingly nervous.

"What?" says Orlov.

"It makes sense, Comrade," says Vanev, in a reassuring tone.

"I don't follow," says Orlov.

The whole group ducks momentarily at the sound of gunfire. Vanev continues, placing a heavy hand on Orlov's shoulder, "If any of us appears in the middle of the square, near enough to get a good shot at the rocket, we will be dead in seconds." He gestures to Volf and himself to denote the ordinary members of the People's Party. "You are the only one who can safely approach the hotel."

Orlov feels his neck and shoulders becoming hot. "I might have half a chance of getting back into Hotel Melikov again in order to take shelter there. But that is not what you are proposing."

"It is not," says Volf, solemnly.

"And I am not a soldier," complains Orlov. "It's years since my national service."

Vanev sighs. "I have a plan. It can work. Do you trust me?" His hand is still on Orlov's shoulder.

Now Orlov sighs. "Yes, but Comrade. This is dangerous. Life and death."

Volf looks deep into Orlov's eyes as though peering into his soul. "Comrade, your country needs you."

The eyes of Volf, Vanev, Smid, and Dinev are trained on him expectantly. Orlov has never felt less qualified for a task than this. He can scarcely believe his own ears when he hears himself saying, "I'll do my best."

Volf waves urgently toward the door. "Comrades. Everyone is in place. They're waiting for the signal. It's now or never."

"This way," says Vanev, steering Orlov through the door and down the stairs.

In the time it takes to dash down several flights of stairs and collect a rifle from a comrade in the kitchen, Vanev has imparted his plan to Orlov, who listens intently and nods to indicate that he understands. The gravity of the moment seems to prevent Orlov from speaking. All his energy is expended in listening to Vanev's words and trying to imagine things playing out just as he has described.

A comrade opens the rear door of Hotel Milekov. Vanev straps the rifle over Orlov's shoulder and guides him outside.

"You can do it, Comrade," says Vanev. "The future of the nation depends on it."

CHAPTER TWENTY-TWO

In which our hero steps out alone

Citizen Orlov steps out into the dim light of the Grand Plaza with a rifle over his shoulder and both his arms raised aloft, just as Vanev had instructed. His heart is beating so hard that he can hear it in his ears.

At first, it is too dark from him to be seen. Slowly and with extreme trepidation, he inches forward, ensuring that his arms remain as high as he can muster, which causes his injured right arm to throb in pain. In the center of the square is a pool of moonlight free from the shadows of the surrounding buildings. He is sure that, once standing in that dim glow, he will be clearly visible to the soldiers guarding Hotel Melikov.

Thrusting his arms aloft, he takes a deep breath and steps to the edge of the moonlight.

Instantly, a crack of gunfire rings out. Orlov ducks, sensing a round fizzing over his head.

"Hold your fire!" says an agitated voice in a stage whisper. There is a pause, and then the voice continues, "Who goes there?"

Orlov stands dead still and clears his throat nervously. He speaks in a whisper. "Minister Orlov. Minister of Security."

There is a pause.

"I can't hear you."

Orlov tries again, a little louder. "Orlov. Minister of Security."

Another pause.

He hears low voices, as though the soldiers are conferring between themselves.

"The ministers are up at the convent," says another voice.

Orlov had anticipated this. "Yes. I was there until this morning. I returned to assist the generals in locating some ammunition."

More conferring.

"You've found ammunition?"

"Yes."

"Where?"

"I will explain it to the generals."

More conferring.

"We have a little problem here in the form of unexploded ordnance." He jabs his rifle in the direction of the unexploded rocket, still lying tantalizingly near the hotel doors.

"Yes," says Orlov.

"No one can use the main entrance at the moment."

"No," says Orlov.

"We'll have to escort you to the rear entrance."

"I am at your disposal."

Now a different soldier speaks. "We need you to surrender your weapon before approaching, minister."

This is exactly as Vanev had anticipated. "Very well," says Orlov. "My rifle is on my shoulder."

"We can see that."

Orlov knows that the most delicate moment of his task is approaching.

He believes he can guide things just as Vanev had proposed, but he is a little farther away from the target than he wants to be. As per Vanev's plan, he wants to reach the precise middle of the square, right in the center of the moonlight, before taking the rifle off his shoulder.

"I want you to be able to see me clearly," says Orlov.

"We can see you."

"May I step forward into the light a little further? Just to make sure there's no misunderstanding?"

"Drop your weapon right there, please."

"I think it will be safer for everyone if I advance into the best light before surrendering my rifle."

Now there is more conferring.

"Very slowly, please, Minister."

Keeping his arms aloft, with the rifle still on his shoulder, Orlov steps slowly forward until he arrives in the middle of the moonlight. As he walks, his eyes remain firmly on the unexploded rocket.

Orlov's voice shakes with nerves. "I think you can see me more clearly now."

"That's far enough. Lay your weapon on the ground in front of you, please. Slowly."

"I'll need to drop my hands for a second."

"Yes. Do it slowly."

Orlov pauses. "Would you mind if I kneel down first? Before taking the rifle off my shoulder?"

It seems to Orlov that this is the key point in terms of Vanev's instructions.

Without kneeling down, the task is possible but much more difficult. A safe and successful completion of the task depends on his being permitted to kneel. He holds his breath while waiting for a reply.

"Why?" The soldier sounds agitated.

"I'd like to be able to lay my rifle down while also keeping my eyes on you and your colleagues. For my own safety, you understand. That will be much easier if I kneel."

There is a pause. "Do it slowly. And keep your hands where we can see them."

Orlov exhales heavily. The moment of truth has arrived.

Keeping his hands up, he drops very slowly onto his good, left, knee.

"I'm going to take my rifle off my shoulder now."

"Slowly."

Orlov can see two of the soldiers in his peripheral vision. But he keeps his gaze trained on the unexploded rocket.

With slow, exaggerated movements, Orlov swings both hands to the rifle, lifts it up high above his head and slowly begins to lower it in front of his chest. Holding the rifle as far in front of him as he is able, he makes sure it is aimed directly at the rocket.

"Slowly," says the soldier, again.

In an instant, Orlov pulls the rifle butt hard into his shoulder and pulls the trigger.

He drops face first onto the cobbles. Rounds of return fire fizz over his head.

There is a flash of light.

An explosion blows the two front doors into the lobby with a ferocious crack, leaving a gaping, burning hole.

The two nearest soldiers are flung through the air, rolling helplessly down the steps of the hotel.

From out of the darkness, Orlov hears shouts and gunfire. The heavy boots of dozens of comrades pound across the cobbles to each side. Some of them jump over his head. He flinches at the thought of being trampled. He is splashed by water from between the damp cobbles as a pair of friendly boots smash into the ground next to his ear.

"Now, now!" shouts the owner of these boots.

"Move!" Another voice up ahead.

Shots ring out in rapid, deafening bursts.

As instructed by Vanev, Orlov keeps his face firmly pressed into the wet cobbles until all the comrades have dashed through the square and into Hotel Melikov through the gaping hole left by the explosion.

He pulls himself up on his elbows just far enough to see the four soldiers he was conversing with lying dead on the steps of the hotel. He pauses for a brief second to admire his work: what's left of the grand front entrance to the hotel is a smoldering mess, spewing dark smoke in all directions.

Leaving his rifle lying on the ground, Orlov turns and dashes out of the square and back around the corner to the rear entrance of Hotel Milekov. His heart is thumping in his chest. A comrade opens the door and bundles him inside.

Orlov dashes back up several flights of stairs—pausing only to rest his complaining knee—and finds Comrades Dinev and Smid still up on the roof. As he emerges through the door, they rush over to embrace him.

"Bravo, Comrade," says Dinev.

"Quickly," says Smid, waving at Orlov to join them at the edge of the roof.

The three rocket operators dash to the front of the hotel, dropping onto their bellies to peek down onto the square and Hotel Melikov opposite. Orlov grips the edge of the roof with both hands. He sees that just two comrades remain outside Hotel Melikov, guarding the door. Everyone else is inside.

Orlov turns to Smid. "What now?" he whispers.

Smid is still looking intently down at the hotel. "Wait," he says.

Muffled shouts ring out, then a woman's screams, then a single gunshot. More shouting.

Something curious begins to happen. Slowly at first, then with a building momentum, respectable couples and family groups begin to emerge, dazed, into the Grand Plaza. Many of them are getting dressed as they run, pulling on formal suits and fur coats as they trip and stumble across the cobbles. The men attempt to guide and shield their wives and children, but they rush to the left and right, apparently with no idea which way to go. It becomes clear to Orlov that most, perhaps all, of the ordinary guests who have been trapped at Hotel Melikov waiting out the revolution are being sent away. It takes several minutes for this process to unfold, perhaps because the comrades are going door to door, persuading guests to leave.

Among the final guests to leave are some more belligerent men who are apparently not happy about their treatment and begin to remonstrate with the comrades. For a moment, it seems this situation might descend into violence on the hotel steps. Then one of the comrades fires two shots in the air and the remaining guests scatter at speed across the square, disappearing into side streets.

Orlov realizes he has been holding his breath. He exhales heavily, wondering what will happen next.

The next person he sees is General Varga, who shuffles down the steps of Hotel Melikov in full uniform, with both hands up high, followed by two comrades with rifles trained on the back of his head. There is a shouted instruction Orlov can't decipher. Varga stops dead, hands still raised.

Varga is followed by another general, then another, then Citizen Galin, then two civilian ministers who—for some reason—must have stayed at the hotel rather than traveling up to the convent. Each new arrival is accompanied by an armed comrade or two with rifles trained on their targets. So it goes on until there is quite a gathering of captives and captors shivering in the middle of the Grand Plaza.

Two vehicles emerge from the government sector and park next to the crowd.

A scuffle breaks out. Someone—a general whom Orlov does not recognize—has dropped his hands and is running away from the group. A comrade fires into the air. The general keeps running. Another comrade fires twice into the general's back. He falls on his face right in front of Vanev and Orlov's fish stall.

More shouting. Some of the comrades jab their captives with the barrels of their rifles. The remaining captives thrust their hands higher into the air.

Several comrades emerge from the two vehicles and begin to approach the captives. It takes a few moments for Orlov to realize that these comrades are equipped with handcuffs, with which they are securing the captured generals and ministers. Now he remembers where he has seen these vehicles before: they are used to transport prisoners from the cells under the High Court.

With more shouting and jabbing with rifles, the captives are persuaded onto the vehicles. Several armed comrades board with them. After some minutes of frantic consultation between comrades, the vehicles are driven away. It seems appropriate to Orlov that members of the government should be held in the cells under the High Court, where he himself was once a captive for having done nothing besides following the instructions of government agents. This reminds him that Zelle and her band of zealots are still very much at large.

Now Orlov spots Vanev for the first time. He is in the middle of the square, waving his arms, ushering comrades back into Hotel Melikov.

Orlov turns to Smid. "What's happening now?"

Smid stares straight down at the action. "They're going to double check the hotel. To make sure no one's hiding in there."

A small group of armed comrades waits on the steps of the hotel while the others go back inside. There follows several minutes of almost total silence. Dinev stands up and begins to pace up and down on the roof. Smid and Orlov follow suit, standing and stretching and waiting for news.

A shot rings out. Orlov ducks.

But this shot is not in anger.

A comrade has emerged from Hotel Melikov and has fired a shot into the air. Another comrade does the same. Then another. Soon there is a multiple gun salute.

In an instant, Comrade Dinev's mood switches from caution to celebration. "Let's go," he says.

The three comrades race inside, down several flights of stairs, and out into the Grand Plaza. Along the way, they are joined by Volf and the small group of comrades who had remained in the ballroom.

By the time they emerge into the square, there is a large gathering of comrades hugging and slapping each other on the back. Someone emerging from Hotel Milekov has brought bottles of slivovitz and begins to pass them around. Someone shoots the top off a slivovitz bottle with his rifle. Someone else breaks out spontaneously into a rousing version of "The Red Flag," and the others follow along.

Then raise the scarlet standard high.
Beneath its shade we'll live and die,
Though cowards flinch and traitors sneer,
We'll keep the red flag flying here.

If Orlov is not entirely mistaken in the semi-darkness of the early hours, some hardened men with rifles over their shoulders are singing with tears in their eyes. Someone hands Orlov a bottle and he takes a long swig, before passing it to Smid.

Orlov sees something he has never seen before: Comrade Volf is smiling. Volf spots Orlov, Dinev, and Smid and walks over to shake their hands. "Good shooting, comrades," he says.

Orlov spots Vanev in the middle of the group, a rifle in one hand and a bottle of slivovitz in the other. Both are raised aloft in victory.

He approaches Vanev, who sees him, hands the bottle off to someone else, and holds out his hand. "Congratulations, Comrade," says Vanev.

Orlov shakes his hand. "What happens now?" he says.

CHAPTER TWENTY-THREE

In which our hero witnesses a new dawn

At six o'clock in the morning precisely, the entire company of People's Party comrades is gathered in the ballroom of Hotel Milekov. They are tired but fueled with adrenaline. In some cases, they are injured and bandaged. In all cases, they are both elated at the events of the morning and apprehensive about what the immediate future holds. The room smells like sweat and recently fired rifles.

On the floor in the middle of the gathering, a wireless crackles into life. Comrade Volf raises a hand and the room falls silent.

After several seconds of harsh static, Orlov recognizes the voice of the same newscaster they listened to in his neighbor's apartment, the last time he was at home. The comrades lean in with focused anticipation as the newscast begins.

Citizens. Please listen carefully to what follows. We begin today's broadcast with news of historical proportions. The government has fallen. I repeat. The government has fallen. We have received reports from credible sources that all minister-generals serving under His Majesty are dead or incarcerated. The fate of the civilian ministers is less clear. We understand most of them are incarcerated or missing. We will endeavor to bring you further news on that as soon as we get it.

Some of the comrades look at Orlov, who looks down at his shoes, uncomfortable to be thought of as a former minister in this company.

As to the fate of the king himself, please listen carefully, citizens. We have credible reports from multiple sources that the monarch has left the country and is en route to join his wife and children in a secret foreign location. We have no reliable information regarding his destination. There are rumors, but we shall not broadcast them until we have confirmation. However, there seems no doubt that the king has fled his kingdom. We are therefore confident in reporting to you that, for all practical purposes, the very short reign of the new king is at an end. Perhaps the monarchy itself is at an end.

This is greeted with shouts, cheers, and back-slapping among the comrades. Volf waves his hand to encourage them to keep listening. Orlov wonders what will happen to the ministers staying at the convent. The broadcast continues.

Citizens, it is a new day for our nation. We do not yet know what the future holds. But we can be sure about this. Citizens are tired and hungry. Many of us have been trapped in our homes with dwindling supplies. So, we send this message out to all merchants and employers. The war is over. The fighting is over. There may be uncertainty, but it will pass. Please, open your doors and your businesses. Citizens need to buy food and supplies. They need life to return to normal, as far as possible. We are all in this together. Thank you.

The group begins to break up. Some comrades continue listening to the broadcast while others walk away, chatting animatedly about what they have just heard.

Orlov spots Vanev, who is standing at the window, looking pensive. He beckons Orlov to join him. Saying nothing, Vanev points through the window.

To Orlov's amazement, some of the market traders are out in the Grand Plaza. In one or two cases, the tarpaulins are already removed as they prepare to open their stalls.

This, however, is not what Vanev is pointing to. It takes Orlov a few seconds to register that, in its usual position right next to the fish stall, sits Citizen Vodnik's fish delivery van. The engine is still running, and Orlov can see Vodnik's arm extended through the window, a cigarette burning between his fingers. This is precisely the position adopted by Vodnik whenever he is made to wait too long before the fishmongers accept his deliveries.

Saying nothing, Vanev looks at Orlov and waves his hand to indicate that they should walk together.

Tired, dazed, but happy, the two fishmongers walk silently down the staircase and out into the early morning sun of the Grand Plaza. Orlov is struck by the normality of the scene. It is just a few hours since his rocket blew the doors off Hotel Melikov but—aside from the unusual backdrop of a gaping, blackened hole where those doors used to stand—preparations for opening the market look much like any other day. By the time the two fishmongers arrive at their stall and take their overalls down from the hook, the greengrocer has arrived next door. Saying nothing, he nods politely and, as he often does, holds out an open packet of cigarettes in lieu of a greeting.

One of the market traders finds Comrade Smid's unexploded rocket lying on the cobbles at the south end of the square. Vanev summons a comrade from Hotel Milekov, who removes it. There is, however, no panic, nor are there any questions about how an unexploded rocket might have arrived at that location. The market traders are, it seems, resigned to the realities of war. They look the other way as the rocket is removed, focusing on folding their tarpaulins and setting out their wares for the day ahead.

The first fish customers of the day arrive at the stall in a state of hurried gratefulness; they are delighted to be able to buy fish in the market once again but, apparently, they dare not linger or chat with the fishmongers for long, just in case something untoward should happen.

"How good to see you both here again," says a regular customer who rushes to buy her usual order—two haddock, two halibut—thrusting the precise coinage toward them on the palm of her hand and shuffling away into a side street the second the wrapped fish are handed over.

Another regular customer asks after the wellbeing of the two fishmongers. "I trust you were able to get away from the city for a while during all this trouble," he says.

Vanev glances at Orlov and back at the man. "Indeed so, Citizen," he says. "We have just returned from a few days in the mountains."

The man grasps his wrapped fish to his chest like a prized possession. "Good for you," he says, before scuttling away.

In the late morning, the two fishmongers enjoy a short cigarette break sitting on barrels. Orlov notices that his barrel is pocked with bullet holes, but decides not to mention this.

"I hope you can manage without me for a while," says Vanev. He nods toward Hotel Milekov. "Some business to attend to."

"Regarding the future of the nation?" asks Orlov.

Vanev stubs his cigarette out on the cobbles with his boot. "Something like that."

Orlov watches as Vanev trundles across the square and into Hotel Milekov. Several other senior People's Party officials are also gathering on the front steps, some of them with bandaged arms or heads. They step inside the hotel and Orlov returns to business, serving a thin but steady stream of grateful customers.

Toward the end of the afternoon, just as some of the merchants are beginning to close up their stalls, Orlov spots a familiar face. Citizen Nowak, his neighbor who owns the first wireless radio in the apartment building, rushes over to buy the last two haddock of the day.

"Since it's the end of the day, let's call it half a crown," says Orlov.

"Thank you, Citizen. Most kind," says Nowak, handing over a coin.

Orlov sees an opportunity to inquire after things at home. "I hope all is well in the building," he says.

Nowak smiles a grim, embarrassed smile. "I am sorry about that unfortunate business. I assume you have been staying with family during," he waves a hand, "all this trouble."

Orlov hesitates. "In a manner of speaking, yes," he says. "But I need to return home now, if you think . . ." The question trails off, because Orlov is unsure how to end it.

Nowak's expression brightens. "Of course, yes. I see no reason why you should stay away any longer. After all"—he glances around to make sure no one is listening—"it seems you are just a fishmonger again."

Orlov opens his hands in agreement.

"I can't be a government minister, if there's no government," he says.

"Quite right," says Nowak, nodding. He scuttles away with the wrapped haddock under his arm.

Orlov turns to the business of packing up the stall for the day but notices several members of the People's Party emerging from Hotel Milekov carrying piles of paper. It transpires that these are fliers, and the comrades proceed to nail a copy of the flier to every lamppost in the Grand Plaza before continuing the task along residential side streets.

Since there is no sign of Vanev, Orlov closes up the stall on his own and bids good evening to the greengrocer. Encouraged by the words of Citizen Nowak, he determines to return home, but first he stops at a lamppost to read the notice.

> CITIZENS! OUR NATION IS ABOUT TO ENTER A NEW ERA. THE MONARCHY AND ITS CORRUPT, UNDEMOCRATIC SYSTEM OF GOVERNMENT ARE AT AN END. SOON WE WILL BE A FREE DEMOCRATIC REPUBLIC. EVERY ADULT CITIZEN WILL BE ABLE TO VOTE. EVERYONE WILL FINALLY HAVE A SAY IN THE FUTURE OF THE NATION. THE FIRST STEP ON THAT JOURNEY BEGINS NOW. THE MEMBERS OF THE PEOPLE'S PARTY WILL APPOINT A PRESIDENT PRO TEMPORE TO OVERSEE THE BIRTH OF OUR NEW DEMOCRACY. GATHER IN THE GRAND PLAZA AT NOON ON FRIDAY TO HEAR MORE.

Although Orlov is very tired and a little disoriented, he is quite sure today is Thursday, in which case this meeting is taking place as soon as tomorrow. Clearly, the People's Party is not wasting any time. Not being a student of political matters, Orlov has no idea what is meant by the strange phrase *President Pro Tempore*. He will ask Vanev about this, as soon as the opportunity arises.

With some trepidation and a little hope that he will be able to return home, Orlov trudges through the side streets to his apartment building, wondering what he will find. Other citizens are gathering around lampposts in groups, discussing the notice. Although he cannot hear the details of these discussions, it's clear the flier is causing a good deal of interest, even excitement.

Orlov turns a corner and sees his apartment building. In what state will he find his apartment? The good news is that the items strewn in the street have been moved. The bad news is that his window remains very much broken.

The doorway to the building is still protected by piles of sandbags. Someone has built a little station for a security guard, but there is no one sitting in it. In the lobby, there are more sandbags behind the windows. There is a rather acrid smell, suggesting that cleaning the lobby has not been the top priority in recent days.

Orlov walks up the stairs and approaches the door to his apartment, nervous about what he will find. The curtains are flapping violently owing to a stiff breeze through the broken window. Shards of glass are scattered on the floor under his humble dining table. Copies of *The Sentinel* that had been sitting on the table have blown all over the apartment, giving it a messy, chaotic appearance. Fighting his weariness but determined not to retire with the apartment in such a state, Orlov sweeps up the broken glass, tidies the newspapers, and nails an old potato sack over the broken window. It is a very ugly solution, but it will suffice until he can arrange for something more permanent.

As is his tradition before turning in for the night, he brews tea on the stove and drinks it sitting by the window, looking out at the lights of the city. On this particular night, however, his normal view is significantly obscured by the potato sack. There is a small window next to it which remains intact, so Orlov shifts his chair to make the best of this partial view.

The fishmonger, former government minister, former mole, and former double agent sips his tea and contemplates the remarkable night and day he has just witnessed. He finds this state of affairs both exhilarating and more than a little confusing. He wonders where the king is now. He wonders what will happen to the civilian ministers up at the convent. He wonders what is meant by *President Pro*

Tempore. He wonders how tomorrow's poll of People's Party members will work. He wonders if he himself is considered by the party to be one of its members. There are so many unknowns, it is taxing on the brain.

There is, however, one important fact lodged firmly in Orlov's mind of which he is certain. He is no longer a government minister. He is no longer a mole. He is no longer a double agent. From today, Citizen Orlov is just a fishmonger. Nothing more, nothing less.

CHAPTER TWENTY-FOUR

In which our hero votes in an election

As befits the occasion, the following morning is as bright and promising a spring morning as Orlov can remember. Expecting that Vanev will be too busy with political matters to appear at the market, Orlov leaves early, receives the fish delivery from Citizen Vodnik, and sets up the stall on his own.

As soon as the market opens, a familiar figure arrives in the square and marches toward the fish stall. It is Comrade Dankova, the administrator of the People's Party.

Perhaps in a deliberate attempt to erase their rather tense history, Dankova is extremely gracious and friendly. She holds out her hand and Orlov shakes it.

"I trust you are well, Citizen," says Dankova.

"I am, thank you," says Orlov.

"Comrade Vanev tells me that you were instrumental in diverting ammunition from the government to the party," says Dankova.

Orlov feels himself blushing. "Well," he says, "I had a good deal of help from Comrades Vanev, Dinev, and Smid."

Dankova continues, "Dinev and Smid tell me yours was the rocket that opened the way to our victory." She gestures at the gaping hole where the front doors of Hotel Melikov used to stand.

Orlov begins to say, "Well, that was perhaps a little fortunate," but Dankova is not listening.

She shakes his hand again. "Thank you for your service, Comrade," she says, eagerly, before strolling away to Hotel Melikov. Based on the comings and goings of various comrades, it seems the People's Party has moved its activity to the older hotel.

Toward the end of the morning, some of the party comrades emerge onto the steps at the front of Hotel Melikov and erect a small platform, complete with a microphone on a stand attached to a loudspeaker. Behind the platform they hang a national flag. Well before noon, Orlov notices journalists beginning to arrive in the square to claim good positions at the foot of the steps. Ordinary citizens begin to follow suit and soon the Grand Plaza is bustling with activity. Several of the traders begin to pack up their stalls early and Orlov does the same. He gives away the last few fish free of charge to delighted customers, secures the stall, hangs up his overalls, and takes his place in the crowd in front of the hotel.

Citizens continue to stream into the square and, before noon, it is a mass of bustling, lively, expectant humanity. A small brass band—dressed in matching suits—arrives unannounced, sets up quickly on the platform, and begins to play a selection of traditional songs. The crowd sings along with some enthusiasm.

At twelve noon precisely, Comrades Volf, Vanev, Dankova, and the rest of the ruling council of the People's Party step out from Hotel Melikov onto the steps. The brass band hurriedly ends its performance in the middle of a song and scuttles away. Looking nervous and squinting into the midday sunlight, Comrade Dankova steps up to the microphone. She taps it to ensure it is working, before taking a deep breath and addressing the crowd.

"Citizens," says Dankova, falteringly. She turns away from the microphone, coughs, and turns back, now speaking more forcefully. "Good afternoon, citizens. Thank you for gathering. I am Citizen Dankova. It is my task to explain today's proceedings." She pauses and takes a moment to look out at the crowd before continuing. "First we will hear brief remarks from Citizen Volf, leader of the People's Party, and from Citizen Vanev, deputy leader. For reasons they will explain, immediately after those remarks, the current membership of the People's Party will file into the room behind me—the ballroom of Hotel Melikov—to conduct a caucus. The caucus will be followed by a secret ballot to elect the President Pro Tempore. That title will be explained in a few moments by the leader of the party."

Apparently unsure how to bring her remarks to a close, Dankova smiles at the crowd and steps aside, allowing Comrade Volf to step up to the microphone. He squints at the crowd for some moments and strokes his unkempt beard slowly, apparently contemplating the gravity of the moment. His voice sounds even thinner than usual via the crackling loudspeaker.

"Citizens, I am Citizen Volf, leader of the People's Party. Yesterday marked the end of the monarchy's undemocratic grip on our nation. Today marks the beginning of our march toward democracy." He pauses for a polite—if not rapturous—round of applause. "The start of that process is to use the democratic systems of the People's Party to put in place a President Pro Tempore, that is, a president for now. A temporary president who can oversee the creation of the laws and systems that we need to march together into a better, democratic future." Now the applause is warmer, and some people in the middle of the crowd begin to sing a faltering version of the national anthem. Volf raises his right hand in the air until the noise recedes. "The People's Party will today choose our President Pro Tempore. But that person will not be me."

A collective gasp issues from the crowd. Dankova frowns and looks at Vanev.

Volf continues, "I will continue to lead the People's Party. When the time comes, I will campaign to be your president following a glorious victory for my party in our first ever national election. For that reason, I cannot be your President Pro Tempore. I cannot be the neutral leader we need." He glances at Dankova. "Therefore, I hereby ask the administrator of the People's Party to withdraw my name from the ballot."

Dankova and Vanev, apparently shocked, whisper to each other. Volf walks off the stage and joins them in an urgent, three-way conversation that no one else can hear. Following a long, awkward silence, Comrade Vanev steps onto the podium.

Vanev looks out at the crowd for a long time before beginning to speak, his voice low and booming. "Citizens, the comments from Citizen Volf apply to the deputy leader of the People's Party just as much as they apply to the leader. Therefore, I too must withdraw my name from the ballot for President Pro Tempore."

Vanev walks off the stage abruptly. He and Volf march with purpose through the blackened hole into Hotel Melikov. A ripple of discomfort runs the crowd. Orlov looks around and sees a sea of confused faces. Looking confused herself, Comrade Dankova steps up onto the podium again.

She speaks in an uncertain tone. "Citizens, please do not be alarmed. The People's Party will now vote for the new President Pro Tempore just as planned, albeit that the names on the ballot will need to be altered. Everything is under control."

Dankova rushes off the podium and into the hotel. Members of the People's Party emerge from the crowd and follow her into the ballroom. The brass band returns to the stage and launches into a traditional medley. It occurs to Orlov that he does not know if he is a member of the People's Party or not. As party members continue to drift into the hotel, he has no idea if he should join them. Dankova appears again on the hotel steps, urgently studying a clipboard. She looks up, spots Orlov, and frantically waves at him to join her. The people standing near Orlov stare at him as he picks his way through the crowd and up the steps.

"Quickly, Comrade," says Dankova, "we are about to start."

The ballroom is full of perhaps one hundred and fifty people. They are milling around excitedly, chatting to each other in groups. The atmosphere is both expectant and nervous. A huge ballot box sits against a wall pocked with bullet holes.

Comrade Dankova calls the room to order. "Comrades! Let us begin, please. We will caucus for one hour exactly, please. When it is time to vote, you will see that the names of Comrades Volf and Vanev have been struck out. At their own request, you may not vote for them. All comrades must write in the name of their choice for President Pro Tempore." She glances briefly around the group before clapping her hands together. "Caucus, please. Caucus for one hour."

The room bursts into life. Comrades instantly begin to huddle, debating fervently and waving their arms to emphasize their points of view. Orlov is unsure what to do or whose name to write in. While he does not fully understand what a President Pro Tempore is or what they will do, nevertheless he was sure that the next steps in the democratic process would be led by Volf and Vanev. Apparently, that is not how things are destined to unfold.

Orlov sees Dankova in deep conversation and it occurs to him that she might be a wise choice. She is, after all, the administrator of the party, someone who seems to understand the rules and procedures of politics better than anyone he knows.

Dankova spots him, and beckons him to join the group she is speaking with.

"Here he is, right now," says Dankova as Orlov approaches.

The other members of the group turn to Orlov and take turns shaking his hand. It seems these comrades know who Orlov is, although he recognizes none of them.

"Is it true you were responsible for the ammunition going to us instead of the generals?" asks a serious woman with thick spectacles.

Before Orlov can answer, a tall man in an ill-fitting suit says, eagerly, "I heard you blew the hole in the hotel doors," while leaning in to shake his hand.

Again, Orlov has no chance to speak before someone else says, "Inspirational."

The other members of the group agree heartily, nodding and saying, "What a patriot," and, "Truly a hero," in hushed tones, more to each other than to Orlov.

Without further ado, this group breaks up as each of the comrades spins away to talk to others. Orlov suddenly finds himself alone again, watching with curiosity as these various comrades look over at him, nodding and smiling. One such comrade points at Orlov while speaking to a new group, causing the other members of the group to rush over, each waiting eagerly to shake his hand.

The noise of chatter around the ballroom is so loud that Orlov can hardly hear what these new arrivals are saying to him. It seems, however, that the story about the ammunition is already well known among the comrades. Someone asks about General Varga, and it seems this comrade believes Orlov had personally captured him and marched him off to the cells under the High Court. Orlov attempts to correct this, but is not sure he has been heard before the man walks away to talk to others.

The remainder of the caucus continues in much the same vein. Orlov repeatedly attempts to engage in conversation about whether Dankova would be a good choice, but each time he is interrupted by questions about the shipment of ammunition or his bravery in venturing into the Grand Plaza to detonate the final rocket. To the best of his ability, he confirms the suggestions that are true and attempts to deny those that are false, but it is not clear whether he has been heard.

Dankova calls the room to order again. "Time is up, comrades. Time is up. Silence, please. Everyone in line."

Instantly, the room falls into silence until the only sound is the shuffling of shoes on the dancefloor as comrades form an orderly line around the edge of the ballroom. Orlov watches on from the middle of the line as, one by one, comrades approach the table with religious reverence, write quickly on a paper, and drop it into the ballot box. As each comrade finishes, Dankova directs them to leave the ballroom and return outside to join the crowd.

Slowly, the room begins to empty as each comrade in turn votes and leaves. When Orlov's turn comes, he sees that a line has been drawn through the names *VOLF* and *VANEV*. At the foot of the paper, he writes *DANKOVA* on the line, folds his paper once, drops it into the box, and walks slowly outside, rejoining the crowd.

The brass band is still playing traditional songs with gusto. Orlov keeps his spot near the front of the crowd until Dankova appears, firmly grasping her clipboard.

"Citizens," she says, her voice shaking with nerves. The sun is now a little higher in the sky, and Dankova shields her eyes with her free hand while she looks out at the expectant throng. She takes a deep breath. "Thank you for your patience. We have a clear result. Please listen carefully." She looks down at her clipboard, coughs, and returns her gaze to the crowd. "Citizen Orlov has been elected President Pro Tempore. Our President Pro Tempore is Citizen Orlov."

CHAPTER TWENTY-FIVE

In which our hero delivers some remarks

It seems to Citizen Orlov that he is no longer outside in the Grand Plaza, but rather in a small, dark room occupied only by Comrade Dankova and himself. To make matters even stranger, his hearing appears to have failed, a harsh whistling the only sound he can hear. Through the gloom, he can see Dankova beckoning someone to walk toward her, but he is unsure if her gesture is directed at him or someone else. He looks around to see if another member of the crowd might respond to Dankova, but—for some peculiar reason—he cannot clearly see anyone else aside from Dankova.

Now Dankova is waving all the more frantically and someone nearby takes Orlov by the shoulders and pushes him toward the podium.

As he walks forward, the whistling sound in Orlov's ears subsides and is replaced by enthusiastic clapping and cheering across the whole of the square. He picks his way through applauding fellow citizens—some of whom pat him on the back as he passes—approaches the podium, and accepts Vanev's hand, allowing his old friend and colleague to pull him up the steps. Vanev claps Orlov on both shoulders and speaks into his ear, but the din from the crowd is now so intense that Orlov cannot hear what is being said.

Orlov leans in to shout urgently into Vanev's ear. "Citizen, I do not think I am the best person for this role."

Vanev seems unperturbed by this. He smiles. "Your comrades have spoken."

Orlov stares directly into Vanev's eyes, in an attempt to convince him of the depth of his concern. "I am serious, Citizen. I had never heard the term President Pro Tempore until yesterday. I have no idea what the role involves."

Vanev grabs his old friend by both shoulders. "It was just a few days ago," says Vanev, "that I was in your ministerial office. You told me you wanted to have a positive influence from inside the establishment. Here's your chance."

Orlov is about to reply, but a frantic Dankova pulls him toward the microphone, positions him in front of it, and steps back to make room for him to speak. Orlov has never before spoken into a microphone and is unsure of the correct technique for doing so. He looks out at a sea of faces, each and every one a fellow citizen now applauding him and awaiting his remarks. Since he has no idea what to say, he turns to glance at Dankova, who waves at him urgently to indicate that he should begin.

Orlov steps up to the microphone and taps on it hard to see if it is turned on. This causes it to make a terrible squealing noise. He steps back, fingers in ears, waiting for this noise to dissipate before making another attempt.

This time, he approaches the microphone more cautiously, stands a few inches behind it, and speaks falteringly.

"Good afternoon, citizens," he says, his voice ringing out through the loudspeaker with a strange, artificial tone. "I am Citizen Orlov the fishmonger."

For reasons not entirely clear to Orlov, he is interrupted by another rapturous round of applause. Someone near the front of the crowd shouts something, but Orlov cannot hear it clearly.

He waits for the noise to die down before continuing. "Normally, at this time of day, I am over there, selling fish." He points at the fish stall as another round of applause breaks out. Once again, he must wait for it to die down. "Bream is particularly good quality at the moment, and on sale for only half a crown for a pair." This time, the applause is deafening.

Orlov is aware that he should say something about the election that just took place, but he is unsure where to start. He decides it is best to be honest. "I am rather surprised to have been chosen to be your President . . ."—he pauses and turns to Dankova, who whispers in his ear; he nods and turns back to the microphone—"your President Pro Tempore. I'm sure I will need assistance from the citizens behind me and from many of you in order to perform the duties of this role." Another rousing round of applause.

Orlov looks around at Vanev and Volf, who nod encouragingly. "I am not an expert in politics. But I promise you I will do whatever I can to make sure the voice of every citizen is heard."

During another round of applause, Orlov notices a man near the front of the crowd, his face glowing with enthusiasm. He waves a hand as if to encourage Orlov to say more. He catches Orlov's eye and—if Orlov is not mistaken—mouths the words, "Keep going."

As he waits for the applause to subside, Orlov scrambles for what else he might say. For a moment, he tries to think of something suitably political, perhaps drawing on his many conversations with Vanev over the years. But in the heat of the moment, he cannot think of anything. He decides it might be better to talk about his family. "My mother is now very senior in years. Just like my late father, she is a patriot; she loves this country and has dedicated her whole life to making it a better place for everyone to live in. But she has never once had a chance to have a say about how we are governed. Not once. I think she should have that chance while she is still alive. And I think each of you should have that chance, too."

Now the applause and cheering are deafening. Unsure what else to say, Orlov turns back to Volf and Vanev, who step forward to shake his hand. Then Dankova and the other comrades shake him by the hand. The brass band, which has hastily reassembled itself at the side of the podium, strikes up a traditional song. Orlov is suddenly surrounded by citizens wanting to congratulate him. Many of them speak to him, but the noise is such that he cannot hear most of what is said. The atmosphere shifts in an instant from formal ceremony to carnival. Many citizens sing along with the brass band; some begin to dance. Others drift away to the restaurants and cafes along the edge of the Grand Plaza, where sausages and ale are ordered in large quantities.

After the shock of what has just happened, Orlov wishes he could slip away for a tankard of ale, but he is unable to leave the steps of Hotel Melikov, as a seemingly never-ending line of citizens arrives to shake his hand and wish him well or, in some cases, to offer advice. He does his best to listen to everyone and thanks them profusely for sharing their thoughts, even if he does not quite follow everything that is said.

Orlov is just about to ask Dankova to rescue him from this long, tiring process when he spots two familiar faces approaching. These faces are surrounded by the traditional, gray habit of the Sisters of Our Lady of Perpetual Sorrow. It is Sisters Sofia and Petra. Their faces are glowing, perhaps with patriotism, perhaps with pride.

Stepping forward first, Sister Sofia grasps one of Orlov's hands in both of hers and says, "Congratulations, Mr. President."

Orlov is so surprised to see them again that he scarcely notices this strange greeting. "How are the sisters?" he says. "Is everyone safe?"

Now Sister Petra leans in, shakes his hand, and replies to his question. "All are safe, thanks to you."

"Have you returned to the convent?" he asks.

Sofia shakes her head. "Not yet. We are lying low in a safe location. We will return there soon."

"I am grateful for your help, sisters," says Orlov. "Without you, things might have turned out very differently."

"We are at your service," says Sister Petra, "as long as you are working in the cause of peace."

"I will do my best," says Orlov.

He shakes hands with the sisters again and simultaneously glances at Dankova to see if she will now intervene to relieve him of this duty. As he does so, he catches a glimpse of a familiar face at the back of the crowd. This person is watching Orlov's interaction with the two sisters very intently. Her head is almost entirely obscured by a large headscarf and dark glasses. A young woman attempting to appear older.

CHAPTER TWENTY-SIX

In which our hero begins a new life

The next morning is even more bright and pleasant than the one before. President Pro Tempore Orlov sits at his small window—the larger window still being covered with a potato sack—sipping coffee and looking out at his beloved nation. He is fighting against tiredness, having slept fitfully, waking up often with countless thoughts racing through his mind. He sinks his first coffee and pours another one.

Remembering the security arrangements put in place at the insistence of Comrade Volf, he delivers coffee to the two armed comrades who have been stationed all night outside the door to his apartment. He also insists that they deliver coffee to their two comrades stationed at the front door to the building.

Back at his window, Orlov's mind is racing through countless questions. How can democratic elections be established in a country whose citizens have never before experienced anything of the sort? How will new political parties be created? What will happen to the generals and civilian ministers currently being held in jail cells?

What will the surviving zealots do next? More specifically, what will Agent Zelle do next? Orlov is grateful for his security detail. He does not think any citizen should ever have to fear for his life simply for fulfilling his or her civic duties, but here we are. Given the uncertainty surrounding Zelle and her band of zealots, he will hang onto his armed security detail for as long as possible.

One of the guards knocks on the door, returns the coffee cups, and informs President Orlov that he is expected soon for a meeting in the ballroom of Hotel Melikov.

Eschewing the offer of an armed vehicle that the comrades found abandoned and have now repurposed for People's Party business, Orlov insists on walking the short distance from his apartment to Hotel Melikov, but he allows the four guards to surround him, per their instructions. He insists, however, that they carry their rifles on their shoulders, so as not to startle market traders and early morning dog walkers.

As this strange little group passes through the Grand Plaza, Orlov instantly spots Citizens Vanev and Vodnik unloading the day's supply of fish. Much to the agitation of his security detail, Orlov insists that they stop and surround the fish stall. They each take a corner of the stall, their gaze outward, surveying the other traders.

With that security precaution in place, Orlov greets Vanev and Vodnik, accepts a cigarette from them, pulls on his apron, and assists in setting out the day's wares in display boxes full of ice.

Once this task is complete, the two fishmongers thank Citizen Vodnik, who departs in his fish delivery van, just as he has done every morning when the market is open for the last twenty years or more. They stand back to admire their work, the early morning sun glinting off beautiful specimens of carp, bream, and haddock.

Vanev takes a long, slow drag on his cigarette before speaking. "Don't you have more important business to attend to, Mr. President?"

"I would prefer to be just plain *Citizen* to you," says Orlov.

"Or perhaps *Comrade*?" suggests Vanev.

"Or *Comrade*," agrees Orlov.

Vanev eyes his old friend with a curious expression. "What would you prefer, Mr. President?"

Orlov sighs deeply, blowing a slow cloud of smoke into the air before replying. "I would prefer to spend the day out here selling fish," he says.

Vanev nods sagely. "The next time you do so, we will be a democratic republic."

"Let us hope so," says Orlov, solemnly.

Vanev stubs his cigarette out on the cobbles with his boot. "You might want to inform your mother that you are not only her son but also her president," he says.

Noticing that his security guards are becoming agitated, Orlov follows suit in extinguishing his cigarette on the cobbles. "All in good time," he says.

With that, Orlov begins the short walk to Hotel Melikov, his security detail surrounding him on all sides.

As the fishmonger mounts the hotel steps, Comrade Dankova emerges through the blackened hole created by Orlov's rocket. She is carrying a clipboard.

Dankova holds out a hand in greeting. "Good morning, Mr. President," she says.

"Good morning," says Orlov.

ACKNOWLEDGMENTS

It has a been a pleasure once again to work with my brilliant editor, Elana Gibson. The world of *Citizen Orlov* would not be same without her.

Thanks to everyone at CamCat Books, including Maryann Appel, whose striking series design has been commented on by many readers.

I'm grateful to be part of the thriller writing community, including International Thriller Writers, which is always creative, supportive, and welcoming.

I'm also grateful to be a member of the Authors Guild, which continues to do essential work representing the interests of writers.

Thanks to the readers and judges at the IBPA Awards and the IPPY Awards, both of which awarded a medal to the first book in this series, *Citizen Orlov*.

Thanks to my gallant beta readers on this book: Micah Abresch, Bill Krieger, Gordon McFarland, Jennifer Loizeaux, and Stephanie Siebert.

Most of all, thanks to my wife, Sonya Payne, and our sons, Stanley Payne and Arthur Payne.

ABOUT THE AUTHOR

Jonathan Payne is a former British government official specializing in national security. He served in London, New York, and Kabul before leaving government service in 2010 and moving to the United States. He soon began to write fiction and published short stories in various magazines, including *Turnpike* and *Fiction Kitchen Berlin*. In 2019, he earned a Master of Arts degree in novel writing from Middlesex University, London. Soon after graduation, he began writing *Citizen Orlov*, which became his first novel, published in May 2023 by CamCat Books. Apple Books named it a Book of the Month. It won the 2024 IBPA Benjamin Franklin Silver Medal for Mystery/Thriller and the 2024 IPPY Bronze Medal for Suspense/Thriller.

If you liked

Jonathan Payne's *Hotel Melikov,*

you'll enjoy

K. L Murphy's *The Great Forgotten.*

CHAPTER ONE

Summer 1988
Nashville, Tennessee

GINNY CAMPBELL SURVEYED the boxes stacked in all four corners of the living room, surprised by how much she'd managed to bring to the new house. Footsteps sounded on the stairs, and she looked over her shoulder. The movers, their faces shining pink with exhaustion, marched down the stairs, arms swinging.

"That was the last of it, Mrs. Campbell," the larger of the two men said. A fresh bead of sweat dripped from his temple and he mopped it with the sleeve of his coveralls. "What do you want me to do with the trunk?"

Her brows creased. "What trunk?"

"The one in the attic." He glanced at his partner and shrugged. "Probably left by the old owners."

The other man, as skinny as a pogo stick, chimed in. "Looks like it's been there a long time."

She thought about it for only a moment. The house was supposed to be empty, cleared of any items left by her grandmother that hadn't already been taken by friends and family, but this must have been missed. "Can you bring it downstairs?"

After they'd gone, she crouched down in front of the trunk, running her hand across the dusty surface. Wiping away the grime, she spied a set of faded gold initials. AMK. Ginny's teeth caught her lower lip and she frowned. Grandma Betty's initials were EJP, not AMK. She studied the curious case again. It was large enough for travel, but there were no stickers or anything to indicate where it came from other than those initials. From the look of it, the movers were right. It was old and had probably been in the attic for ages.

"Who do you belong to?" she asked the trunk, her voice a whisper. Reaching out, she caught the antique brass lock in her hand and drew in a breath.

The sharp trill of the phone made her gasp and fall back on her heels with a thump. Shaking her head with a laugh, she scrambled to her feet and hurried to the phone hanging on the kitchen wall.

"Hello?"

"Did they break anything? Movers always break something, you know."

Ginny's grip on the phone loosened. "Hi, Mom."

"You have to watch them like hawks." Ginny couldn't help but smile. Her mother might be short on pleasantries, but she was long on opinion. "When we moved to Tallahassee, they broke an entire place setting of Grandma Betty's china. Do you remember it? The plates had those tiny pink flowers in the middle with gold trim along the edges. Maybe you don't though. I can't say I ever used it except when Grandma Betty came for Christmas which wasn't often—thank the Lord. It wasn't my style. Not modern at all. Please don't tell your father I said that. His mother was a dear when she was with us, of course, but we never did have much in common."

Ginny choked back a snort and dragged a chair closer to the phone. Her mother liked to imagine that she and Grandma Betty were quite different, but they definitely had one thing in common. Both women could talk and neither cared to whom—as long as the body was warm and even that wasn't absolutely necessary. It was no wonder Ginny's father was a quiet man.

"Anyway, I hope none of your china has broken like Grandma Betty's. Though I guess yours is plain enough that you could probably replace it with any old white plate, and no one would notice the difference. Now, if it were one of the Florentine patterns or the Scandinavian designs we considered, that would be quite upsetting. I really wish you'd gone with that Wedgwood. Can you imagine how gorgeous your table would be during the holidays? And with the crystal that—"

"Mom, stop." Ginny's fingers tightened over the phone again.

Maggie Piler made a clucking sound. "Surely, I'm entitled to my opinion, Virginia."

"I know your opinion." Ginny heard the sharp inhale over the line and groaned. "Please, Mom. Can we talk about something else?"

"Maybe you'd like to talk about that husband of yours. I swear, Virginia, I don't understand that man. Letting you move all on your own. He should have told his boss no, that it wasn't a good time for him to go to London. I still can't understand why he had to go halfway around the world. Couldn't they have done one of those conference calls? Your father did them all the time before he retired."

"No, Mom." Ginny raised a hand to her temple, massaging the soft flesh. "We've been over this."

"Well, in my day, a man would never let his pregnant wife move alone. It's not right."

"I'm not due for almost six months, Mom. I'm fine. Perfectly capable of handling a move by myself."

"It's still not right." The words were spoken in a way that made Ginny know her mother's chin was lifted to the sky, her red-stained mouth puckered in disapproval. "You can't tell me I'm wrong about this."

Ginny had no intention of discussing Shawn with her mother. "I'm hanging up now."

"Wait. I haven't even had a chance to ask how you're feeling or how the baby is."

"The baby's fine."

"You would tell me if anything was wrong, wouldn't you?"

Ginny looked up at the ceiling. "Yes, Mom."

"Good, because I would get on a plane if you needed me. I'd do it right now. All you would have to do is ask. Your father, too. We could be there in a few short hours."

Ginny's lips parted. "You hate flying. You're terrified."

"I'd still be terrified, but for you and the baby, I would do it. Promise me that if you need me, you'll let me know."

"I promise."

"Good." Maggie changed the subject again. "Well, how's the house? Is it as dreary as I remember?"

Ginny's gaze swept past the counters cluttered with half-emptied boxes to the large window overlooking the small backyard. The grass could stand to be cut, and the fence needed to be repaired, but there was room enough for a swing set and a patio. A huge oak shaded the front porch, and there was a fireplace. Now that her grandmother's heavy furniture and brocade drapes had been removed, the house felt brighter. The wallpaper would have to go though. "It's not dreary, Mom. It needs a little updating, that's all. But you can help me with that when you and dad drive up next month."

"Will you let me help you with the nursery?"

Ginny hesitated. It wasn't like her mother to ask permission for anything. Maybe it was being a grandmother that was softening Maggie. Either way, Ginny wasn't one to argue. "I would love your help."

"I've got so many ideas. What do you think about pink and yellow with—"

"Why don't we wait until you're here?"

"Yes, we can do that. I've been going through boxes of your old things. Make sure you save room in the attic for the baby's clothes as she grows older."

"Mom, we don't know the baby's a girl."

"It's only a feeling, Virginia. Don't make too much of it. But I do have some dresses of yours I've kept stored all these years."

"That reminds me," she said and told her mother about the trunk.

"One of your grandmother's?"

"I don't think so. It has the initials AMK."

"AMK . . . AMK. I can't think who that could be." Ginny heard the clink of a spoon against a teacup over the line.

"Well," Ginny said with a sigh. "I guess I'll have to decide what to do with it."

"What's to decide? It's probably filled with spiders and mouse droppings by now." Ginny laughed imagining her mother shuddering at the idea. "Toss it in the trash before you regret it, Virginia. I'd do it today."

"But what if it's filled with family heirlooms or," she paused, her lips twitching, "very valuable china?"

"Well," Maggie said, dragging out the word. "I suppose you could open it and see, but I'm telling you, Virginia, if you don't find jewels or money, you need to get rid of that thing."

"How sentimental of you, Mom."

"Ha! Being sentimental is dead these days, or haven't you heard?"

"Whatever you say, Mom. I'm hanging up now. For real this time."

Ginny went back to the living room, stopping when she passed a small carton covered in pink hearts. Shawn had laughed when she'd drawn them, but she'd countered, "I'm being efficient. I could label it wedding albums, but this saves time." He'd grinned and wrapped his arms around her. That had been three moves and three apartments ago. The hearts were faded now, nearly invisible. Her hand dropped to her growing belly, and her chin fell to her chest. This was supposed to be a happy time. The gift of Grandma Betty's house. Shawn's new job. A baby. So, why was she fighting back tears?

"Stop it," she said to the empty house. "You can do this."

Across the room, late afternoon sunbeams poured through the large window, spotlighting the leather-wrapped trunk. Sun-speckled particles of dust danced over the case, reminding her of fireflies on a hot summer night. She forgot about the heart-covered box, forgot about Shawn.

Falling to her knees in front of the trunk, she breathed in the musty scent of dried leather and dead flowers. In an instant, she was transported back to her childhood and playing in Grandma Betty's cedar closet. How many times had she hidden among the heavy woolen coats and perfumed gowns? Her heart swelled with the memory as she stared down at the old case. There was no telling what could be inside. Her mother was wrong. Sentimentality wasn't dead. It couldn't be. Besides, there were other reasons to value photos, books, or artifacts. Those things were someone's story, and more importantly, history.

She sneezed and knew her mother wasn't wrong about one thing. The trunk was dirty, and she leaned closer, inspecting the case for spiders or rotted wood or splits in the seams, but saw nothing. Hands trembling, she unbuckled the bindings. The leather straps split as they fell away. Dust clouds rose and tickled her nose again. Who was AMK? Had he or she searched for the trunk only to give up?

Ginny considered whether the case could contain family heirlooms or valuable books or any number of things. Squaring her shoulders, she told herself there was only one way to find out. She turned the key.

GINNY PULLED INTO the small lot, slowing at the sign. Welcome. Nashville Home for the Infirm. Hands resting on the wheel, she studied the three-story building. Dark streaks stained the concrete from the roof line to the lowest window. Cracks and broken pavement marked the lot and sidewalk, and dandelions pushed up through the weed-choked front lawn, their yellow faces the only bright spot to be seen. There's nothing welcoming about it, she thought. Not for the first time, she wondered if this was a good idea.

"Are you sure it's the right lady?" Shawn had asked when he'd phoned.

"Yes. Well, no. I suppose there could be another woman with the same name, but it doesn't seem likely."

"Gin, I'm not sure this is such a great idea. I don't have a good feeling."

She'd wanted to laugh but thought better of it. "What do you think's going to happen, Shawn? I'm going to see an old woman in a nursing home."

It had been an easy argument to win, but she wasn't sure if it was because she was right, or because they were both too tired to make the effort. In spite of her brave words, she had doubts of her own. What if it was the wrong woman? What if the trunk did belong to her, but she didn't want it back, or worse, didn't want to be reminded of it? Images of the things inside flashed through her mind. Everything in the old case had been so carefully wrapped and preserved. It didn't make sense that it had been abandoned. A new idea struck her. Maybe the trunk wasn't left but lost.

Ginny got out of the car and raised her sunglasses on her head. At the front doors, she peered through the glass. Inside, a woman in a white nursing uniform sat behind the front desk of an empty waiting room.

"Good morning," the nurse said when Ginny walked in. The nametag she wore read Jean. "Visiting?" she asked.

"Yes."

Nurse Jean flipped a page in her book and pointed at a wooden clipboard. "You can sign in there. Who are you seeing today?"

Ginny picked up the pen and wrote her name. "Anna Mae Kennedy."

The woman's head came up. "Anna Mae Kennedy?" She closed her book and tented her hands, eyes narrowed. "Are you family?"

"Daughter." Ginny hadn't planned to say that, but the lie popped out of her mouth before she could take it back. The nurse lifted one brow. Realizing her mistake, she forced a laugh. "I mean, granddaughter."

"Granddaughter, huh?" Jean pursed her lips and looked past Ginny to the mostly empty lot. "Are you alone?"

"Yes." Ginny's face flushed under the woman's scrutiny. It occurred to her that maybe she shouldn't have shown up without having sent a letter first. What if other family showed up? How would she explain herself?

"Anna Mae doesn't get many visitors," the nurse said. "Actually, she doesn't get any visitors."

"Oh." While Ginny was thankful she wouldn't be running into actual family, she found the nurse's declaration sad. "Then I'm glad I came."

Jean tapped her fingers for a minute, as though considering. "She gets tired," the nurse said. "She's one of our oldest patients."

Ginny exhaled. "I won't stay long."

"Fifteen minutes," the nurse said, handing Ginny a visitor pass. "Second floor. Room five."

On the second floor, another nurse sat behind a larger desk. Ginny waved her pass in the air and kept walking. The door to Room One was open, the interior dark. A man in a wheelchair was parked outside of Room Two. Ginny slowed. The crown of his head shone pink and white under the unforgiving florescent lights. The hair he did have fell in a grey sheet to his shoulders, partially obscuring the cracked lines of his face. With his chin tucked close to his chest, he twisted his hands in his lap, half-talking, half-ranting, his words rising and falling in a droning hum.

"They're coming, I tell you. Coming. Watch for the night. That's when they come." His hands moved faster, his body rocking. "They're coming, I tell you. Coming." Spit dribbled down his chin. He repeated the same words and his head snapped up, his pupils searching, unfocused in the light. "Watch for the night. That's when they come." Ginny backed away and his head dropped down. "They're coming, I tell you."

At the door to Room Five, she tapped lightly on the door. Silence. She knocked louder, glanced around once, and pushed the door open.

An elderly woman sat in a wheelchair; her face angled toward the window. Wispy white hair like soft-spun cotton candy floated around her head. She wore a high-necked nightgown with pink lace trim and pearl-colored buttons. A colorful quilt lay across her lap, and pink slippers poked out from under the coverlet.

"Mrs. Kennedy?"

The old woman shifted toward Ginny. "You don't look like a nurse. Where's your white uniform?"

"I'm visiting." She lifted the pass again.

The woman in the chair blinked. "Oh, my. Did they tell you the wrong room?" She tipped her head to one shoulder. "Who are you here to see? I might be able to tell you the room you need."

"No. I'm in the right room." Ginny's arm dropped. "At least I think I am."

The woman's forehead wrinkled, her expression a mix of surprise and doubt. "Do I know you?"

"No. We've never met, but I found something of yours, at least I think it's yours."

"How mysterious." The lines that fanned out across her cheeks softened and she settled back. "Why don't you sit down?" She lifted a graceful hand toward a wooden chair and Ginny sat, perched on the end, her purse in her lap. "And what is it that you think you've found?" the woman asked, her pale lips turned up in a small smile.

"A trunk. It was in the attic of my house."

The woman made a choking sound, and Ginny sprang to her feet, panic rising in her belly. "Oh, my God, are you all right? Should I call someone?"

Waving her other hand, the woman's breathing steadied. "No, no. I'm fine. You surprised me is all." The old woman, still deathly pale, pointed at the chair again. "Sit down. I'll be fine in a minute."

"I'm sorry. I didn't mean to upset you."

"Nothing to apologize for," she said, "but I must ask. What makes you think this trunk belongs to me?"

Ginny swallowed. "Well, there are initials on the outside of it, AMK, or I think that's what it says. And there were some letters inside, addressed to Anna Mae Kennedy."

"I see." The woman's gaze drifted to the window, and a stillness fell over the room. Ginny didn't know what to think. Was the woman angry? Sad? Both? Maybe Shawn and her mother had been right. It occurred to her that this was one of the few things those two had ever agreed upon.

"What else did you find?"

Ginny looked up to find the woman watching her now. "Some photos, hats, a diary. Oh, and sheet music." There was more, but when the woman nodded, she knew she'd said enough.

"And where did you say you found this trunk?"

"The attic of my house. I moved here a couple of days ago."

"What house?" the woman asked, her voice arched.

"On Sunset Place, not too far from Vanderbilt. It was my grandmother's house."

The old woman blinked and sat back slowly. "Sunset Place. I don't think I've ever been there." She tilted her head to her shoulder, openly studying Ginny now. "What did you say your name was?"

"Oh, I didn't," she said. "Ginny Campbell."

The old woman stared at her so long, Ginny's cheeks flushed. "Is something wrong?"

CC
CamCat
Books